A HEART BEYOND

Book Description

Leigh Ann Eden had a great life in New York as a partner in a public relations business she'd helped to build—and lost it all when her father was charged with financial crimes. She wasn't involved in his business or the fraud, but her very public role as the face of the PR firm made her a target for media, federal investigators, angry investors, and even the merely curious. She couldn't withstand the pressure. She went into hiding, and avoidance became a way of life.

Her cousin, Florence, offered her a place to hide in her home in the Fan District of Richmond, Virginia. She was a lifesaver for Leigh for almost two years, but Florence died, and now Leigh's alone and doesn't know how to un-hide herself, how to find the courage to get a public life again—until the day an unexpected event occurs during her weekly trip to buy groceries and she comes home with a cat—an unfriendly cat who's just as unhappy with the situation as she is. Her careful routine disrupted, Leigh is swept along as fate seems determined to force her out of the narrow life she's constructed.

She must act. But reemerging into everyday life won't be that simple, because the sins of the past—even though she wasn't a party to them—will come back to harm her.

Published by Grace Greene and Kersey Creek Books

ISBN-13: (eBook) 979-8-9910543-0-0

ISBN-13: (Print) 979-8-9910543-1-7

ISBN-13: (Large Print) 979-8-9910543-2-4

ISBN-13: (Hardcover) 979-8-9910543-3-1

Cover design by Grace Greene

Printed in the United States of America

Dedication

My sincere thanks to everyone who discussed this story with me as it was being developed and written. Thank you for your advice and your time. Special thanks to my cousin Teresa who introduced me to Hanover Avenue years ago (when we were much, much younger), to the shops on Cary Street, and to the absolute delight of being able to step out of the front door of her home and take the short walk to the Virginia Museum of Fine Arts. Thank you, Terry! I grew up in the county, in a more rural area, so walking the city sidewalks of the Fan District was truly an adventure. In fact, she helped me appreciate the importance of traffic lights for pedestrians crossing intersections, and saved me from injury more than once, so I dedicate this book to her, and to my other family members who helped tell this story.

Special thanks to the kindle of kittens in *A Heart Beyond*—who represent the many cats and kittens I've known and loved throughout my life, and who made my life so much richer, but this dedication would not be complete without mentioning two very special gingers, Matthew and Pumpkin, who greatly influenced and inspired the ginger in this story. *Meow to you too. Thank you for being purrfectly perfect as only a cat can be.* And a shout-out to my granddogs. They are pretty cool guys in my world, and in some of my books too.

Thank you all.

A Heart Beyond

My heart within
These walls,
This narrow house,
A haven found,
This home
That kept me safe
And hid me well,
No longer fits.

This narrow house,
These walls,
I love them yet
They cannot block
This song
That calls my heart
And leads me to
The path beyond.

—Grace Greene, July 2024

A HEART BEYOND

GRACE GREENE

Chapter One

On a Wednesday morning in mid-May, I went to the store to buy groceries and came home with a cat. It wasn't even a friendly cat—not a single purr to be heard from the creature—but to be fair, I wasn't feeling happy about the situation either.

I'd made this trip every week on foot for two years, only skipping the walk when the weather was atrocious or if I, myself, was under the weather. I carried a vinyl tote bag that my cousin, Florence, had given me. Home was only a few blocks away. Today, the sun was bright, the sky was blue, and the huge trees lining the old city streets created a dappled shade on the sidewalk that shifted gracefully in the breeze. The weather was perfect—perfectly worthy of taking time to breathe in the scents of newly blooming flowers and enjoy the birdsong in the heart of this city neighborhood.

I knew each step along my preferred routes, each crack in the sidewalk, and every root working hard to break through the concrete. I also knew the houses that lined these particular city streets—their faces, anyway. When Florence and I had been making this walk together, she'd identify the birds by their warbles and remark on the houses, the people she'd known in this house or that one, calling out which buildings were being kept up properly and which were aging not so well. Then she'd laugh and say that, as regarded aging, she was in much the same case herself. She'd remind me to slow down, that not only was I twenty years younger than her fifty-eight but my legs were longer than hers too.

Without Florence, this was a quieter trip, but more often than not, I still heard the echoes of her voice and our conversations as I walked along.

The houses here were generally two- or three-story brick, stone, or wood with an occasional small turret or other decorative elements that were favored back when these houses were built. Most had wide front porches and distinctive woodwork or decorative ironwork.

Florence was proud of this neighborhood, more broadly called the Fan District because of the shape created by the layout of the streets. She was especially proud of the part she lived in, the Museum District.

It's mostly Victorian era, you know, she'd said with delight.

The homes were old—I could see that with my own eyes—and represented most of the architectural styles that were popular during the latter 1800's through the early 1900's. Many were delightfully colorful or more sedately done—whichever best suited the individual architectural features of the houses and fit within the guidelines of the neighborhood historical committees. Many people worked to protect this pocket of time and architecture—to make it a thriving neighborhood while preserving its special flavor despite being surrounded by commerce, industry, and even abutting the huge, ever-expanding Virginia Commonwealth University. My cousin had been an ardent supporter of the preservation effort.

From my perspective, the energy and variety of people living here, many for generations, mixing with the newcomers and temporary residents, made it the perfect place for me to hide in plain sight. It was easy to mind my own business here yet blend in when I needed to be out and about. Plus, almost everything I might need—from grocery stores to museums— was within easy walking distance. When I'd arrived here two years ago, I'd parked my car in Florence's garage and hadn't moved it since.

Today, as I left the store and headed toward the intersection to cross over to Floyd Avenue, the hard edge of a can began digging into my side. My wallet and phone were also tucked in the bag with the groceries, and I didn't want to drop any of it. I managed to make it across the intersection, barely reaching the curb before stopping to adjust the bag while breathing a sigh of relief that I'd made it without dropping it altogether, when just at that moment a car came fast and close. I felt the heat from it, the nearness. Startled, I jumped forward and lost my grip on the bag.

It fell, yes, but I was able to control its landing. An avocado and a can of tuna bounced out. The avocado plopped over the curb's edge and stopped, but the can of tuna landed on its side. It took off like a tiny tin tire, rolling down the sidewalk until it hit an uneven joint between the concrete slabs and popped up into the air. It took flight, heading off toward the second or third house before it disappeared from view.

Wow. It was an amazing sight. It stirred my curiosity—

something I'd rarely felt since the awful debacle with my father. Bottom line—if the bag had spilled, the mess would've attracted attention. As it was, the incident had simply been awkward, but no one was in sight and I could shake it off and move along.

But the can . . . Where did it go?

First, I knelt to retrieve the avocado, then picked up the tote bag again. The can of tuna couldn't have gone far.

Normally, I'd cross again to the other side of Floyd to continue walking the remaining blocks to Hanover Avenue, but I could easily stay on Floyd and cross over at the next intersection instead to reach home.

Smiling fondly, I remembered what Florence had often said —*In the Fan, you can't get lost. All roads lead to home . . . eventually. Just mind which way you turn.*

I settled the tote bag straps back over my shoulder and went forward, unsuspecting and unprepared to come face-to-face with the unexpected.

****

As with most old neighborhoods, there were pockets of houses where the upkeep was struggling. *Struggling* had been Florence's polite way of saying shabby or rundown. But these houses looked pretty good. The one directly in front of me, a brown-stained stucco with a wide porch, needed a facelift and the bushes cried for the attention of a pair of clippers. As for the small patch of lawn, I couldn't tell whether it had been left to go to seed or if it was a failed attempt at a butterfly and bee garden. They were popular here. Overall, the place looked . . . quiet, if a little forgotten.

A small glint of something shiny—perhaps sunlight hitting

metal—caught my eye. It was on the ground near the passageway between this house and its neighbor.

Some of the houses in the Fan adjoined, but others had narrow alleyways between them. That was the case here. The entrance to the alleyway between this house and the next loomed ahead as a shadowy opening redolent of moist odors and dank air. And the glint of light I'd seen? It was only a bit of foil. I nudged it with the toe of my shoe, annoyed. But as I stood there, I heard a voice, soft as it funneled up the walkway, a fragile voice that communicated urgency.

Despite myself, I moved forward, listening. At first, there was nothing more, but then I heard it again . . . not a soft voice, but a weak one, crying, *Help, help.* I hurried now, pausing only to ease my tote bag down to the ground and to peek around the corner of the building before venturing into view of the back-yard itself. But as soon as I could see around the house, the elderly woman saw me too. She called out more loudly, waving her thin pale hand in earnest. She was seated in a wheelchair beside an old wrought iron table.

A fragile-looking white-haired woman in a wheelchair? Not a threat.

I stepped fully into view, asking, "Are you okay?"

The woman's thin voice cracked as she said, "Thank goodness, you're here. Late, but in time." The woman then pointed down toward a crocheted blanket lying on the patio bricks. "Can you get that for me? I'm freezing!"

She did look frail and a little shivery.

In recent years, I'd grown accustomed to not volunteering for anything, but to refuse such a small request . . . I moved forward to retrieve the blanket, and the woman gestured at her thin, hunched shoulders. I complied, carefully draping the blanket like a shawl around her. She finished the job by drawing it snugly across her chest. I noticed she had a black orthopedic boot fastened with Velcro closures on one leg that went from the sole of her foot almost up to her knee, and leaning against her knees was a cane that she clutched tightly.

This patio, this backyard, was a miserable place. Not the worst I'd seen, but not welcoming. Neglected. Tall, skinny weeds grew between the cracked and mossy bricks. A privacy fence worked with a huge tree and overgrown bushes to screen this small yard from the world. Who would leave this old woman here alone? In this damp, dark, seedy place?

Who would? Well, *someone* had, and I, Leigh Ann Eden, currently going by my grandmother's maiden name, Sonder, would too because whoever had brought the elderly woman out here would be back any moment. I wasn't needed. I didn't belong here. I could go home.

Even as the thoughts passed through my head, I was turning to go back to the passageway to reclaim my groceries and move on. This place, this odd situation, gave me an increasingly uneasy feeling. A creepy-crawly flesh-tingling feeling. Like an electrical charge brushing my skin just before a lightning strike.

Before I managed more than a step away, a door slammed behind me. I spun around and saw another woman. This one was middle-aged, with a headful of curly auburn hair pushed back with a headband. She was a larger woman, sturdy look-ing, and her face wore a decidedly disgruntled expression as she descended the porch steps to the patio while clinging to the railing, but when she saw me, she jabbed a pointing, accusing finger in my direction and called out, "You. Wait. Stand right there. Don't you move!"

The woman clambered back up the steps to the porch.

I was out of my element here. The woman had ordered me to wait, but all I wanted was to go home. I don't know why I didn't run, but I didn't. The woman only went as far as the porch and returned in a quick minute, this time carrying a large beige pet carrier. Again, she let the porch door slam as she descended the steps, even more awkwardly than before. The plastic case banged against the wooden railing several times, and the creature inside howled, angry and objecting, and surely frightened.

The woman, gripping the handle with both hands, pushed it toward me. Reflexively, I put my hands out to stop her, to ward off the carrier.

She gave the case a little shake, clearly impatient. "Here. Take it. We're late."

I shook my head. "I'm sorry, there's been a mistake. I wanted . . ." *My can of tuna.* How could I say that? How odd it would sound. I should just leave. Thinking that, I stepped backward.

"Doesn't matter," the woman said, dismissing me rudely. "We're late. We must go." She tried to force the handle of the carrier into my hands.

I resisted. This was absurd behavior. It felt like a brawl between strangers for no rational reason, and I wanted *out*. But when the woman released the handle abruptly, I grabbed it because otherwise the carrier, and the creature inside, would've crashed to the ground. Even so, I moved directly to the patio table to set the case there. I would divest myself of it and leave before this ridiculous situation proceeded further.

The old woman fixed her faded blue eyes on me. She asked hoarsely, "If not you, then who?"

Her whispery tone was sane and solemn. I heard her and understood her as if we shared a pocket of time wherein the action had stopped cold and allowed absolute, unemotional clarity. But for all that, the woman might as well have been speaking a foreign language, because every cell in my body refused this—this insanity.

Harsher words came from the sturdy woman who was now moving behind the wheelchair releasing the brakes. "The pound will."

I gestured back toward the passageway where I'd left my bag. "I went to the grocery store and—"

The sturdy woman frowned. "We're behind schedule. You're late, so we're late." Her words dripped with an *I-couldn't-care-less-and-you're-in-my-way* overtone.

Late? Shades of the White Rabbit?

This wasn't Wonderland, and I wasn't Alice. I couldn't think of anything sensible to say in the middle of this . . . whatever this craziness was.

The sturdy woman told the elderly one, "Keep your feet on the footrests and your hands on your lap. We'll fit, but barely," as she pushed the wheelchair past me, toward the passageway and the bag of groceries I'd left there.

Leaving the cat carrier on the table, I scurried around the women, wanting to reach the passageway first. "My bag . . ." The last thing I needed was for my groceries to be scattered across the dirty, dank bricks. I snagged the tote bag and dragged it out of the way, all the while grabbing for items as they rolled free.

The woman pushed past me, moving the wheelchair with force. The old lady shouted back at me—or to someone—something that sounded like, "Better late than never, Suzie Q. The cat is hungry!"

I stood there in disbelief, maybe in shock, but wasting precious seconds as I clutched the handle of the grocery tote still sitting between my feet. I stared blankly ahead at the passageway and then over at the cat. The cat yowled. I dropped the bag handle and stepped forward, stumbling over the tote and sending more items rolling as I ran after the two women, calling out, "Wait! There's been a mistake!"

A van was pulling away from the curb as I reached it. There were no other vehicles in sight, and this one looked handicap accessible—a van with a wheelchair ramp. *Had to be them.* I chased after it, catching glimpses of the women's dark silhouettes inside, but the van kept going and I couldn't keep up.

The woman had said they were late. Maybe a doctor's appointment or such? The old woman had said something about being late too.

Better late than never . . . Yes, that's what she'd said. *Suzie Q? What the heck did she mean by that?*

The cat's hungry. She'd said that too.

Dazed, I scratched my head, mussing my neat ponytail. I looked up and down the street. No one else was around. I stared back at the house. The windows were dark. I hurried up to the front porch to press the doorbell and try the doorknob. It was locked and there was no response.

Slowly, stunned, I returned to the passageway and the backyard to reclaim my groceries, checking to make sure my phone and wallet were still there in the tote. The carrier was on the table as I'd left it. A cat's face was pressed against the metal wire door. A dirty nose and tufts of dusty, drab-looking orange fur poked out between the wires of the metal door grille.

The animal hissed.

I didn't blame the cat. I didn't like this either. Not the craziness. Not this feeling of being taken advantage of. And I was most definitely *not* in the market for a cat.

The neighboring houses were close on each side, though obscured by the foliage and fence. A detached garage, maybe in use as a shed, but in an advanced state of deterioration, was at the back of the tiny yard. But there were people in the houses, and surely some of them knew the old woman . . .

assuming she lived here, and my instinct said she did. One of the neighbors might take the cat in until its owner returned.

In that instant, the key to this puzzle hit me. The explanation bloomed in my brain like a full-color image—or in shades of gray like those sweet, intriguing Bogart or Grant classic movies from the forties and fifties. This was a simple case of mistaken identity, and at any moment the canned laugh track would play in the background.

These two women had been expecting someone to pick the cat up, to take it somewhere. For a while or forever? Who knew? But they hadn't *met* that person. The coincidence of the timing and me showing up while they were waiting for the person . . . the pet-sitter . . . was the unexpected event that had triggered the rest. That was it. That made sense. Except what had the sturdy woman said? That if I didn't take the cat, the pound would?

My breath caught. Okay, but that wasn't my problem, was it? This wasn't my cat.

Not my cat. Not my business.

Feeling slightly desperate, I went up the steps and to the back porch. The screen door was unlocked. The porch was empty, except for the peeling paint and city grime. The back door of the house was solidly locked. I peered through the dirty glass of the back door's window but saw only a dark interior, too dim to make out anything, but no one was in there. I could tell by the overwhelming sense of emptiness.

I didn't want a role in this movie, classic or not. Could I leave the cat on the porch? Would it be safe here until the women returned?

But when would they return? Would it even be today? This week?

As I descended the steps to the patio, I glanced up, noting

the clouds rolling in. The day had been lovely but not overly warm. Tonight would be chilly, especially if it rained.

Guilt rose in me. Was I truly capable of abandoning the cat —helpless and caged—for my own convenience? I shuddered.

Okay, so I would consider my options logically.

This cat wasn't my responsibility. I didn't have food for it. Not even that stupid can of tuna I'd lost.

The cat glared at me through the bars, its face smashed against the grille. I had already heard the claws scraping against the plastic carrier and I could see those sharp teeth when it hissed at me. Two blazing amber eyes were fixed on me from between those tufts of drab orangey fur.

What should I do? I sighed, suddenly exhausted by all this. I wanted to be home.

The fidgety feeling I dreaded had started. Anxiety built inside me when I was out of the house too long and felt too exposed. And no wonder. Look what had just happened . . . which totally validated my fears.

I looked at the cat again and then the tote bag. I couldn't carry both.

But then, past the patio and the straggly grass beyond, and next to the shed, I saw an old wagon. Perhaps bright red long ago, now it was rusty, dented, and scratched. It was a typical kid's wagon, but old and abused. A few twigs and leaves littered the bottom.

I pulled the wagon over to the patio. The solid rubber tires rolled well enough to serve my purpose.

The wagon bed wouldn't hold both the tote full of groceries and the cat carry case, yet managing the very full tote bag on my shoulder while pulling the child's wagon with my free arm would be terribly awkward.

But I had a plan. Having a plan always made the difference.

Keeping my fingers well away from the cutouts in the plastic, I settled the carrier in the wagon. For the first time, I noticed a name scrawled on the back end of the carrier in black marker. The ink had mostly worn off, but it clearly said *HARVEY*.

"Okay, Harvey," I said. "I guess we're in this together for the present, but not for long. That I promise you."

The cat, Harvey, ignored me. I could do the same, right?

I emptied as many grocery items as I could fit into the remaining space in the wagon bed. I hoped the canned goods and boxed products would help anchor the carrier. I could carry the now-lighter tote on my shoulder more easily and manage the wagon with my free arm.

Being so tall . . . the juxtaposition of me versus the low-riding kiddie wagon would look ridiculous—which meant I would be more visible, more noticeable than I liked. Being forgettable had served me well since Dad's schemes had crashed three years ago and I'd been pulled into the chaos of it. Avoiding notice had become a habit—that's what Florence had said.

It occurred to me that this—me taking the cat for tonight—could be viewed as a good deed. It had been a while since I'd done something nice for anyone other than Florence. Maybe it was time. Past time. That's what Florence had been telling me when she got sick. *Time to get out more often, Leigh Ann. Time to get closer to people again.*

So today could be the good deed (acknowledging that I was only doing this because I could think of no better plan), but come morning, I'd return the wagon along with the cat and carrier to this house on Floyd Avenue whether the act was in keeping with good deeds or not.

I shivered. The cat looked mean. It was probably just scared. *Maybe.*

As I pulled the wagon behind me, softly apologizing to the cat for the rumbly, bumpy ride along the brick passageway, I emerged from the shadows between the houses and into the sunshine. My shoe kicked something. I looked down.

I'd kicked a can.

Of tuna.

Chapter Two

I knew how I looked to those who saw me—a tall, thin woman pulling a beleaguered wagon loaded with a beige cat carrier and an assortment of groceries, with a large tote hanging from her shoulder that bumped awkwardly against her hip as she walked along the sidewalk of a residential city street. I stood erect and kept my eyes focused ahead. I was bound to get stares.

If I'd had any pride left, I might not have been able to manage this odd parade with dignity, but I knew how to do this. Even as people gave me looks, I kept my expression mild and didn't acknowledge their stares, in effect saying I was slightly above the humdrum, not someone to trifle with, and certainly not someone singular enough to remember.

It was the runway view that, when focused enough, could override present reality. I didn't smooth my hair. Each strand was in place and I knew it (even if it *wasn't*). I didn't adjust my sunglasses. They were perched perfectly atop a nose that photographers had once declared worthy of envy. I took no personal gratification in my high cheekbones or my long neck —deemed graceful and classic by those in the industry who decided such things—because those features were no more than an accident of birth and DNA. And when life went way wrong, those things couldn't console or save you.

The focus and self-control I'd learned in my childhood had translated well into my short career as a model, but I'd polished that image to a shining gloss as the public face of a PR firm in which I was a partner for ten years—a better fit for me than the modeling. My light brown hair had grown long over the past two years and had lost its perfect cut and any hint of dye or highlights, but the advantage of such benign neglect was that I could clip it back out of the way easily—and the change in my appearance added distance between how people had seen me then and how I looked now. I kept my public face impassive, remote, and vaguely aloof. That aloof façade had served me well when I lived in the public eye. It had continued to do so as privacy and anonymity had become essential to my sanity. I wore that remote, yet benevolent expression like a mask, shaped to control what others could read on my face.

Emotionally, I was badly damaged. Inside my head, I was a mess, terrified of the unexpected, of strangers, of everything that might be beyond my control. But my exterior disguise as *forgettable* had been perfected. The better I performed this role, the calmer I felt inside. When I was home, behind closed doors, I could let the angst out, though the usefulness of that release was questionable.

At the end of this block of Floyd, I turned left. Only a few blocks yet to go. *Head up. Eyes ahead. And keep moving.*

As I (and the cat) turned the corner onto Hanover Avenue, my street, I breathed more easily. Almost home. We were almost safe . . . and then the cat started yowling.

The noise was a repeated hoarse shrieking that even I couldn't pretend wasn't happening.

Nothing had changed from the prior moment to this one. I

stopped to check the cat as best I could with it crouched in the carrier—a huge, largely indistinguishable mess of orange fur except for the paw hooking its claws in the wire mesh of the door.

How did one pretend this horrific racket was okay? Just shake it off as one of those things? Only in the land of psychopaths and serial killers. People would hear the shrieking and get curious, and they'd stare at me and ask questions and . . .

Panic hit me. *Not allowed,* I told myself. I pressed a hand to my midsection and tried to bring the panic down to a manageable level with slow, even breaths.

"Leigh Ann? Hello there."

I jumped. Mr. Marshburn offered a reassuring smile. My neighbor. An older man, fatherly, gentlemanly, who was always pleasant. I tried to smile politely, but the cat continued to howl in outrage.

"Sounds like he's upset." He bent over, his hands on his knees, and spoke to the cat through the door grille. "Hey, fella." He glanced up. "Is it a fella? Most ginger cats are, you know. What's its name?"

I should know its name. I was so busy hiding my distress that my brain wasn't working in any useful way. I shook my head, seeing nothing more helpful than the women's faces and the brown stucco house and . . . the name on the carrier. "Harvey," I said, thinking I'd need to get into the bizarre story about what had happened . . . but Mr. Marshburn seemed instantly satisfied, so I shut up.

"Nice," Mr. Marshburn said and smiled again. He returned his attention to the cat. "Hello there, Harvey."

The cat's shrieks hadn't altogether stopped, but the screeching effect had softened and diminished to more like a series of strident cat complaints.

"The cat's not mine."

"No?" He nodded, saying, "I didn't recall seeing a cat at your house." He smiled pleasantly. "They are fond of sitting in windows, you know."

"Sitting . . . Yes, I'm cat-sitting. For an old woman I met. She had an urgent appointment."

He nodded again. "An emergency?"

"Yes. I'm not prepared for it. For a cat, I mean. Sorry for the noise." I forced myself to smile again.

"Very kind of you to help your friend. Harvey is probably off-kilter, missing his person and being away from home."

For a split second, I tried to remember who Harvey was. The cat, of course.

Mr. Marshburn frowned ever so slightly. "Have you ever cared for a cat?"

"No," I said and felt better admitting to at least that nugget of truth. "I've never had a pet of any kind."

"How long are you expecting Harvey to be visiting you? I see you have groceries, but did your friend give you a litter box? Food?"

I nearly gasped. "No. It happened so quickly."

"Urgent appointment? Was she sick?"

He noticed a lot. He was asking a lot of questions.

"I really should get him in the house. Help him calm down." Help myself to calm down too. My heart was about to slam right out of my chest and shatter this controlled mask that was seriously faltering.

"Quite right, Leigh Ann. You should call me Samuel, you know. We've been neighbors for a couple of years now. If you don't mind, might I suggest that you talk to Marla?"

"In the blue house? Ms. Johnson, you mean?"

"Yes. Marla has several cats. It would drive me bonkers,

but she loves them. Anyway, she probably has food and litter to spare."

"That's an excellent idea. Thank you, Mr. Marshburn."

"Samuel."

"Samuel. Thank you for the suggestion."

"I'll be on my way. I'm meeting an old friend for lunch." He nodded, and raising his hand to his forehead, he executed a fake tipping of a nonexistent hat. "Let me know if I may be of assistance."

He walked away, and I realized that Harvey had stopped making those dreadful noises. I'd better move now and get him inside. And then I'd break a rule, the one that said I never asked anyone for a favor.

I'd made the rule. It was mine to break. I might pay an anxiety price, but better that than not having toilet facilities for . . . Harvey. Thank goodness that Samuel Marshburn had suggested Marla. Marla had cats. Her house was directly across the street from me. I'd seen them in her windows quite often. I wasn't chummy with her, but we'd nodded in passing a few times. Florence had considered her a good friend.

But first, Harvey needed to be inside the house, for both our sakes—before he started howling again. Hopefully, he'd feel more *on-kilter* within the safety of the house.

I always did.

****

I hauled the cat in its carrier up to the porch and into the house, then left the carrier and groceries in the foyer before hurrying across to Marla's house. If Marla could help me, that would be the best possible outcome for today. Tomorrow morning, first thing, I'd load that cat carrier, complete with cat, onto the wagon and transport Harvey right back to where he'd come from.

But meanwhile, I was standing on Marla's porch and the sound of the doorbell's ring was still fading as she opened the front door. Before I could speak, Marla said, "Samuel called. He told me you have a cat now?"

"Temporarily," I said carefully.

"Come on in."

"I can't stay." I nodded back toward my house as if that explained why.

"This will only take a minute. Do you need litter and supplies? I've got plenty."

"That's very generous of you."

Marla looked surprised. "No problem. I'll be right back."

She disappeared briefly in the direction of the kitchen, then returned with a plastic kitchen sink tub. Kitty litter was already spread in the bottom of it. Both the tub and litter were clean and fresh. Marla handed the tub to me and set a plastic bag on top of the litter. She smiled brightly, saying, "There are several cans of food and a small container of dry food. Some kitties are picky. Not sure which type of food yours prefers."

"Thank you. What do I owe you?"

Marla's eyes opened wide. "Oh, not a thing. My pleasure."

"But—"

"Don't fret about owing me anything. I promise I'll call on you when I'm out of town and need someone to feed and water my kitty crew."

"Oh. Of course." I nodded. "Even so, thank you."

Marla moved suddenly, diving forward in alarm, which startled me almost into dropping the tub, litter, and food, but in the next moment, I realized she was moving to intercept a black cat who was attempting to escape through the gap left by the open door. Having retrieved the cat, and now holding it one-handed and close to her chest, she smiled again.

"Got him. Badger's a tricky one. Always so eager to get out, but then when he does, he hides in the bushes afraid of every noise." She rubbed her cheek against his head, smushing his ear. He didn't seem to mind, but he did meow, and she made baby talk noises in return. She said, "I'd best close this door before the others make a break for it."

"Thanks again."

****

My home was two houses up from the Marshburn residence and directly across the street from Marla's. Looking at my home from the vantage point of Marla's front steps, the difference between mine and most of the other homes on this block was unmistakable. My house was narrower and smaller, yes, but I wasn't talking about the size. There was something else.

Did the house or the plantings look seedy or unkempt? Like it was *struggling*? Perhaps verging into invisibility? I hoped not. Simple and understated was the goal.

The porch had a large potted plant and a wicker chair set with a table between them, but I rarely sat there. Porch-sitting was too much like being on stage, like encouraging personal interaction. I'd left the friendly-neighbor activity to Florence. Now the wicker chairs could use a bit of a washup. The plant might be too far gone to save.

How would Florence judge my efforts at upkeep? I'd been greatly blessed when she took me in. I was meticulous about the state of the interior. I should do a better job of caring for the outside of her house.

I'd have to think about that later. Just now, I had a cat

named Harvey waiting for me, captive in that carrier and probably hungry. Hadn't the old woman said the cat needed to be fed?

****

Harvey howled in a loud, demanding voice when I entered the foyer.

I stopped just inside the door to slip off my sneakers. I carried the cat supplies back to the kitchen as he continued his howling meows . . . *meowling* . . . until I hurried back to let him out of his carrier. Even as I tried to squeeze the latch to unlock the door, my fingers were under assault. I received only one tiny scratch, and I might've done that myself in my clumsy fumbling with the latch. The door swung open maybe an inch, and I stepped back quickly, expecting him to rush me. But no, he hung back now, his amber eyes glowing and looking almost possessed as he stared. He moved slowly toward the opening and paused to hiss at me.

Was he feral? Was he housebroken? How big a mistake had I made in bringing him here?

Suddenly, the wire mesh door flew open as he barreled out at a fast clip. He ran past me, keeping his eyes fixed on me, accusing me, and then he scurried down the hallway toward the kitchen at the back of the house.

Calm down, Leigh. Not great, but also not terrible. At least he'd find the food and water dishes and the litter box back there.

The foyer opened into the small living room on the left. In between the living room and kitchen was an even smaller dining room, but from the foyer the hallway was a straight shot back to the kitchen, passing a guest half bath fitted in under the stairway. As I walked along the hallway, I knew the cat would likely run the other way, but that was okay too. At least he'd know where to find what he needed when he needed it.

For now, my objective was to make sure no *mistakes* happened on Florence's lovingly maintained dark wooden floors. I was particular in how I kept them, just as my cousin had been. Some things were easily fixable, but urine-stained floors weren't in that category.

When I reached the kitchen, I chose a can of savory chicken cat food. *Thank you, Marla.* I tapped the lid with my fingernail until I sensed the cat was near, then I flipped up the lid key and snapped it open. The metal pulled back with a slight hiss. And yes, there was Harvey, crazed eyes and all, staring at me from around the corner of the doorway to the dining room.

I went to the litter box and pointed. "This is for you." Then I returned to the counter and spooned the food into a dish.

He continued glaring, staring at me as I set the dish on the floor and placed a bowl of water beside it.

He's waiting for me to leave.

So I took a moment to unlock the kitchen door and the door to the back porch, and then I donned my shoes again and left. I needed to stow the wagon anyway.

The front yard was tiny, and the backyard wasn't much bigger. At the very back was a privacy fence between my yard and the alley. On the left side was the ancient single-car garage that opened front and back. The back of the garage opened directly into the alley, as did a small gate in the privacy fence.

The garage was in decent shape, considering how old and forgotten it was. And while it was chock-full of years of junk, plus my car, it was not currently in use. The bushes back here needed trimming. But I assured myself that, while overgrown, they weren't as monstrous as those at the brown house on Floyd.

The wagon was already chipped and battered, so there seemed little point in putting it out of the weather into the garage. No need to open the garage.

I pulled the wagon up next to the porch. Tomorrow morning the cat and I had a date to return to that house, to confront either or both of the women who'd made this cat my problem. He would be returned to where he belonged.

****

Harvey wasn't in the kitchen, but the food had been nibbled at.

The litter landscape had little hills and valleys. It looked like he'd pawed at it, which was good I thought, but it didn't appear to have been used, which worried me. Florence had kept her wood plank floors pristine. If the cat preferred to do his toilet business behind the sofa or in a corner—that would be unacceptable.

"Harvey?" I searched the first floor, seeking him, even though I could hardly expect him to respond to me, a stranger. Illogical. But then this whole frustrating, confusing series of events was bizarre. Unfortunately, it was also reality.

I paused in the foyer at the base of the stairs. Might he have gone upstairs to hide?

In his world, I was the bad guy.

This was going from bad to worse.

What should I do? Go up and try to find him? That would probably scare him more. I could ignore him. Maybe he'd get curious and that might draw him out.

I went back to the kitchen, this time to fix *my* food. Maybe lunch would help my attitude. It occurred to me that the sounds and smells of cooking food in the kitchen might draw him back out.

Or what about that can of tuna fish?

I laughed. Only a little, yes, but I was surprised to hear even a chuckle coming from me. I hadn't laughed out loud in . . . how long?

Okay. Tuna fish, then. It might be pungent enough to draw him out. If he was still hiding later, I'd give it a try. If it didn't work . . . well, I'd think of something else.

Frankly, there wasn't anywhere much to hide, upstairs or down. I hadn't changed the house since Florence had died. She'd kept the furnishings lean and the house tidy, and it suited me well to go on as she'd done. But then I hadn't anticipated taking in a furry boarder, had I?

****

Tidy and lean décor. Simple. Minimal. Nowhere to hide.

Tell that to the cat, I thought.

As the day progressed, I gave up trying to find Harvey or even draw him out with appetizing smells. I would ignore him, letting the vaunted curiosity inherent in cats bring him out of hiding. And eventually he did come out, sort of, as a low-crouching form silently slinking from one shadowed spot to the next.

So the scruffy creature had snuck down, nibbled at the food, and used the litter box. But the food, the litter, and even the folded blanket I'd put on the floor as a welcome to reassure him had failed as overtures of friendship, because Harvey had chosen a dark corner in the room, mostly hidden by the bulk of the sofa, from which to hunch and glare, clearly not open to fraternization.

I stayed away from that corner of the room and pretended not to see my feline guest. I sat in the padded rocker. This gooseneck rocker had been Florence's. The other chair, she called the guest chair. Normally, I'd put my feet up on the ottoman and read or watch a movie while I ate. But something about the cat, or this stand-off, made it impossible for me to relax.

Frustrated, I went to clean up the already clean kitchen, all the while slamming a drawer or two and banging a cabinet door.

Because of the cat.

I wanted to open the door and shout, *Go for it. Run free. Get out of my house.* But I didn't because Harvey wasn't my cat. Tomorrow he'd go back to where he belonged. No question.

In my usual late-afternoon routine, I'd go to my desk in the small study off the end of the living room, do my usual sorting, reading, whatever, and I resolved to do exactly that. Harvey had everything he needed to safely maintain his hostile, miserable attitude without being allowed to ruin the rest of my day too.

But as afternoon moved into evening and darkness set in, the cat made weird rumbly, growling noises.

"Hush," I said to the shadows, deeper now such that I could hardly see him. He hid even better than I did.

He hissed.

So be it, then. "Have it your way," I said aloud.

This cat smelled. He needed a trip to the vet and a serious day of grooming. Between his hiding and that thick, unkempt fur coat he wore, I wasn't even certain he was a he. Might be a she. Might be neutered . . . or not.

In frustration, I slapped the arms of my chair. It didn't matter. *Nothing* I could do at this moment mattered whatsoever. Switching off the television, I said, "Suit yourself, Harvey. Be a grump. You're going home tomorrow anyway."

The cat poked its head just past the doorframe between the

living room and the dining room. It looked directly at me and meowed.

For the first time. A meow.

The sound was rough and coarse.

I frowned. Had he injured his voice box somehow? Maybe it was an old injury? Or had he strained his voice with all that yowling and howling?

Why was I speculating? It didn't matter.

Even so, I tried to entice the cat into the carrier for bedtime but wasn't surprised when the attempt failed. If I were him, I wouldn't willingly go back in there either.

When I went upstairs to bed that night, I shut my door. No cats were welcome here during the night, thank you very much. Harvey had food, water, and a litter box in the kitchen and seemed to know what to do with them. I'd moved that cozy, worn blanket to that dark corner he seemed to prefer. He'd have a spot to sleep where he wouldn't feel confined or trapped—if he chose to use it.

My parting words to the cat, wherever he was hiding now, were, "You're on your own, Harvey. Be as grumpy as you like, all by yourself."

How much trouble could he get into?

I was willing to take the risk. After all, it was only for one night.

Chapter Three

My father's fall from success had happened fast when his fraudulent financial schemes became known. State and federal investigators swarmed, the media did likewise, and I was blindsided by all of it. After the investigations were complete and Dad's trial and conviction for . . . well, numerous counts, most of which centered primarily around investment fraud, New York no longer loved him, and their angry disdain included his ex-wife and daughter, and the daughter's fiancé—now ex-fiancé. I'd abandoned my apartment in the city, driving straight through to Florida to stay at my mother's home, but that hadn't lasted long, and I'd ended up here in Richmond with Florence. Two years ago now. And except for Dad being in prison, nothing had changed for the better.

After I'd adjusted to the change in night noises from New York to Richmond, my predictably sound sleep resumed. That night—my first night with a cat in the house—went as usual until three a.m., when Harvey let loose with the yowls again.

I sat up abruptly, staring and seeing nothing but total darkness. That pitch dark aligned with the yowls nearly tipped me over into full panic until I remembered I was wearing a sleep mask. To the tune of Harvey's howls, I ripped the mask off and tossed it aside as I kicked the coverlet out of the way.

The cat must be in agony, perhaps even fatally wounded. Something dreadful had happened to the poor creature.

I dashed to the bedroom door, flipped the key to unlock it, flung the door wide, and ran out to the stairs, intent on rescuing Harvey from whatever was hurting him. The noise had stopped. I listened and heard nothing. Had he died? Could I reach him and save him before it was too late? And then I saw him.

Harvey was at the base of the stairs. Just sitting. Maybe waiting. He seemed unperturbed.

Breathing hard, I stopped to catch my breath and gather my wits. Harvey was no more than a dark, silent form as he stared up at me. His eyes picking up reflected light from the foyer lamp were unnervingly bright.

"Harvey?" I dared to take one step down. "Are you hurt?"

If he isn't hurt, I might hurt him.

Grimacing, I shook my head. Angry or not, that threat was bluster, pure and simple. So far, I hadn't even been able to catch him.

Keeping my hand on the banister, I descended two more steps, taking them carefully and feeling the old wood, smooth and cool beneath my bare feet. As I passed the halfway mark, Harvey ran, vanishing down the hallway with surprising speed.

He wasn't injured or sick, it seemed.

I wanted to feel relieved, and maybe I did a little. But since no emergency was apparent, it was becoming clear that this cat's caterwauling had been outrageously unnecessary. Spiteful.

Caterwauling. I hadn't known I knew that word.

By now, I'd reached the bottom step. I stopped in the darkness of the foyer and looked back along its length. The cat was sitting at the far end of the hallway, positioned just inside the open doorway to the kitchen. The moonlight filtered in through the kitchen window, backlighting him and spilling around him. The bluish light created a feathery outline of his fur and cast his form into a dark silhouette.

Whatever his game was, I wasn't enjoying it.

Maybe he'd eaten the food or finished the water and had summoned me to refill the bowls? *Great.* Now I was *truly* annoyed.

I walked down the hallway, staring at the cat who was staring at me. I might not've seen the hazard in time even if I'd been watching my step because it was very dark in this area of the hallway and I hadn't turned on other lights. When the sole of my foot planted itself on the soft, still-warm body, I may have screamed. I screamed inside for sure, and bright spots danced before my eyes in the dark around me. I jumped a foot at least. When I landed, it wasn't done gracefully. My foot hit the rodent's body a second time. Its corpse slipped. I slipped more. When I landed, my shoulder hit the wall. I bounced off and slammed flat on my back. I lay there in pain, trying to draw air back into my lungs.

In the kitchen, Harvey was lapping at the water dish, and then I heard him shifting the litter around in the box. When I opened my eyes again, finally able to get a full breath without big pain, it was to see Harvey watching me with his golden eyes and staying just out of reach.

He meowed.

I thrust my arm toward him, not really sure of my intent, but he scooted back a few more inches. I let my arm drop back down to the floor, then rolled over very slowly and began the gradual process of getting to my knees and to my feet. When I made it upright, I put my hand flat against the wall and leaned there for a long minute.

City houses. Country homes. Many buildings had mice. One never saw them until one did—or a cat caught one and brought it to you as a gift or a trophy.

Florence had lived in this house for most of her life. I'd come to live with her after the . . . the defining event in my life, the disaster that had ended my way of life as I'd known it. Her taking me in had been a sanity-saver. She'd gotten ill about nine months ago and passed three months later, but before she died, she deeded the house to me. So pests were my problem.

Florence had talked about her beloved cat Cookie, who'd been a great mouser. Back then, when she'd told me, I'd scanned the room, had all but picked my feet up from the floor to tuck them up into the chair with me, safe from mice. Florence laughed and assured me that all the mouse holes had been filled up and there hadn't been a problem in years.

It seemed that had changed. I needed to call a pest control company specializing in rodents. For now, the mouse disposal was up to me. *Yuck.*

Thanks, Harvey.

****

When the disposal was completed, I ignored the cat, wherever he was, and went back up to bed. This time, in addition to my eye cover, I found the earplugs I'd used to block out Florence's snores still tucked into the corner of the nightstand drawer. They were old, but they'd do. I closed the bedroom door and slept the rest of the night without disturbance.

In the morning, my shoulder and elbow ached, but it was nothing I couldn't deal with.

This morning, I would resolve this problem that had been thrust upon me—literally. Harvey was going home. Whoever was there at the house, I'd refuse to take no for an answer. To that end, I brought a bath towel downstairs. I'd considered this carefully and had envisioned exactly how it should go. Bracing the back end of the carrier against the wall, I opened the metal door as wide as it would go. When Harvey's back was turned to eat or drink, I intended to swoop down with the open towel for a swift grab. I'd wrap him up, both to protect him from injury and likewise myself, and then I'd shove him like a sausage into the cage.

Apparently, Harvey had slept comfortably, having spent the night in my rocker. I knew because he'd left a quantity of orange hair half-woven into the upholstery and the lap blanket. He'd probably heard the boards creaking upstairs as I dressed and planned his capture, and thus had resumed hiding from me.

But not entirely. I'd catch him peeking around corners or from shadowed areas like from behind chairs as I oh-so-casually walked through the first-floor rooms holding that towel. He kept his eyes on me and kept his distance.

I conceded we'd reached a stalemate.

Fine. Okay.

So I was back to the part of the plan I could control—confronting Harvey's owner.

I refilled his water and gave him another scoop of food. Aggravated, I said, "So now I need to make an extra trip to the store for a lint roller, in addition to confronting those women, all thanks to you." Then I grinned unpleasantly at him, in effect baring my teeth. He just stared at me from the other side of the doorway between the dining room and the kitchen. I responded by venting my frustration in more words—my form of hissing, perhaps. "As a matter of fact, Harvey, when I tell that woman to come and fetch you, I'll also tell her she needs to pay for the lint roller."

Hah. Told him.

Complaining to a cat. How sad. For me, that is. The cat didn't care.

I rubbed my arm and tested my shoulder.

Harvey stared. He'd moved into the open doorway. I watched as he swished his tail and then took off again.

He'd been out in the open this time, and I'd gotten the best look at him that I'd had thus far. He was one big ball of thick, dirty orange fur. Crouched as he'd been, I couldn't see where his sides ended and his thigh bones began. With an elderly owner, I could imagine he didn't get enough exercise. They probably napped all day. And yet . . . I had a moment of doubt, and then just as quickly dismissed it.

Not my cat. Harvey needed a serious visit to a vet. *Not my problem.*

Even so, I felt a stir of sympathy. None of this was Harvey's fault. Nor was it mine. We shared at least that much. And I couldn't explain any of it to him.

Florence had talked about her cat until my eyes had glazed over. I'd tried not to let my cousin see because I appreciated her kindness. Marla had given food and litter out of kindness to me. And Samuel Marshburn, with his polite hello, had directed me to Marla.

Harvey didn't understand their kindness or appreciate any of it, though he would surely have meowled all over again if he were lacking the food part.

He just took, as pets did, limited only by what was offered. And without the least display of gratitude. The most I got back was those eyes fixed on me in accusation and the tail-swish dismissal.

But I couldn't explain the problem to him, or the unfairness of it—for either of us.

Complaining to a cat was a fast track to being reminded that I, myself, was easily dismissed.

Yes, even a cat's dismissal stung.

****

I believed in setting the stage. Planning was the best way to ensure the desired outcome. I'd learned that as my parents' daughter, had strengthened that process in my modeling career, and it had served me well, especially when I moved to the public relations arena. For today, the slacks and blouse I chose, my neatly pulled-back hair, and my controlled demeanor would communicate sincerity and seriousness. I hoped for a polite exchange but was prepared to use sharper words if necessary.

When I reached the house on Floyd Avenue, I marched straight up the front steps to the porch to knock on the front door—and then did a double take. Half-hidden in the bushes was a sign—*For Sale.*

What?

The sign didn't look new, but not ancient either. Safe to assume the sign wasn't where it was intended to be; otherwise, I would've seen it sooner.

I rang the doorbell but there was no response, so then I knocked. I knocked again very firmly before finally grabbing the rough, worn knob and twisting it for all I was worth.

Locked, no question about it. The front windows were easily reached from the porch, so I peered through the dirty glass.

The interior was dim, but bare walls, bare floors . . . that's all I could make out.

This house was *totally* vacant.

No, this can't be. I tried the door again. No change.

This house hadn't been emptied overnight. This made no sense. Much as the day before hadn't.

Now what?

A phone number was handwritten on the For Sale sign in big, scrawled digits.

I pulled my cell phone from my tote and called the number. It rang once, then went to a series of tones that finished with a tinny message.

The number was no longer in service.

Rummaging in my tote, I found a slip of paper and a pen, and wrote the house number down. Perhaps I could call the city or state property tax or land offices with the address and find out some info that would help me identify or locate the women.

Before giving up, I walked down that nasty passageway and into the backyard. The patio was as I remembered it, complete with weeds. The patio table was the same, with peeling paint and large areas of rust.

But this time there was no one in sight.

****

I went straight across to the grocery store and purchased the lint brush and a few other items, including some cat essentials. I didn't purchase mousetraps. It had been a decision, not an oversight.

Reality was reality. I tried to believe a random mouse had wandered inside all on its lonesome, but I couldn't. Maybe it wasn't too late to prevent an infestation, but I wasn't the gal to do it. When I got home, I'd look online or ask a neighbor for a reference.

Returning from the grocery store, as I waited for the *Walk* light, I urged myself to stop at the brown house one more time.

I should knock on the neighbors' doors. Just that. So simple. I would ask if they knew anything about the two women and their cat.

My shoes took me there, but I was stuck on the sidewalk, staring at the houses, unable to do more.

Yes, I could ask my neighbors about exterminators. Some of them, anyway, because I sort of knew them. I knew what to expect from them.

But it was different here. I had no idea who'd be in these houses.

And that was also reality.

I was pretty sure I saw a curtain move at the window of the house next door.

I pushed myself to boldly go up onto that porch. Perspiration broke out along my hairline and the back of my neck as I pressed the doorbell. I waited, my panic growing and me trying to control it with slow, even breathing. When no one answered the door, I closed my eyes, grateful.

Walking around these neighborhood streets had been a big step for me early on. Going with Florence had eased me into it. But strangers . . . talking to strangers . . . not knowing who might be on the other side of the door . . . that was a double risk. It was too much for me.

I'd tried, right? For now, so be it. Trying would have to be good enough.

Just call me a *coward*.

Chapter Four

Defeated. Was that the word for this heavy feeling in my heart?

Cowardly. Yes. I couldn't even knock on a freaking door because someone might actually answer it.

What a failure I'd become. My prior life must've been as fake as a façade on an Old West saloon movie set because everything I'd built, everything I was proud of, every stick of which had come crashing down around me, had blown away like a tumbleweed on the wind in an instant of time. And I was making no effort to reclaim that life. I'd given up.

As I walked home, I tried to keep my usual controlled expression on my face but found it difficult. When I turned the corner onto Hanover Avenue, Mr. Marshburn . . . Samuel . . . was getting out of a car at the curb. Before closing the door, he leaned back inside as if speaking to the driver. He'd seen me coming before leaning back in, and I'd seen that car before, so I guessed Sam Jr. was behind the wheel. Too late to avoid him now.

A year ago, Florence had schemed with Mr. Marshburn to set me up with his son. Yikes—the matchmaking machinations between Florence, a woman who'd never married, and her neighbor, Mr. Marshburn, a widower, was a wasted effort. Anyone with any sense could've seen it wouldn't work out well. Even if all other conditions had been right, I was struggling, still deep in my misery. And Sam Jr. had recently had a broken engagement. I knew the pain of such breakups. It amazed me that otherwise caring, honest people could be so oblivious, and devious, for a cause they saw as good.

Today, Mr. Marshburn waved as he moved away from the car and turned toward his house, and at that same moment, his son, Sam Jr., stepped out of the vehicle. He stood there as tall as ever, which, I was convinced, was the reason my cousin and Mr. Marshburn thought we were destined for each other.

"Leigh, how are you?"

Sam Jr. smiled. I returned it politely, fully intending to continue walking, but he kept smiling and I had to stop or seem deliberately rude.

He nodded at my tote bag. "Out for a walk? Nice day for it."

I shrugged. "Nice day. Needed a few things at the store."

"Yeah. I hear you have a cat now."

"Your dad told you?"

He nodded. "I was surprised."

"It's not a big thing. Lots of people have pets. Cats and dogs . . . whatever. Plus, he's only with me temporarily. Pet-sitting, you know."

He nodded again. "Nice of you to help his person out."

"Sure."

"Need any help?"

"With what?"

"The cat. Are you all set? I'm pretty good with animals."

"I didn't know that."

"Well, we didn't discuss that during our date. We might've gotten around to it, though, in time."

He sounded as lame and awkward as I felt, and I decided a little mercy was called for—for both of us.

"Take care, Sam. I do need to go. I'm sure I'll see you around."

He pressed his lips together. I noted how the light hit his cheekbones. He had the best cheekbones and jawline, no question. Silently, I nodded and moved on, feeling a little lighter. It was sufficient to know that despite feeling like a failure a short time ago, I still had some dignity and self-control. And Sam seemed good. I was glad to see that.

I hoped the cat would allow me to keep the slight uptick in my mood for, at least, a little while.

As for Sam and me—on that one date a year ago, we'd gone to a nice restaurant. We'd hung in through dinner trying to make conversation and had stumbled through one awkward dance together, but I'd known as soon as we met that *no* special something would spark between us. Sam felt the same, I was sure.

I was still too damaged from all that had happened—the horror that had taken me from a successful career and had stolen my confidence and made my too-recognizable face more broadly recognizable in a not-great way—all due to my father's poor decisions. And we each had an engagement that had ended badly. Sam's was even more recent than mine.

Since that blind date, both Sam Jr. and I had avoided each other, if for no other reason than to discourage our families' matchmaking efforts. It wasn't hard. Sam didn't live with his dad. He had his own full life elsewhere in the city, and since I'd come to Richmond, I rarely ventured far from home.

****

Harvey didn't greet me when I walked into the house. Not

that I'd expected an actual welcome, but after a few minutes of going about my usual routine, I finally spied him crouched under the end table. He looked . . . serious. Unapproachable.

Fine with me. I said aloud, "Good to see you too, Harvey."

I went to the kitchen to check the litter box, wishing there was a better spot for it, but next to the kitchen door was the best I could do.

The litter box had been used. *Good.* Next, I checked the water dish over by the fridge. There was a trace of water left, so I refilled it. The food dish was full. Seeing that, I did a double take. Yesterday, Harvey had eaten—no, he'd gobbled his food without hesitation once he'd gotten started. Judging by his circumference, he wasn't at risk of starvation, but I had limited experience with cats, so perhaps this eating behavior was normal.

Between the cat food Marla had given me and what I'd added to the supplies today, I had a few days to figure out what to do. But then what?

To the pound, the woman had said.

There was a feline smell in the house, or maybe it was due to the cat food? But regardless, it was an unaccustomed odor here, so I opened some windows front and back to let a breeze blow through.

I stripped the packaging from my new lint roller brush and went to work on the chair Harvey had slept in. Was that what this would come to? This cat leaving hair everywhere and me scrambling to clean it up? He didn't belong here. He wasn't mine, and I wasn't in the market for a pet.

Could I just leave a door open? He wasn't happy here. Let him . . .

I was horrified. It hadn't even been two full days. Was I seriously considering letting that cat slip out the door for my convenience? No.

So perhaps the pound *would* be the best option. That's how someone who wanted a pet, who was prepared to care for a dog or cat, would find the perfect one to adopt. A different kind of matchmaking? Yeah. Perhaps the people at the shelter would take him to a vet, get him bathed and up-to-date on whatever inoculations cats were supposed to have. All that would have to be done by someone other than me, because it just wasn't . . .

Harvey howled. One long, seemingly endless yowl that hurt my ears and echoed in the house and in my head even after he'd stopped.

Where was he? The sound seemed to have come from everywhere. The house was so narrow that the height in the stairwell acted as a funnel for noise. I'd closed the bedroom doors to keep that orange fur machine out of those rooms, so he was down here on the main floor somewhere.

I looked behind the sofa, then searched the tiny side library I used as an office and found him nowhere. Another noise came. Not as loud this time. Stepping quietly through the living room, I checked the hallway. Nope, not there. The door to the half bath in the hallway was ajar, but I'd probably left it that way. It was a small powder room tucked under the stairs.

I approached it slowly, whispering, "Harvey?"

The door shot back as Harvey dashed out. A manic look lit his eyes. His movements, as he tried to pass me, weren't fluid like before. Convinced he'd gone rabid, I screamed and stumbled backward, but then he fell, twitching as he rolled, ending on his back.

Shocked. I was beyond horrified. His forelegs and hindlegs pawed at the air, and I saw Harvey's belly.

Not a boy.

The fur was still thick and dirty, yes, but thin on the

belly . . . and the fullness of that belly was due to more than overeating.

Harvey's body was preparing to give birth, to be a mom, and be ready to nurse.

Guilt assailed me. How had I not realized sooner?

Because Harvey had mostly stayed out of sight? Or because I hadn't wanted to engage with this whole topic and think it through? I'd been more concerned with ditching this cat.

Harvey rolled side to side again, her forelegs moving in the air, and then . . .

Get Marla, my brain shouted. *Yes,* I thought. There was no time to find a vet. Marla knew cats well. I'd beg her to come and help because I was way out of my depth here. Yet all the while that I was panicking, a soft voice in my head was assuring me that cats gave birth unassisted all the time and there was no need for hysteria.

Harvey's frantic movements ceased. The mama-to-be cat was busy.

On Florence's gleaming, perfectly maintained, century-old wooden floor—Harvey was very busy indeed.

I gasped and ran to the stairs, grasping the newel post as I spun into the climb and dashed up the steps faster than I'd thought I was capable of. The worn but clean towels that I kept for emergencies were stored in the closet, and if this wasn't that—an emergency—then I didn't know what this was . . . except I *did* know, and if I objected to caring for *one* cat . . .

What was I going to do with a family of them?

Clutching the stack of towels, I tripped and nearly fell running down the stairs. I grabbed the railing to stop my descent, but the towels continued without me. Meanwhile, Harvey seemed to be busy, but not in distress. Looking down between the spindles in the railing, I saw something dark and wet on the floor near her. My knees buckled and I sat on the step. The creature was tiny, though a little larger than the rodent Harvey had gifted me with less than twelve hours earlier.

I was struggling to get back on my feet when someone knocked on the door. *Who?* This was the final straw—the piling on that would break me, surely.

Shame hit me again for worrying about the floor and a visitor, and not my cat.

She's NOT MY CAT.

From where I stood, still a few steps up above the floor, looking straight ahead the top of a dark head of hair was visible through the arching windows high on the front door.

That could only be Sam Jr.

I gave up and gave in. I had no control over this situation. Any pretense of control over my world seemed to have flown the day before.

"Hey," I said, opening the door only a couple of inches. I tried to block his view of the foyer with my body.

"I heard a scream." His eyes examined my face. "I couldn't just . . ." Tension suddenly hardened his look. He was trying to see past me, even around me. "Is there . . ." He seemed to be sending a message with his eyes. He left the sentence unfinished.

"I'm sorry, Sam. Can't talk now. Gotta go."

His hand was on the door, his fingers wrapping around the edge. I felt his energy, his body braced to push, to force it open.

"Are you . . ." His voice changed, the tension in it suddenly sounding entirely ordinary, but in a very odd way. "Dad sent me to ask for a cup of sugar."

My mouth gaped open. I accepted that I now lived in an

upside-down world of nonsense. My strained defenses couldn't withstand the pure illogic that my life had become.

I closed my gaping mouth and released the door. It opened as I stepped back. "I can't chat. Harvey is giving birth." I turned away from Sam Jr. to look at Harvey, now seeing *two* little dark, wet forms near her. "Kittens are being born on my floor."

"Oh, thank God," he said with such a rush that I couldn't doubt his sincerity, though it mystified me . . . along with many other things these days.

"Why?" I asked, gathering up the scattered towels. "Why do you care that Harvey is becoming a mother?"

"No, not that." He stopped and wrapped his arms around me hard, impulsively and briefly, before releasing me gently and moving toward the birthing cat who was doing what nature compelled her to do on Cousin Florence's beautifully cared-for wood flooring.

His voice was as gentle as his actions. "I thought you might be in danger, like being held hostage. Asking for a cup of sugar was the only excuse I could think of in the moment." He dropped to his knees, keeping a few feet away from Harvey. "I don't want to scare her. She's pretty busy." He smiled. It was the kindest smile I'd ever seen from a man.

There were now three dark forms. Amazingly, one baby was squirming as Harvey licked it briskly, washing the kitten until it uttered a tiny cry, then she moved her ministrations to the second baby before pausing to push out a fourth, and then she seemed to need a moment to breathe.

Sam's voice was soft, much like his smile. "Good job, Harvey. Excellent job." He didn't reach toward her, just offered her encouragement in his soothing voice. Giving her a feeling of friendly safety? It was working for me too.

Still cradling towels in my arms, I knelt beside him and whispered, "Is she okay?"

Harvey raised partway up and twisted to reach the second two babies and began to bathe them, sharing her attentions back and forth between them.

I sagged, half falling against Sam's arm. My cheek hit his shoulder, and I let it stay there.

"I was so blind," I said.

"About me? Us? We can go out again if you like."

"Please. I mean about the cat. Suppose . . . I mean . . ." I couldn't finish.

"You can only know what you know, Leigh."

"I was close to turning him . . . her . . . out. The woman who pushed the cat off on me . . . I went to the house. No one is living there. There's a For Sale sign out front." I breathed. "I considered taking Harvey to the pound. Maybe even just . . . letting her escape out the door." I shook my head, not minding the feel of Sam's cotton shirt against my cheek. "You don't have to tell me how awful I am. I already know."

"You're too hard on yourself." He said it in the same soothing tone he'd used with Harvey.

I forced myself to sit upright. I pushed the strands of hair that had escaped from my ponytail clasp out of my face. I needed a task. A goal. "What can I do to help her?"

"Do you have a box? A cardboard box about so big?" He moved his hands to show the size he had in mind. "We can cut the sides down to a few inches. She'll want it for the kittens."

"Sure. There's a box in the storeroom."

"Maybe put it, with a couple of those towels in the bottom, under the bathroom sink. I'm assuming that you don't have any kind of cabinet arrangement under that sink?"

"No, it's just as it's always been."

He nodded. "She'll feel safer there. If she doesn't feel safe, she'll move the babies elsewhere. Cats have amazing instincts."

"Should I do something for her? Now, I mean?"

"No, just let her focus on the task at hand. No need to scare her. When she's done, and she may be now, we'll have the box ready for her, and I'll help you clean up the floor."

"Why?"

"Because you shouldn't leave the floor like that. The longer you wait to clean it, the greater the possibility of damage."

"Smart aleck." But I wasn't really annoyed. "Can I ask a favor?"

"Go for it."

"Do you mind getting the box and cutting it back? I feel like maybe I should sit here with her." I cleared my throat. "With Harvey."

He looked me in the face and brushed a last stray hair from my cheek. "My pleasure."

He was already rising to his feet as I asked, "Do you know where the storage room is?"

"Remember, I helped Florence with odd jobs back in the day."

I nodded, fresh out of words, and returned my attention to Harvey and her four babies.

Sam Jr. cut down the sides of the box, but before putting it in the half bath, he put a large plastic trash bag on the floor, spreading it carefully and neatly. He said, "I found this newspaper in the kitchen. Mind if I use it here?"

"Please do."

He laid a couple of layers of newsprint over the plastic, then added the box. The job was neatly done and fit nicely under the sink. It was my turn, and I smoothed the towels into the bottom of the box, and then Sam suggested I move one kitten at a time carefully into that box—under Harvey's watchful gaze—so she'd know what we intended. Using a small hand towel, nearly threadbare, to pick them up, I moved each one, and then I scooted out of the way again, though I didn't go far.

I stared at my hands.

Who had the towel been intended to protect? Even through the cloth, I'd felt the life in those bodies, but they weren't as warm as I'd expected, and so very fragile. Harvey joined them in the box within seconds of me finishing my task. She went immediately to licking them, nosing them, touching them with her paws, almost as if she didn't trust these were the same babies, or didn't trust my actions in moving them.

Meanwhile, Sam was wetting towels and grabbing the floor cleaner from the cabinet under the kitchen sink. But me . . . I sat near the open bathroom door. Harvey had given me a look —only one—and then had settled into the box under the sink to tend her babies.

Sam said, "You don't want to be too helpful or make her worry about your intentions, else she'll take those babies one by one to a spot that seems safer to her. What seems safer to her may seem incomprehensible to you . . . and may be inconvenient too, so hopefully she'll be content to care for them right here for a while."

"I'll leave the door partway open so she can get to the food and litter box as needed."

"Yep. Luckily, it's quiet in this house and along this hallway. That will help her relax." He offered his hand. "In fact, why don't we go sit in the kitchen? I could use a cup of coffee or tea or whatever is handy. I think you could too. Harvey will appreciate a little alone time with the kids."

I accepted his hand, and with an easy tug, he pulled me up

from the floor. It felt good to stand and to stretch. I hadn't realized how much tension I'd been holding in me, in my muscles.

"A break sounds wonderful."

Still clasping my hand, he asked, "You good?"

"I'm good." I glanced back into the bathroom. "One cat and four kittens. What am I going to do?"

"Let Harvey take care of them for now. You have some time before they'll be underfoot."

"By then, maybe the women will return?"

He was shaking his head.

"You don't think so?" I put my hand on his arm. "Oh, you think they knew she was expecting?"

"I don't see how they wouldn't. It seems like it would be obvious."

"Harvey was so skittish," I said, shaking my head. "I couldn't get a good look at her."

"Well, but she was their cat, presumably for a while, at least, so . . ." Sam grinned. The lines at the corners of his eyes deepened, and he looked like laughter was about to bubble up right out of him. But after a long look at me, he swallowed it back down. In a solemn tone—though one that didn't sound altogether sincere—he said, "Well, now you'll get a good long look, if my guess is right."

Chapter Five

The air around us felt companionable. My tension over realizing I was stuck with someone else's cat—and now that cat's offspring—was easing. My legs were feeling a bit weak. I put my hand on the back of the kitchen chair and simply sat.

Sam didn't speak. He didn't ask any questions. He found the glasses, the ice, and filled them from the pitcher in the fridge.

"Looks like you do still know your way around here."

He shrugged. "It's just iced tea." After a pause, he added, "You haven't rearranged much since Florence passed, from what I can see."

I shook my head. "Florence had years to work out the best places for things. Those places work for me. She's only been gone six months. It feels longer." I shrugged. "There's no reason to rush to rearrange." Or redecorate. The worn vinyl on the floor . . . the faded paint on the kitchen walls . . . I'd never suggested updating them to Florence. She didn't see *old*, she saw *home*, and that had been good enough for me.

Home. A big part of my brain, my attention, refocused on what was happening a short distance down the hallway in the half bath. Except for the clink of ice cubes as we drank, I could almost pretend that none of that had happened . . . except Sam was here with me in my kitchen. And he was staring at me.

"I need to ask," he said. "Was it me? Something I did or said?"

I frowned, trying to fit his words into the context of what we'd just experienced. But no, he was speaking of our one date.

"Oh, Sam. No. It was all me. I wasn't in the right state of mind at that time to deal with relationships. It was too soon."

"You mean the thing with your father?"

"Yes. That thing with my father that led to everything else." I breathed in quickly and held the air in my lungs for a couple of seconds to interrupt the fear reflex before answering. I said, "Yes. Florence took me in and gave me a place to hide. She and your dad . . . I guess they thought I could just step out there and get my life back on track, but I was more than derailed." I shook my head. "And you . . . you'd just gone through a breakup."

I stopped. Sam didn't respond. He seemed to be waiting.

"I appreciate your help with Harvey."

"You're welcome," he said, but then he frowned. "You're alone here too much. Not my business, I know. But you have some great neighbors, Leigh."

I looked aside, wanting to be annoyed, but knowing he was right. "Everyone here in the neighborhood . . . they're nice. They respect my wish for privacy. Honestly, Sam, I went through too much, tried too hard to get out of that spotlight, to be able to get cozy with people even now, two years later. Cousin Florence was different. She was family, yes, and not a total stranger. Almost my mother's age. I didn't remember her, but she remembered me. She welcomed me. She, Florence, was pure gold." I shrugged. "As far as our date went, I didn't mean to be unfair to you. I felt that I was doing both of us a big favor, you especially, by not prolonging it."

"Are you in a better place now?"

"I hope so. What about you?"

"Everyone has something they carry around. Sometimes visible, sometimes not." This time, he shrugged. "What happened between Brie and me was for the best. Neither of us was overly upset about ending our engagement—which was a clear signal that we made the right choice."

I nodded in agreement. "Ultimately, it was the same for *my* breakup. Andrew and I, our relationship, couldn't survive what happened two years ago." My sigh was involuntary. "By the time we made the break official, it felt anticlimactic." And how sad was that? I started to move, to rise from the chair, to escape the memory. If I stayed in place, all the ugly memories would roll back in and swamp me.

Sam asked, "Do you have what you need for your new tenants?"

His quick switch back to my cat troubles startled me.

Sam assured me, "Harvey will take care of things. It isn't until the kittens get mobile that they'll become a headache for you."

He didn't fool me. He'd read my face and had tried to rescue me by this change of subject back to the cats. I was happy to go along.

"Should I take them to a vet?"

"Harvey could use a checkup because she doesn't look well cared for, but I'd guess that this is not the time. Interruptions could interfere with her bonding with and caring for her babies. Maybe talk to a vet and get their recommendation?"

"Sam, how did you get so smart about animals, specifically cats?"

"We had a few pets over the years when I was growing up.

The last was my mom's cat. The Empress." He flashed a quick smile. "A long-haired blue. Not purebred. Mom insisted that mixed breeds have a better disposition, but you couldn't prove it with that creature. Scary cat." He paused to laugh softly, then he shrugged. "I was interested in veterinary medicine years ago and gave it a try but dropped out of the program." He went silent for a moment.

I said, "I thought you worked as a risk manager."

"Yes, risk management consulting." He stopped, then added, "Seems like a lifetime ago."

"Seems like a big switch. Moving from veterinary care to managing risk."

"True." His expression changed, brightening. "As a matter of fact, one of my classmates completed the program and has his own practice. I could ask him to come by and check out Harvey and the quads."

I shook my head. "The quads? Thanks, but no—I don't want to put anyone out." *No favors and no strangers . . .*

"Reconsider that, Leigh. Harvey looks good, considering that she also appears to have been neglected. She's resting now. The kittens are tiny, but probably good for now. But the neglect? That could not only hurt her, but there could also be pests and illnesses that infect the babies. It's tricky. New mom. Unsettled around strangers in a strange place. Don is good with cats. Like a cat whisperer." He paused, then added, "I could come with him."

My sigh was much more dramatic, much louder than I expected. I closed my eyes, then looked back at Sam. "Okay, if you recommend him. I would appreciate you being here too. I'm uncomfortable around strangers. You may have noticed . . . it's like I get so scrambled that my brain stops working properly." I breathed. "*But* I feel responsible for Harvey and her little family and want to do the right thing."

Sam's expression softened, and the light in his eyes was warmer. "I'll give him a call. I'll let you know the timing."

"Thank you," I said, then added, "I am sorry, Sam. Sincerely."

He frowned. "For what?"

"That date. We should never have tried it. Not then."

He shrugged. "Maybe we'll try again? But if we do, this time, don't ghost me."

I frowned. "I called you."

"After not responding to my calls and texts for three weeks."

He had a point. I nodded.

He moved to stand. I rose to my feet too, a little disappointed.

I walked him to the door. We stopped to check on Harvey and her babies.

Sam said, "One of them is very pale, one is orange."

"The pale one is peach-colored. Looks smaller than the others." I pointed in the general direction of the kittens. "That one is a mixture, and the other is darker. Gray."

"The mixture is called tortoiseshell, or tortie. Or a calico. There's some kind of difference between the two. The gray is actually called blue." He made a low, thinking kind of noise, almost a whistle. "Quite a variety. A DNA chart of kitten possibilities would tell us with a good likelihood of accuracy what flavor of cat the father was."

DNA chart? *Hah.* But flavor? Yeah. I liked that turn of phrase.

After Sam left and I'd closed the door, I stood there for a long moment, my hand still grasping the doorknob. Something was sparking in my brain.

Maybe we'll try again, he'd said.

I smiled at the door. I leaned my forehead against its

smooth, finely grained wood. He was willing to try another date. He wouldn't have said that otherwise.

How did I feel about that?

Yesterday—maybe even just this morning—I wouldn't have considered dating anyone anytime soon as even a remote possibility.

I cautioned myself not to assume that getting close to Sam, or anyone, would be different now. But maybe I was better now. At least a little.

Things seemed to be changing, kind of weirdly. I had a cat and kittens in my care, after all. And I'd agreed to allow a stranger inside my home to examine them because it was the responsible, appropriate action . . . and I had been able to agree without falling apart. And still wasn't falling apart. Only a smidge anxious.

Having Sam there when the vet came, someone I knew, would help immensely.

Sam as a friend . . . I liked that. It didn't have to get romantic.

Glancing down the hallway, I couldn't see directly into the bathroom, but judging by the silence from which occasional soft, snuggly noises could be heard, for now, this moment, all was well in this house.

For how long? I shook my head. I wouldn't think about that right now. I'd take a page from Scarlett O'Hara and think about the future tomorrow. For tonight, I'd give my anxiety a rest.

And yet I lingered there, near the half bath, not quite ready to walk away.

What had I not done that I should have? Did the cats have what they needed?

Nothing and *yes*—those were the answers.

I didn't pray much and never had—nor had my parents—

but tonight, before going to bed, I offered up a few awkward words asking God for help doing what I had to do, regardless of how scary I might find it. It felt kind of strange, or maybe unaccustomed, but it also felt oddly, unexpectedly, comforting.

****

My mind and heart were overfull as I prepared for bed that night. I was accustomed to being alone, even among people, including my parents. With Florence, it had been different, but by the time we were truly comfortable together, her health was declining.

Florence was the daughter of my mother's elder sister. She was closer to my mother's age than to mine. The age difference, plus the fact that I was away at school or involved in activities as a child, and later, as an adult, living in New York pursuing my career, meant our paths didn't cross—at least not as far as I remembered. It was during that time that Florence lost her father and then her mother.

Unmarried and with no children, Florence stayed in the home she'd grown up in and settled into living alone, except for her cat, Cookie. She'd lost that cat several years before my troubles started.

When Dad's crimes made the news, Florence thought of me and what I might be going through. She discreetly communicated with my mother, extending an offer to me to hide out at her place.

I hadn't done anything wrong, except to be the daughter of an embezzler. A con man. A liar. A cheat. And, yes, I was desperately in need of a hiding place.

Chapter Six

My father had cheated people in a big, very damaging way. I was shocked when his house of cards caved in, perhaps because I'd given up any real relationship with him years before and had moved on to make my own life. He hadn't been much interested in me when I was young. As I grew older, he began to push me to engage in his businesses but by then I didn't trust him and knew he wasn't someone I could, or would want to, count on.

Even so, maybe if I'd been braver or tougher and had had the guts to look deeper into his business, I would've figured out that he was running Ponzi schemes and who knew what else. I might've saved some investors heartbreak. And that knowledge continued to weigh on me.

At the PR firm I'd helped start, where I was a partner, I'd recently begun an ad campaign that splashed my face on city buses and media ads promoting our business. So when the news broke about Dad and the media zoomed in on his villainy, and the photo ops of him became common viewing and clickbait news online—like videos of him being arrested and assailed on the courthouse steps and the press calling out questions and holding gotcha stakeouts at his Manhattan home, and door knocks at my mother's property down in Florida—which she ignored, repeating only that they'd been divorced for years—well, I was on my own, very recognizable, and conveniently within the crosshairs of anyone who could shout a question or an accusation.

I could only be thankful that I'd never worked with, or for, my father, or at any of his businesses.

My natural course when I escaped New York and public scrutiny was to flee to my mother and ride out this storm with her. But no, it didn't work that way in my family.

How had Mom broached the subject when I arrived unannounced at her home in Florida? She'd mentioned Florence's name. I'd hardly been aware of Florence's existence. She was a barely known cousin who figured nowhere in our lives. In fact, Mother had to say her name several times before it finally penetrated the dark place I was in.

I asked, "What? Who?"

Mom said, "Florence . . . your cousin. My niece." When I returned only silence, she said, "You know *of* her even if you don't know her well personally. I've spoken of her to you over the years. I'm sure you must've met her at some time in the past."

"Why are you speaking of her now?" I asked, but not because I wanted to know. I was looking to escape the world, not for more connections.

"I'm telling you about her because she suggested that you visit her. She said you can stay with her as long as you need to."

"Seriously? If you want me to leave that badly"—*and she did, I knew that*—"then say it outright. No need to come up with distant relatives or other excuses to get me out of here." I stood. "I have options." *Options? Maybe.* But none of them were good, and all of them ended with me being alone. I didn't want to be alone.

Mom had lived in Florida for years—many miles and states away from Dad. Their marriage had ended when I was a child. Mom had kept her life separate from Dad's except for the contacts required by shared custody of me. That custody had ended many years ago, thus severing what little remained of their interactions. She wanted to keep it that way. However, for me, as an adult and living in New York, it had been almost impossible not to have a relationship with him—and he'd seemed to want that, especially after I neared adulthood. For Mother, having me at her home now was a risk to her peace of mind . . . or her peaceful, self-focused life. Being there with her, I was trying to claim some of her distance from Dad for myself—to use it as a shelter from the media or against the curious.

"Visit Florence," Mother said. "She lives in Richmond. You don't know anyone there. It's a big enough city to get a little lost in without getting lost entirely. She lives in a quiet neighborhood, a lovely southern town where people are pleasant and mind their own business." She stared at me. "Besides, Florence is all alone. She's a quiet woman, a gentle sort. No one will connect her to any of us." She smiled slightly. "In fact, she suggested you use my mother's maiden name, Sonder, temporarily. Said it would throw anyone off who might think you look familiar from all of the . . . recent ugliness in the media. I think that's a good idea."

In the end, I'd done as my mother advised. I'd arrived in Richmond bereft of expectations, wondering only how soon I'd be moving on again, because one thing I did know for absolutely sure was that my present sanity hinged upon having a private life and staying out of the spotlight. The years when I'd moved confidently within that spotlight were gone, along with my nerves. Being hounded, even targeted, for activities that had been no part of my life . . . at least not knowingly . . . had changed me.

Had damaged me.

And my fiancé too.

Despite my urging Andrew not to go to work for my father, he had. My father had wooed him, or maybe he'd wooed my father, but that connection in addition to me being Marcom Eden's daughter was doom. My face in the media, my father, my fiancé—my entire life—kaleidoscoped into focus with the speed of light for law enforcement, financial regulatory agencies, the press, and all manner of media. No wonder the questions had persisted, the constant attempts to draw me in, but truly I hadn't known what was going on. My distrust of my father was more instinctive than based on knowledge of corruption. Distrust, yes. Suspicion, maybe. Knowledge, no.

I'd tried to keep a civil distance between us. When Andrew came into my life . . . Had my father wooed Andrew with promises of financial success in hopes of bringing me back into his orbit? Not because he loved me, but because he wanted to leverage his daughter's success to draw more victims into his financial trap? I'd warned Andrew that something wasn't right. I'd argued with him over it. But he'd been excited about being in business with my father, and I'd let my better judgment soften. I wanted to make Andrew happy. Maybe if I'd had hard facts instead of just that instinctive mistrust of my father, I would've been more successful at persuading Andrew to stay away from him.

Dad went to prison, in part because Andrew turned

evidence against him—which in some part probably saved me from worse scrutiny—or maybe it was my nearly mute grief over all of it and the lack of actual evidence of my involvement. Even so, my career was ruined. The PR firm bid me farewell without fanfare, though with a significant check to buy me out, and we mutually agreed to part without more embarrassment for anyone.

They had wanted to protect the firm. I understood that.

Mother wanted to protect herself. Nothing new there.

But Florence had offered. She'd watched the public spectacle play out on her TV screen in real time and had reached out to my mother, her aunt. During the year and a half that I lived with Florence—until her death—I never once perceived that she regretted having made the offer.

I'd arrived in Richmond on a rainy day in May and drove my car directly into my cousin's tiny garage by way of the alley, as she'd instructed. She'd left the garage door open so I could cruise right in. I was still working my suitcase out of the back seat, made awkward by the narrow space around the car, when she arrived in the opposite doorway that opened into the backyard. She was a bit breathless and holding an umbrella, with a welcoming smile on her face.

She said, "We'll come back out for the suitcase when the rain slackens. For now, tuck under here with me and we'll scoot across the backyard under cover." She gave me a one-armed hug and giggled. "Get it? Undercover?"

I recognized her, sort of. We must've met, or at least been in the same room, when I was very young. I was older and taller now. She was older and still petite, and mostly gray. When she smiled, I was overcome with gratitude.

Florence kept her straight gray-brown hair short and pulled back on the sides with a variety of hair clips. The clips tended to slip in her fine hair, which gave her a scattered look until you looked straight on into bright, keen brown eyes.

She watched all the crime shows, from the improbable to the cliché. She recalled all the details, and she loved having company now to share them with, but she was always careful to avoid financial crimes. Out of consideration for me.

I found her delightful and at times rather alarming, but I had to admit she had a lot of good ideas about present and future possible problems. She loved to chew all that over with any willing listener. I gathered from what she said that until her cat died—she called him Cookie—he was her most receptive audience. She was delighted that I listened without complaint and occasionally contributed comments and ideas. It was the least I could do. She sheltered me and saved my sanity.

When her health was failing, she deeded me her house. For that, I had to use my legal name, but by then, as Florence had predicted, all the hubbub about my father's crimes was old news. No one blinked when the legal papers were executed. And yet . . . I knew that meant my legal name was now on official records directly connected to this address. For the next month, I woke in the night with cold sweats and heart palpitations.

Tonight, on the day that my unexpected cat had presented me with unexpected kittens, and despite me having resolved *not* to think about worrisome things, yet I'd wallowed in these memories as I plumped my pillows and turned out the lamp, the past was still trying to play in my head. Like movie clips. I thought of them that way because it felt less personal. Just some poor schmuck's story. The girl who'd learned to wear blinders. But in the end, blinders hadn't saved me. In fact, it may have guaranteed my downfall. So when I settled under the covers and could only lie there staring into darkness, I shouldn't have been surprised that sleep eluded me and the memories kept rolling.

I dozed. Some sort of light may have flashed outside my bedroom windows at some crucial point in a dream. Suddenly, I was blinded by the flash and click of cameras, harried by the shouts of people asking for information, some accusing me of being part of the embezzlement as I struggled to descend the granite steps of the courthouse without falling and making things worse.

The flash and click of cameras and the shouts and honking horns disoriented me. Leland Graves, the attorney my mother had insisted I hire, was there beside me, his hand on my elbow, shepherding me past the lights and shouts and crowds.

One woman in particular was shouting at me. Many people crowded nearby and were held back by security, but from among them, her voice was the one that reached me out of the midst of the noise and anger, saying, "You're part of it. Even if you, yourself, didn't take one dime of our hard-earned money, you got a good school, good job, good tee—"

I didn't hear the rest because Leland hurried me away and out of the limelight.

Good teeth . . . Those were the words I thought I heard as I was hustled away. *Good teeth.* I hadn't needed braces . . . but that hadn't really been the woman's point. And she was right, in some ways. Had my father's crimes paid for my advantages growing up? How much of what I'd benefited from had come from ill-gotten gains? I'd worked hard in my careers. But I'd never know how well I would have done if I'd started with fewer advantages. And I felt the weight of it all.

So, yes, I'd moved in with Florence on a rainy day, my identity disguised under a rain hat and umbrella, and thereafter, I seldom left. My car . . . well, it was still in the garage and not used. I didn't worry so much about being recognized now. I was content here in my contained world with my peace and quiet, and my routines. Friendly nods to neighbors in passing were enough interaction for me. Weekly walks to the corner grocery or an occasional hired car when shoe leather wouldn't suffice were my outings. Florence had tried to push me to do more, but then she'd gotten sick and our focus had shifted to managing her health needs.

At some point, I drifted into a deeper sleep, but it was small wonder that I woke in the wee hours of the night in a sweat, frantically fighting the sheets. That woman screaming at me in nightmare land was in the room with me. The side of my face burned as if I'd been slapped. I fled from the bed and landed with a crash on the floor.

The fall stunned me. My heart racing, I scanned the room as if I might need to defend myself. The woman before me was nothing more than the shadow shape of my robe hooked over the bedpost finial. As the remains of the terror subsided, it all resolved itself, shedding the dregs of the nightmare. My bedroom became my familiar bedroom again. I was safe in Florence's narrow house.

Had I screamed out loud? If I'd frightened Harvey, she might've left her babies, and they would die and . . .

Crap. No more of this brain spinning.

I stood and made my way to the hallway and down the stairs by moonlight. In the quiet of the peaceful night, it was easy to let the lingering effects of my disturbed sleep fall away. The moonlight spilled from the kitchen and down the hallway. I stepped carefully in case any other gifts had been left for me to find.

The bathroom door was open a foot or so, as I'd left it.

This first-floor world was asleep. I switched on a small lamp Florence had left on the top bookcase shelf in the study. Its weak but soft, warm light gave the room an air of grace, a dignity that daylight didn't, spreading across the living room and filtering into the foyer. Softly, I walked through the living room and paused by the bathroom. I peeked into the room, not touching the door or making a sound.

Harvey looked up at me, her eyes keen and not moving so much as a hair. The kittens were still too, snuggled against their mother's warm belly, sleeping, at least for the moment. And something about Harvey's eyes seemed to ask that we please do not disturb the babies, that their mom needed her rest.

I sat on the floor in the wide opening between the living room and the foyer hallway. It was maybe five feet away from the bathroom where the cats were. Because of the angle and the bathroom door, I couldn't see into the room and I wouldn't be visible to them, but I was quite sure Harvey knew I was nearby. Hopefully, I wasn't close enough to disturb them, but near enough for me to feel the . . . What was it? Good feelings? Good energy? I held my breath and listened.

Was that a tiny squeak? Then a shift of some sort, of the sound of terrycloth brushing against the inside of the cardboard box?

Was that low, barely there vibration purring? The sound was so very faint, but I believed my rough and tough Harvey was indeed purring again.

My Harvey? My eyes stung. My chest warmed. And I thought it might be true that whether I'd wanted this or not, had not volunteered for this, that somehow, in this nonsensical, bewildering, non sequitur world—an often cruel world—this cat family was now *mine*.

What would Cousin Florence say?

I leaned my cheek against the doorframe and pulled my robe closer around me.

If Florence were still alive, she would be right here beside me, spinning stories as she speculated about the women, about Harvey's past, her babies, and reminiscing about her own lost Cookie.

In the dim light, I remembered her voice with the backdrop of soft purrs coming from a few feet away. My heart took on an easy rhythm and my eyelids grew heavy.

****

I fell asleep there, which I only discovered when I woke before dawn on that hard floor. Somehow, I'd gone from sitting to lying down, curled up on my side with my knees pulled close to my body. My robe was bunched up under my head like a pillow, leaving the rest of me quite chilly. The distant, rather delicate sound of water being lapped came to me, soon followed by the swish and push of litter being used, and then the whispery pad of cat feet on the hall floor as Harvey returned to her babies.

Cat litter. Harvey. This had truly happened. It hadn't been a dream.

Whiskers brushed my face ever so lightly, along with a puff of warm breath that smelled of cat food.

I opened my eyes. We were practically nose to nose and eye to eye as she stared at me intently. But it seemed that whatever concern or curiosity drove her was now satisfied because she turned, her tail brushing my cheek as she returned to the nursery.

Nursery. That sounded much better than *the box under the sink in the bathroom.*

Pushing myself up from the floor, I stood and made my way up the stairs. I needed my mattress, blankets, and pillows. I needed proper rest.

Judging by the text Sam had sent late the prior evening,

he'd moved fast. I'd be seeing him today, probably late after-noon, and he'd have his vet friend with him. Only heaven knew what this day might bring.

The nicest thing of all was that despite being apprehensive, I was also looking forward to finding out.

Chapter Seven

"I hope she won't mind," I said.

Sam gave me a look. He'd dropped by about lunchtime with a covered dish his dad had sent. He offered it to me, saying, "It's a pot pie. Dad has taken up cooking in his retirement years. You are today's lucky beneficiary."

I accepted the gift. "Thank you. And thank your father for me, please. Won't you come in?"

"I can only stay a few minutes. Have to go to the office for a few hours before coming back here to meet Don."

"I'd offer to let you off the hook, but I do want you here . . . you know, for the vet check."

"It's not a problem. That's the nicest thing about being a consultant and not a direct employee for a corporation."

"I think it's fortunate for me and Harvey. I doubt she'll agree about the vet, but I hope she won't mind too much."

Sam frowned. He stepped inside and I closed the door.

I asked, "Did you text so late yesterday because you thought I'd flake out? I won't change my mind about the vet visit, I promise."

"You give me more credit for strategy than I deserve. I

texted as soon as I heard from Don. And I texted *because* it was so late. I didn't want to disturb you, especially since you'd already said you were okay with this." He paused before asking, "How's Harvey and the quads?"

I laughed. He'd said that before, but it struck me as even funnier this time. *Quads.* But I was so startled to hear myself laugh that I choked and bent over coughing, nearly dropping the deep pie dish. Sam immediately moved to put his hands over mine to steady them lest the pot pie go flying.

"Are you okay?" he asked.

I released the dish into his custody, then pressing a hand to my throat, I nodded, saying, "I'm fine. Sorry."

"I'll put this in the kitchen."

"Thanks," I said, following him. "I surprised myself, hearing myself laugh. How silly is that?" And I smiled, surprising myself again.

He didn't respond with words. His expression was unreadable as he turned away to set the dish on the counter. I stared, wondering, but longer than intended, and when he faced me again I broke off my gaze.

"The vet is a good idea." I added, "Hopefully, we'll find it was unnecessary. Harvey and the kittens are doing fine as far as I can tell, but I don't know what to look for." I shook my head, then whispered, "I'm worried because I don't think she'll cooperate. I don't know whether she's simply unfriendly or actually feral."

He didn't speak, so I added, "She hissed at me from the first and wouldn't let me near her, but maybe that was because she was in a new place and expecting. She was protecting herself, right?"

"Makes sense."

"But then she caught the mouse."

This time he laughed. "Caught what?"

"A mouse. Her first night here?" I gasped. "Was that only two nights ago? Wow." I shook my head and gave a little shudder. "She woke me in the middle of the night, howling, and then waited for me at the bottom of the stairs." I rubbed my arm, remembering the fall in the hallway where I'd hit the wall. "I came downstairs and found a dead mouse on the hallway floor. She *watched* me find it. Like it was a gift." I sighed. "Unpleasant, yes, and at first I was annoyed, but then I remembered Florence talking about her cat bringing her gifts."

"Okay."

"Yes, and I'm wondering if it's because I gave her food? Maybe it was an overture . . . a friendly move on her part? What do you think?"

Sam touched my arm. I stayed as I was, refusing to allow myself to pull away, but I did look him squarely in the eyes.

He said, "Anything is possible with cats, but yes, it could be that she meant it . . . in a friendly way." He smiled. "As for having the vet check her, Harvey may not cooperate, but don't worry. Don won't push her. He'll judge the situation and act accordingly."

"Okay."

Sam's offer of help felt like a lifesaver. I didn't want Harvey or her babies to get sick and certainly not while in my care. And I couldn't imagine myself shoving her back into the carrier—if I could catch her—and putting the kittens in their box in my car and hearing their anguish and knowing I was doing damage to them all the way to the vet's office. Just thinking about it . . . I had to focus and breathe slowly to calm myself.

"Hey," Sam said. "Whatever you're imagining in your brain . . . quit it."

In that moment, I'd almost forgotten he was here. I grabbed his forearm and squeezed like a lifeline. The connection helped me breathe and focus. I didn't know whether Sam understood that, but he waited quietly while I borrowed his calm to help me.

As the panic began to clear from my head, he may have understood by the slacking of my grip or the taut expression easing on my face.

Softly, he said, "Someday, I hope you'll feel comfortable talking to me about all that stuff in your past. As a friend, if nothing else. Despite our history, after our successful joint delivery of four kittens, I think we should qualify as friends, at least."

I said, "Harvey did all the work."

"But we did the cheering and the cleanup. That matters."

I looked away, not wanting to meet his eyes, but I nodded. I agreed. We should be able to be friends. But I wasn't sure that a connection to me, even as a friend, would be in Sam's best interest. So I squeezed his arm again, but gently this time, and then, with a nod and a forced smile, I released him.

"Thank you," I said.

****

Don was great. I knew he would be the instant I met him at the door and Sam introduced us. He wasn't as tall as Sam, but broad-shouldered. He wore a button shirt and jeans and was calm and capable looking.

He extended his hand. I accepted it as we murmured the usual *Pleased to meet you*, and I added, perhaps too warmly, "Thank you for coming." Then I stepped back. His blue eyes—they felt insightful. He radiated an understated, assured calm. If Harvey would tolerate any human touch, I believed she would allow his. The feeling of connection that made me uncomfortable might work very well with Harvey. I hoped so.

The anxiety that made my brain stop working properly was rising. I didn't want to look foolish in front of these two well-meaning men.

I clasped my hands together, and with a swift glance at Sam, I stepped back, saying, "She's in the nursery—" I broke off, and added, "Sorry, the half bath. Under the stairs. Right there." I nodded toward the partly open door. My face got hot, so I was surely blushing. Truly, I wanted both him and Sam to redirect their focus. We needed to move on and get with the task at hand. But instead of doing that, Don said, "Tell me about your situation."

My situation. I went blank. I thought of Dad, of Florence, even of Mom . . . none of whom would I discuss with this stranger.

Softly, Sam prompted, "About Harvey."

Such relief flooded me that for another moment I was speechless. Don hadn't wanted to know about *my* situation.

Don continued, "For instance, how did she come to be here with you? Do you know her history? Sam said that you'd given her a home, but unexpectedly, and that you were concerned for her well-being and that of her litter. Is there anything you can tell me that might help?"

Where to start? I said, "Two days ago, I met two women. Totally unexpected and by chance. One was elderly and in a wheelchair, the other was middle-aged, and she seemed to be in charge. She insisted I take Harvey—rather, the cat carrier that Harvey was in—and then she left with the older woman." I shook my head. "I know it doesn't make sense. It didn't make sense to me either. I returned to the house the next day, yester-day, but she, or they, seem to have moved away because the house is totally vacant. Before I could figure out the next steps, Harvey went into labor."

I wouldn't tell him that I'd assumed Harvey was a *he.*

"She was so skittish. I didn't realize she was expecting because she hid and wouldn't allow me near. To be honest, she may be feral. She looks rough, dusty, and uncared for. I have no idea about vaccinations or such." I added, "I appreciate you coming like this. I hope I haven't wasted your time."

"Not at all. How much I can do for her is another question. It's not uncommon that when people must leave their homes and move, a pet becomes inconvenient."

"To be fair," I said, stumbling over the words, "I suspect that they didn't intend to abandon her, but had planned for someone to pick Harvey up, someone who didn't arrive and I did, and thus the confusion. The women didn't say much that made sense to me except that if I didn't take her, she could go to the pound."

Don nodded. "Well, that's the likely explanation, then."

Sam had been silent since he and the vet had first arrived. He touched my arm now, saying, "Why don't you introduce Don to Harvey now?"

A fierce protectiveness rose in me, surprising me. "Of course," I said, "but you'll be careful? Don't upset her."

This time Don didn't smile, but I sensed approval in his expression and in his light blue eyes as he said, "I promise."

Chapter Eight

After Sam and Don left, I stayed near the bathroom door as if only my presence, nearby, offered reassurance to Harvey—which was silly. And yet, as the kittens nursed, kneading their tiny paws against her belly, and as mama purred and pressed her paws against their bodies, perhaps to adjust their positions or to reassure her babies, I sighed. Maybe I was the one seeking reassurance. I needed to know that I'd done the right thing.

Harvey had been suspicious of Don, had allowed him to look, but not touch. When his hand had come too close, she'd reached her paw out in unmistakable warning. He'd withdrawn his hand, and she'd done likewise. She kept her eyes on him, and he stayed about two feet away.

I held my breath the whole time, worried.

Don spoke softly in a warm, even tone. "From what I can see, your assessment is pretty spot-on, Leigh. You've got good instincts. Harvey has not been properly cared for, but overall she seems strong, her eyes are bright and clear. She is an attentive mama, and the kittens look good, based on observation."

He smiled at me. "I don't think she'll accept me touching

them, and I don't see the need to add stress at this point. They are suckling well, with no apparent trouble breathing. But it's early days yet and things can go wrong with newborn kittens pretty quickly, even if you and Harvey do everything right, so don't panic if they seem off, but trust your instincts and give me a call."

Kindness. That was it. Don was all but alight with kindness and competence. He'd said the words I needed to hear, and I suspected he'd done that with deliberation and intention.

"Thank you. I will."

I thanked Sam too before he left to join Don, who was waiting outside by his car.

I waved to them both and gently closed the door.

Sam had seen my nervousness, as Don had. He'd been kind too.

I hoped Sam understood that I hadn't always been so neurotic.

No, *neurotic* wasn't the right word. Defensive. Protective. Those were better words.

I saw that protective instinct in Harvey too. Not for herself, as mine was. For Harvey, for now, it was all about protecting her babies.

In the soft, satisfied closing of her eyes, the occasional lazy-looking half-peek at me, I read watchfulness, but not distrust. If I reached my hands toward that bubble of maternal peace, even desiring no more than to touch the soft fur of one of her babies, I believed the response would be different. We weren't on a hands-on basis yet. So, for now, I stayed seated on the floor, my back against the wall, and let Harvey see that no further human intrusions would trouble her family this day.

Plus, and I didn't know how to quite describe it, but there was a feeling of peace like an aura around Harvey and her little ones, and maybe I craved sharing even a little wisp from the fringes of their bubble.

The *nursery. Hah.* I smiled to myself. I'd said it aloud during the visit, and both Sam and Don had heard me, though neither had remarked on it. I liked Don—what little I'd seen. He had good hands for animals. Calming hands. An overall vibe of assurance laced with a strong dose of intuition and empathy.

Harvey must've sensed a change in my tension as I was remembering, because she not only opened her eyes, but she lifted her head—though still not to the point of disturbing her babies—and eyed me with a steady glare.

Trying to relax, I rested my head back against the wall again and closed my eyes. I focused on breathing slowly. After a few minutes, I said softly, "That's it for now, Harvey. I have to move around before my legs fall asleep. Don't be alarmed when you hear me getting up." Carefully, I stood and quietly left the area and went to the kitchen.

I fixed a cup of tea and carried it back to the living room, taking the route from the kitchen through the narrow dining room and into the front room, the route that avoided the foyer and hallway. I turned the TV on but kept the volume low, more for background noise than anything else. A nature show was playing, which was perfect, so long as it wasn't about animal food chains or survival of the fittest. I sat in my gooseneck rocker, where I had a slice of a view of the bathroom door across the hallway, but not so close I'd disturb the maternity ward.

Was calling my guest half bath a maternity ward better than calling it a nursery? Didn't matter. It was all good. Time enough to fret when those kittens got bigger and bolder and were ready to separate from . . . *Oh my.* Chills swept my body.

How damaged was I, truly? How much more damaged was I because I'd been hiding for so long?

I wanted a real life again. But I was scared I might not be able to handle it.

Tiny snuffling noises, then high-pitched barely there mewing, and then Harvey emerged, having dislodged the nursing mouths, to answer her own needs. She headed to the water dish and then to the litter box. Those sounds had so quickly become utterly familiar to me.

When Sam smiled at me . . . When he spoke in that way, he was . . . friendly.

Like a friend, maybe. That would be good. For now.

Little noises resumed as Harvey returned to the kittens. I heard those sounds—the mewling, the soft brush of terry against cardboard, purring—and understood them. The sounds meant they were together, generating a special pocket of energy that enfolded them and made them feel so safe they didn't even think about whether they were truly safe or not because everything was good and complete in their world.

I rose as quietly as I could from my rocker. It squeaked as it had since my first day here when Florence had welcomed me and we'd sat in this room to talk, to get to know each other, she'd said.

Moving across the thin carpet to the bare wooden flooring in the foyer and hallway, I stepped softly and paused at the open bathroom door. The nursery. I whispered, "Good night, Harvey."

****

Before going to bed, I texted Sam a thank-you, saying Harvey and her kittens showed no signs of upset after Don's visit. I added that I appreciated his help. I hit Send. Then I sat there for a long moment looking at the screen, but of course there wasn't a response yet.

It made me feel connected. Such a little thing, but it proved how disconnected I was from other people, and how much I wanted that to change.

It gave me a warm, fuzzy feeling inside—sort of like my own energy bubble. I recognized the feeling as that of hope. Hope and potential.

Would I still feel that warmth in the morning?

Maybe it was time to take it a step further. I should get the car checked. Two years of disuse . . . It was ridiculous to keep it if I wasn't going to use it. I should sell it. Buy a newer vehicle.

I couldn't help the smile that formed on my face, like my lips were volunteering to join in on the hope party too.

The text was noted as delivered. I turned off the ringer and laid the phone face down on the nightstand. I needed my sleep. And maybe I'd be gifted with some sweet dreams too. Two nights in a row of broken sleep, whether disturbed by Harvey or my own memories, was two too many. Tonight it would be sweet dreams all the way.

That would be especially nice.

****

Sweet dreams? That night, I couldn't recall any dreams before the one with my dad in it. And it was most definitely *not sweet*. It was a nightmare. We were in a small dark room with gray walls and a metal table between us. One of us was in trouble. In the nightmare, I couldn't tell which one. I wanted *out* of this dream but couldn't move because my feet were stuck somehow—there was a problem with the floor—and just then a dark figure entered the room and I realized my feet were stuck in quicksand . . .

It was roughly two thirty a.m. non-dreamland time when I tumbled out of bed, caught up in my covers and fighting them for all I was worth. When I hit the bedroom floor with a loud bump and a pain in my leg, I knew, instantly, it hadn't been real—it had been an unpleasant dream—and seeing the clock on the dresser . . . ouch. Way too early to start the day. I rubbed my hip and thigh.

It hadn't just been Dad in the dream. Andrew had been the dark figure who'd walked in just as I realized I was trapped in quicksand.

And that made a lot of sense—*not*.

Or maybe it did—*if* I was worried about not getting free of the mess, but I *had* gotten free. After two years, the only things keeping me tied to the past were my fears and this habit of hiding.

Three nights in a row of this nonsense. Of this nightmare terror. Was this the penalty I had to pay for trying to find that new life? For engaging with life?

At this rate, I'd better beef up my first aid supplies, especially for analgesics, because I was getting too old for this rough treatment.

Okay. I could grab a few hours more of sleep if I could relax and let it happen. I went to the bathroom and got a drink of water, but the bed still didn't look inviting, so I tiptoed downstairs to make sure I hadn't disturbed Harvey and her family when I'd crashed to the floor, and maybe I could snag a bit of that good-feelings bubble to help me find sleepyland again.

The night-light in the foyer cast enough light to see well enough, except gifts of mice. Hopefully, that was a one-time event and there'd be no more of those. Again, I smiled. I was developing a strange sense of humor, but at least it was humor.

By the low light spilling into the half bath through the partly open door, all seemed well with Harvey. As far as I could make out, her eyes stayed closed, but she was aware, of that I was certain. She was becoming accustomed to me, and I to her. I liked the feeling.

Very different from how I'd felt less than a day ago.

Like a kaleidoscope refocus.

I liked that idea.

Beyond the front part of the hallway, the foyer night-light wasn't effective. On nights when the moon was bright, I could maneuver quite well into the kitchen without switching on artificial lights—which was good, since tonight I'd neglected to switch the back porch light on. I flipped the light switch and discovered I hadn't forgotten. The light simply hadn't come on. The bulb seemed to have burned out. I'd put a new bulb in tomorrow, first thing, and be thankful tonight for the moonlight to navigate by.

I needed a snack. Maybe crackers? Or oatmeal raisin cookies?

I followed the moonlight to the cabinet on the far side of the kitchen sink and window to grab a small plate. As I passed the sink, I looked out into the night, and I . . . I stared. In the dark and the shadows of night, the thin strip of light outlining the garage door was shocking.

Chapter Nine

Light would only show in the garage if the interior light was switched on.

From the kitchen window, I could see the thin bright lines across the top and bottom of the sliding door. The garage was at the back of the yard, but the yard wasn't that deep.

Okay. So the light was on out there. But how had that happened? I hadn't been out there today or any day recently. The thin bright edge of light probably wouldn't be noticeable in the daylight, but if it had switched on sometime in the last few days, I would surely have noticed after dark. So today, then? I'd been busy today.

The garage could be entered from the backyard or the alley. Someone, decades ago, had installed a manual roll-up door on the alley side. On the front, an extra-wide barn-type door slid sideways on rollers, allowing access from the yard. The alley was narrow, as was the garage. It was awkward, but not impossible, to drive in and out of. After all, I'd driven my car in there when I'd arrived.

Anyone could be traipsing around back there in the dark.

I should replace the porch bulb now. I wouldn't go out to

the garage in the night and alone, but the porch light was right next to the kitchen door. It would be safe enough, wouldn't it?

My phone. If I had my phone, I could call someone. The police? For a glowing overhead light in my garage and a burnt-out bulb on my porch? It was probably the result of a power surge, like maybe a surge or a backward short in the electric line. Was that a thing? If Florence were still here, I'd have her wait at the back door while I changed the bulb and then went to the garage to check it out. But me here alone? No.

First, I would go upstairs for my phone, then I'd figure out the next steps. I'd been gripping the edge of the sink without realizing it. My hands shook a little as I flexed my fingers. I drew in a deep breath and went for my phone.

It was a good move. By the time I'd grabbed my phone and returned to the kitchen window, I'd calmed down. It was a stupid light in a garage that would interest no one. Even the car was probably past saving, at least without expensive repairs. Mice or other rodents had probably made many meals out of the softer parts of the car engine and burrowed in the upholstery.

Shiver. Yikes.

I reassured myself that this was no more than a fluke. Weighing the risk of going out at night while I was here alone? The risk could be off the charts. Tomorrow, in the light of day, would be soon enough for the garage. But fixing the porch light was very doable tonight.

Back in the kitchen, I stood at the window again, staring. I rubbed my eyes and looked again. I saw no indication the interior garage light was on.

Had viewing the phone screen made it harder to see? Maybe my vision needed to readjust?

Or had I imagined it? Maybe I'd been half-asleep and had only dreamed . . .

No. I'd seen that bright sliver of light around the garage door.

It was likely to be a bad wire or a failing connection. Could it be a fire hazard?

Oh goodness. Enough guessing already.

I found a flashlight in the kitchen drawer and a replacement bulb. The bulb fit snugly into the pocket of my roomy pajama pants, leaving my hands free to carry the flashlight and stool. It was a stool with a flip-up seat and pull-out steps. It was Florence's and so old that it had probably belonged to her parents or grandparents. But it worked fine and was reliable so it was still here and available for me to use.

I stepped out to the small porch. The porch was screened in, but that thin layer of screening was an illusion of security because it couldn't even stop a ticked-off cat from clawing their way in or out if they had the motivation. That image allowed me to smile and feel rather more confident—until the flashlight gleam caught the locks on the porch door and showed me that the hook was dangling and the bolt lock was disengaged.

Quickly, I swept the porch with the light and saw no one, and the area outside of the porch that the torchlight could reach revealed no one.

Could I have forgotten to lock the door? Not likely, but not impossible. There was no way to dislodge the hook and the upper latch from outside without doing actual damage to the screening material. The screening looked unmarred.

I locked both the bolt and hook immediately.

Not a big deal, I told myself. But I wasn't sure of it.

Focus, Leigh. I was out here for the burned-out bulb. The bulb would be changed. It would only take a minute, and then I'd go back to bed and leave other worries for tomorrow.

The bulb was screwed up into a decorative lantern, and the

surface of the bulb was mottled by the shadows created by the moon and flashlight as the light passed through the decorative cutouts, almost camouflaging it. Holding the flashlight at the best angle I could, I reached up through the open bottom of the lantern to grasp the bulb —and something sharp bit into my fingers.

In horror, I snatched my hand back and the stool rocked beneath my feet. Reflexively, I grabbed for the doorframe and felt my fingers slip along the shingles and wood trim as the warm, slick wetness transferred from my injured fingers.

Revulsion made me queasy. I leaned forward, managing to keep one hand clutching the top bar of the stool. I assured myself I was fine. A little blood from cut fingers—that's all it was. Adhesive bandages were in the kitchen drawer. That's what I needed. Meanwhile, I was making a mess. I needed to pull myself together. To think.

A broken bulb. Something had caused the bulb to shatter. Maybe the same power surge that had lit up the garage?

Now down from the stool steps, I held my hand at shoulder height trying to keep my fingers from dripping everywhere, but it didn't work. I hurried into the kitchen, wishing now that I'd turned on the room light so I could see better, but not pausing to do so now because the cleanup was already going to be bad enough. No more blood drips or smears, please . . . Images from every true crime drama I'd sat through with Florence flashed before my eyes. I sacrificed a hand towel, wrapping it around my bleeding fingers, and then crossed to the light switch. I needed light.

Yes, light helped. My initial shock gave way to annoyance —the angry, frustrated kind. The adrenaline rush made the bleeding worse. I held my fingers under the running faucet, examining the cuts. I didn't think stitches were needed, but yes to some serious bandaging, yet how would I manage that one-handed? The hospital? What about transportation . . . ? Middle of the night . . . ? It added up to one huge headache. I could call a taxi or one of those ride services, but somehow I had to get out of my pajamas and into traveling clothes . . . or go dressed as I was.

Was that wet spot on my lashes and touching my cheek . . . was that a tear? No. No crying. I had to be an adult.

I'd *always* had to be an adult, hadn't I? Even when I was a kid.

I was tired.

I was pouting.

I heard the pebbly sound of litter shifting and looked down. Harvey and I met eyes.

"Yes, it's another one of those days. And nights." The truth of the thought hit me with a shock—that this week the universe had suddenly conspired with all its parts to force me from my hiding place. But compared to bringing Harvey home . . . this felt like an unwarranted escalation. I wasn't equal to this.

"Not fair," I said.

Harvey meowed as if responding directly to me. She swished her tail and left the room.

Oh crap. My finger had bled through the towel. This wouldn't do.

I had a knee-length all-weather raincoat I could slip on over my pajamas and casual shoes I could slip my bare feet into. I'd look like a grab bag of clothing, but it was the middle of the night. Who was going to see and judge? Especially with the bleeding.

The nearest emergency room that would be open this time of night was at Retreat Doctor's Hospital. On a nice day, and uninjured, I could've walked the distance in ten minutes or a little more. But not tonight. With the phone on the kitchen counter, I used my good hand—and good fingers—to order a car via a ride app. For when I needed transportation, I typed *NOW*. Continuing to keep my injured hand raised aloft, I grabbed an extra towel from the kitchen, found my purse, and still had enough functioning brain cells to remember to lock the kitchen door. For no rational reason, but only because I wanted to, as I passed down the hallway, I paused to whisper into the half bath, "I'll be back as soon as possible."

Irrational? No, I had reasons—and whether they understood it or not, all of them were depending on me to find my way home again. So no, speaking those words aloud wasn't irrational at all.

It was chilly on the front porch. I stood at the top of the steps, holding my arm across the front of my coat with my good hand under my elbow to elevate my arm and thus the towel-wrapped hand, while trying to keep watch in both directions. It had rained at some point because the street was highly reflective with the city traffic lights going through their red, green, and yellow rotations. I shivered. Maybe I could've just called 911 . . . For broken light bulb cuts? It felt like overkill. I didn't want to look more foolish than I already did.

Oh, so is that why you're standing on your porch in the chilly night's mist in your pajamas in your all-weather coat with a dish towel wrapped around your hand and held aloft like an unlit Statue of Liberty torch?

My lower lip trembled, and my eyes watered again.

"Leigh Ann?"

I jumped, nearly tumbling down the steps as I dropped my purse to grab for the railing. Sam Sr. was there in a few quick steps to steady me. He moved fast for a senior, especially being hampered by holding his dog's leash.

"You're hurt?"

"Cut myself. I called a car. It should be here any time."

"Standing out here in this drizzle in the middle of the

night? We'll leave Maisie at the house, and I'll drive you myself."

"Oh no, I couldn't ask that of you. As you said, middle of the night and all that."

"No, I insist." By now, he had his hand under my elbow supporting my arm. I had no choice but to follow. In fact, we were being led by Maisie, who seemed to understand the situation and wasted no time moving us forward. Since the Marshburn house was only two doors down, it was a quick trip, all things considered. No car had yet arrived, so I said, "Thank you, Mr. Marshburn . . . Samuel. I'm grateful for the ride, but it's not like I'm bleeding to death or anything. Just . . . messy." I was shivering for real now and my jaw was tight. It was difficult trying to speak through chattering teeth.

He opened the front door. "Come inside. I'll get the keys."

As he walked away, I noticed that, like me, he was wearing a coat over his pajamas. Flannel, a lot like mine, but mine had pandas. His pajama pants were plaid.

The Marshburn house was bigger than Florence's, and as my mother might've said, it was well appointed, with tasteful, yet comfy décor. In a jiffy, he had the keys in hand and was leading me back down the steps to his car at the curb. He settled me into the passenger seat, then closed the door and climbed in himself.

He named the nearest hospital, and I agreed. "We'll be there in no time," he said, and we got underway. "Does it hurt?"

"No. It aches. It was unexpected. A shock."

"You don't need to tell me anything. I'm happy to help and glad of the chance to do a good deed. But I am curious . . . I know why I was out and about at three a.m., and it was only because Maisie insisted she had business to do. But shouldn't you be sound asleep? Sam told me about the kittens. Lots of excitement going on over at your house." He grinned. "Harvey was full of surprises!" And then he laughed, loudly and genuinely. I couldn't help smiling too.

"Yes, *he* was."

"So do you mind me asking?"

"About the fingers?"

He shrugged.

"I don't mind. It's embarrassing, though. Stupid."

"I've done some of that in my lifetime. More than I'd like to admit."

"I woke. An unpleasant dream. Nothing big, but just . . ." I shrugged. "So I was thirsty and thought a snack might help me settle down again, but when I went down to the kitchen, well" —*no need to mention the garage or the unlatched screen door* —"I realized the back porch light was out." I took a quick breath. Nodded, then continued, "So I thought I'd change the bulb. A quick job, right?"

"Okay."

"So I grabbed the flashlight, the old step stool, a new bulb and went out." I was feeling better. This sounded reasonable. Sort of. "But when I reached up to untwist the old bulb, the lighting wasn't great and I didn't see it was broken."

"Ouch."

"Yes, exactly. It surprised me, you know? I nearly fell off the stool, but then I got myself together. When I got a better look at the cuts, I realized I might need help with the first aid, maybe even a stitch or two."

"Next time you have a problem, call me." He grinned. "I'll either help—I can change a bulb—or advise sensible choices, like waiting until morning when the light is better."

I let that go unanswered. I'd kept my arm up for a while now. It had grown heavy. My head too. My eyes felt gritty and tired.

"Here we are." He pulled up at the curb.

"You can't park here."

"Just long enough to get you inside."

I fumbled with the door handle. "I can manage."

"Not so sure of that. I'll get you inside first." And he was out and around the car before I managed to put my feet on the pavement.

I did feel a little lightheaded. When he took my arm, I didn't protest. When I stood, I paused to get my balance.

Softly, Samuel said, "The adrenaline has probably dropped. Likely that's what you're feeling."

As he was speaking, a man in blue scrubs came out of the entrance doors, probably wanting to say what I'd already said about parking. But he saw us and stopped, stepping back inside and coming right back out with a wheelchair. I didn't argue with him either.

Samuel said, "She cut her fingers on a broken light bulb. She's bleeding." He leaned toward me. "I'll park and be right in."

"Thanks." I nodded, but I seemed to be speaking in slow motion, and we were already moving.

"I'm okay," I said to the man, and I repeated those words to the person at the admittance desk, but it didn't feel like my voice. I saw the toes of my taupe flats peeking out beyond the hems of my panda bear lightweight flannel pajama pants and my navy all-weather coat and felt confused. It felt almost otherworldly.

"Ma'am?"

"Oh, sorry." I tried to focus.

She asked my name and stuff, and I told her, but when she wanted my ID, I cried. I couldn't get my ID out or my insurance card—not one-handed. Not with my purse balanced on my knees and my hand still elevated in its towel wrap with blossoms of red still growing, though more slowly now. The man behind the chair said, "The person who brought her is parking. Said he'll be right in, that her fingers were cut by a broken light bulb."

The desk attendant said, "Go on to triage. I'll talk to him, and we'll get her info after they check the status of the bleeding."

I caught a glimpse of the waiting room as we moved toward a door beyond the desk. Mostly empty. Some of those folks might be waiting for others. Hopefully, I wasn't skipping the line and leaving someone else untreated because I'd done something foolish.

Like changing a light bulb in the dark.

Adrenaline drop, Samuel had said. Maybe so. Or maybe it was something as basic as feeling naked in public. Not because I wasn't wearing clothing, but because I felt stripped of my disguise and wearing my vulnerability for all to see. I wasn't sure I could handle that.

I was worried about the wrong things, including that I'd have to give them my real name.

Altogether, this was a stupid and embarrassing failure on my part. But one that couldn't be avoided.

Chapter Ten

It was a quiet-ish hour at the ER. The nurse told me that was unusual. I was grateful. No one here seemed to understand or notice that I'd dropped the ball on my usual put-together sleek image. They were more interested in my injury—which again spoke to how quiet the night was in terms of accidents and mishaps that my cut fingers were of such interest. And thus far, no one had shown any interest in my name or my once-familiar face. Perhaps I could credit that to my unbrushed hair and makeup-free face and panda pajamas.

"Ms. Eden, how are you doing?" The nurse brushed around the end of the half-pulled curtain. She took my hand and looked at the cuts again. "The bleeding is much less. Those were remarkably sharp, so the doctor wants to put a stitch in each." She looked at me as if asking a question. I nodded.

"I'll be back in a minute to numb the fingers."

"Thank you."

"There's a man who came with you? He's asking about you. I can let him come back for a minute before we do the stitches if you like?"

The folks at the ER desk had thought Samuel was my

father. She probably thought so too. I started to tell the nurse that, no, he was a neighbor, when I thought better of it. If he was still out there waiting—and he'd already seen what a mess I was—then maybe it would be a kindness to let him come back for a moment to break the tedium for him.

"Sure. Thanks."

She nodded and left.

A minute or so later I heard a voice from the other side of the curtain.

"Leigh?"

"Yes, it's me. Come in." The answer was pure reflex, spoken as realization dawned more slowly that this was not the voice of the elder Mr. Marshburn. As Sam Jr. stepped around the curtain, I wanted to hide under the covers, but he was here now and it was too late. Better to just keep my discomfiture hidden behind my public face.

He frowned slightly. "Are you okay?" He nodded toward the hand resting on a white cloth on the bedside table. "Are you in pain?"

I bit my lip. This would not do. Should I try honesty, maybe? Acknowledge the obvious? Sam was in jeans and a T-shirt with a jacket hanging from his hands, and his dark hair was tousled as if he'd been roused from bed.

"No. Not much now. It bled a lot." I shook my head. With my good hand, I touched my messy hair. "Middle-of-the-night kind of thing. Thankfully, your dad showed up at the right moment and drove me here. Is *he* okay?"

"Yeah. Fine. He was worried I'd call and not reach him at home . . . where he left his phone. I came over and sent him home."

"I'm sorry."

He laughed softly. "Don't be. He didn't mind. He was glad to be of help. So am I."

"You don't have to wait around here. I can get a taxi or an Uber." And then I remembered I'd sort of ghosted one ride already. In the chaos, I hadn't thought to cancel the order. Well, there'd been a lot of blood, so the driver, if he'd ever shown up might well have been grateful. I sighed. I'd figure it out later. I added, "I don't know how much longer this will take."

Just at that moment, the nurse returned. "Not much longer. We'll have you out of here soon."

Soon was a relative term. Despite the nurse arranging my hand and the implements, I spoke directly to Sam, saying, "Truly, I can get myself home."

"No worries. I'm here now. It's no problem." He grinned. "Dad will have a lot to say about it if I abandon you here, and he'd be right." With a nod, Sam vanished back around the curtain.

The nurse was washing my fingers with an antiseptic and applying a numbing agent. She said, "Nice man. The desk said something about him being your father, but he looks too young." She gave me a conspiratorial look as if I was in on some sort of deception. "Maybe a brother?"

"A neighbor," I insisted. "His father brought me into the ER."

"Uh-huh."

My first reaction was that she didn't believe me, but then I realized, no, she was just focusing. She'd already moved on conversationally.

Better that way, anyway. I put my head back on the pillow and counted the ceiling tiles to distract myself from all the thoughts. The fears, the worries. The switch of the Sams.

"Pardon?"

I looked at her. The doctor had arrived.

"Sorry. I thought you said something."

The doctor said, "This shouldn't hurt. If it does, let me

know."

I focused again on counting the tiles. Now that he was working on my wounds, it brought the whole episode back. I *would* go out to the shed today and check. If someone had been messing in there, I'd know. I'd take a look at the overhead outlet too. It was probably old and worn, and the likely culprit.

Unless the porch bulb had been broken on purpose.

If someone had come onto the porch to disable that light.

No. Ridiculous.

But was it?

Was that Florence's voice? Florence and her many crime shows.

"All done."

I stopped counting the ceiling tiles and returned my attention to the nurse and the doctor.

"Thank you so much."

"Keep the bandages dry for a week. Should heal fine if you don't reopen them or get them infected." The doctor stood. "Do you have a primary care physician you can see to have them checked? The sutures will come out on their own, but if there's a problem . . ."

"Sure. Yes." I didn't, but I'd get one.

"All right then, Ms. Eden. Watch out for broken light bulbs." He smiled. "And those . . ." He pointed at my panda-print PJs. "Nice." He left.

****

They insisted I leave by wheelchair. For injured fingers. By now, the lightheadedness I'd felt when I'd arrived was long gone. Truthfully, though, I was glad I'd come here, that I'd had my fingers taken care of properly, which I might not have done if they hadn't bled so much.

Sam stood as we emerged through the automatic doors. "Done?"

The orderly never paused as he asked, "Are you parked out front?"

"Close to it."

I put my feet down, literally and figuratively. "Stop. I'm good now. Thanks for your help. Truly."

I stood, taking Sam's proffered arm. "Thanks, Sam."

As we walked out the door to the outside where a chilly dawn greeted us, I paused and drew in a deep breath.

"You okay?"

"Fine. Truly fine."

He stared at my hair and the mismatched clothing.

"Yeah. A mess. Remember, it was the middle of the night." I laughed it off.

He didn't laugh. He said, "You look amazing."

I turned away.

Gently, he said, "Let's get you home. Harvey's probably wondering where you've vanished to."

That made me smile. I must be insane, but honestly, who could think of Harvey and her babies and not smile?

"You're right. Thank you again. And your dad too."

"You mean that?" He opened the car door. In a different tone, he said, "Watch your fingers."

"Of course I mean it. Why wouldn't—"

He closed the door, cutting me off, and walked around to the driver's side.

I was still frowning, annoyed, as he climbed into the driver's seat and started the car.

He looked at me sternly and said, "Good. Remember that gratitude when I start asking questions about what went on at your house last night."

Chapter Eleven

Rude. So rude. His manner and his question. And intrusive too. Where had the friendly Sam—the one who'd helped me with Harvey and fixed my iced tea—where had he gone? I tightened my jaw and pressed my lips firmly together.

I was grateful. That said, I hadn't asked for anyone's help. It had been offered. So, yes, I appreciated the help both Sams had given me, but the details behind what had happened? What business was it of theirs to question me?

"I am grateful," I said, staring straight forward. "I told your father what happened. Apparently, he didn't choose to relay the details to you."

He made an *mmmm* sound, like a low, one-note hum under his breath, and that was it.

I insisted, "I did."

"What you told him was that in the middle of the night you decided to change the light bulb on your back porch." He skewed his head around, looking at something across the street. "Hey, are you hungry? Doughnut shop over there. Maybe coffee?"

"No thank you," I said, but the words were heavily laced with annoyance.

"Have it your way."

"I will." I didn't want to be annoyed. I wanted to simply be gracious and move on. But I couldn't shake this vulnerable feeling, and it made me feel exposed.

By now, we were only a couple of blocks from my house.

"So, Leigh, this is the thing. Granted that people can make unexpected decisions at odd times or under stress, and maybe you weren't sleeping well, but you are sensible. I just don't see you undertaking bulb changes in the dark without a better reason than that the light wasn't working." He turned onto my street. "And"—he flashed me a quick sideways grin—"my dad has pretty good instincts. When I was a kid . . ." He laughed. "Even now, he sees through my evasions and omissions often enough. He doesn't always call me on it, but I can tell he's choosing to let it go.

"And he told me you skipped over something." He shrugged. "Now if it's just a personal thing, then say so, and I'll quit pushing you." He pulled the car over and came to a halt in front of my house. "But," he said, turning to face me squarely, "if you have some sort of problem—I don't know . . . maybe something serious or even just mechanical—I hope you'll take me into your confidence because you don't like to ask for help . . . or advice . . . and for now, you're gonna be a little hampered by that injury, so let's talk before the problem gets bigger or you risk undoing all the good work the doctor did on your hand."

"My *fingers*."

"Your fingers."

Heavens, but I felt petty. And ungrateful. But asking for help, or even accepting it when offered, was never easy for me. I came from a home where nothing was given—not a gift or favor—without exposing a weakness or incurring an obligation.

But the Sams—both of them—were different. I knew that.

He broke the silence. "Sit tight. Let me get the door for you. Focus on protecting your hand." He pulled his door handle.

"Wait," I said. "I *am* grateful."

"I know, Leigh."

"I did omit something, but it wasn't a big deal . . . it was just . . . rather perplexing. If I mentioned it to your dad, he might've felt the need to look into it himself, and I . . . Not that I think it's a dangerous thing, but he doesn't need to get dragged into something that's probably nothing." I stopped.

"Thanks. I appreciate that you were concerned about my father. But here I am. If there is anything I can do for you, now is the time to tell me. For instance, I'm assuming you didn't get that light bulb changed? So how about I come in with you and I'll finish the bulb job."

"Oh. That's true." I stared at him. "You sure?"

"Positive."

"Okay, then. Thank you."

"But only if you don't mind me fixing some coffee. I'm overdue."

"Well . . . I'm not sure about that." Then I laughed. "Okay, it's a deal. Make a cup for me too." I waved my hand, but carefully. "I don't know how I'm going to manage with this."

"Too bad it's your right hand."

"It would be worse if it was my left hand."

"A leftie? Okay, sit tight." He came around and opened the door.

Exiting the car without the use of both hands was awkward, but Sam took my arms and helped propel me to my feet. I handed him my purse.

"You can dig out the keys. They are in that side pocket." This one-handed thing was going to be a total pain in the butt.

****

We were barely in the foyer when Harvey welcomed us with a loud meow. As much as I might like to think it was a genuine welcome, I suspected the food dish was empty. And it was.

Sam stopped to peek at the kittens. I managed the food refill promptly and without undue awkwardness.

"Sam?"

He joined me in the kitchen.

"Are you going to fix that coffee you mentioned? If so, I'm going upstairs to change. Do you mind?"

"Be careful of that hand. The fingers, I mean."

"Will do."

But when I reached the second floor, I went to my room and sat on the side of the bed. To catch my breath? To give myself a moment to think? To recenter, maybe.

I wished Florence were here.

And that was a totally extraneous thought.

Why would I miss her at this moment? Because she would talk about it all, chew over the aspects of it, and make it seem like just a thing. An interesting thing that didn't reflect on me in any negative way.

Life. Just life. No bad guy. No failure.

Onward, I told myself.

Because of my hand and the bandage, I hadn't belted the coat but had put it over my shoulders, so it was easy to shed with a shrug. I managed to ditch the PJs without difficulty. Washing one-handed was tricky, so the benefit was limited. I'd figure out bathing later. Hair-brushing and tooth-brushing were manageable. I could figure this out.

Florence's hairdresser would probably be willing to help me wash my hair. She'd come to the house a few times when Florence hadn't been able to go to her salon. Maybe I'd even get a trim while she was here.

Coffee. The aroma wafted up the stairs. I kicked into faster gear.

Was that bacon? My guilty pleasure. I didn't eat bacon until Florence. Now, I rationed it—one slice and infrequently. I was guessing Sam had violated the ration rule.

I opted for stretchy pants. Donning them was tricky with one hand, but with no zipper or snap to finagle it was doable. I pulled a loose, wide-necked T-shirt over my head and then added a lightweight cardigan over that.

Good enough for a dawn breakfast.

Keeping my good hand on the railing, I descended. So many charming smells greeted me, along with the sounds of life—of other lives within this space. Sam and the kittens. So tiny—I watched them for a moment. Mama Harvey was absent, so I knelt and touched the gray one and then the calico. There was an orange baby too, just like mama. What Sam had said was likely true—a geneticist could probably map a chart of this and figure out what color the daddy must've been. I stroked the backs of each of them gently before Harvey returned. She meowed and pushed past my arm, using her body to move my hand away from the little ones.

"Sorry, Harvey," I whispered.

I stepped back as she settled in with them. She was ignoring me, maybe. At least she didn't seem upset that I'd touched them.

"That you, Leigh?"

"Who else?" I answered as I joined Sam in the kitchen.

"Perfect timing."

He'd even set the table.

"Wow," I said.

"I'm putting the eggs on now. Do you prefer scrambled or fried?"

Sam and the kitchen were in full breakfast-production mode.

"Doesn't matter. Only one egg for me."

"Cooking is going to be awkward for a few days. Thought I'd get you off to a good start before leaving you on your own to slowly starve."

I stared. "Uh, thank you?"

He laughed. "Seriously, just don't be angry that I took this job on without asking."

"I'm grateful, remember?"

"Then have a seat."

I did and I watched. I'd never watched a man cook. Dad certainly had not. And Andrew didn't cook—at least he hadn't in my presence. Why watching Sam fascinated me, I couldn't have said, but it did. His movements were focused and efficient. When he was done and the food was on the table, he apologized for not having toast.

"I couldn't find the bread," he explained.

"This is wonderful. I don't eat that much. This is like a week's worth of breakfast, as it is."

"Eat while it's hot." He took a bite himself, and while I was chewing, he said, "I already checked the bulb. It's stuck up in the socket—that's why it broke when you tried to unscrew it. I'm going to need some needle-nose pliers to work it out. Do you have any?"

I was slow to answer. Either he thought I was mistaken about what had happened or I hadn't been clear.

He added, "If not, Dad has a pair I can borrow."

"No, I do have a pair. But, Sam, I never got that far. It was when I reached inside the lantern part to unscrew the bulb that I was cut. The bulb was already broken."

He wanted to insist that I must've tried to unscrew it and caused it to break. I could see the struggle on his face between simply accepting what I'd said or not.

"Seriously, Sam. I know it was already broken. Not that it matters." Except that it did. To me, anyway.

"It was the middle of the night, Leigh. You were probably half-asleep."

I interrupted. "Stop right there or I'm not going to be grateful anymore."

He frowned.

"I was wide-awake, and I remember clearly what happened."

He sat back. This felt awkward now. But I couldn't drop it. I was a grown woman, competent and not given to delusion.

"Okay," I said. "So please listen. This is what happened. I woke in the night from a bad dream, came down for a snack, and walked into the kitchen. The moon gave me light to walk by. I checked the switch for the porch light, thinking I'd forgotten to flip it before going to bed, but no, I'd turned it on and now it wasn't working. When I looked out the kitchen window, I saw the light was on in the garage."

His expression changed.

"I haven't been out there in a while, and I'm confident that the light has not been on, yet I could see it rimming the garage door." I breathed. "So I considered going out there to check . . . but didn't because I was here alone and the porch light, as you know now, was out."

"That was smart."

I nodded. "I suppose so. But after I went upstairs for my phone and returned to the kitchen, the garage light was off again." I shook my head. "At that hour, being alone and not knowing what was up, I wasn't going out there to investigate the garage but the porch bulb was within easy reach with Florence's old step stool, and I had my flashlight.

"A little light on the porch would give me some security, especially since the porch door wasn't latched." I shrugged, adding, "I must've forgotten to lock it with all the Harvey stuff. It felt important to change that bulb."

I shook my head, remembering. "When I went out there, though, it felt creepy because of the garage thing, I suppose, and the porch door not being locked. When I reached up to grab the bulb, my fingers were cut. That was my first touch. I could *not* have mistaken that. The only contact I had with the bulb was when it sliced into my fingers."

He nodded. "Did you consider calling the police about the garage light?"

"Not seriously. Likely, it's just a wiring issue, but I do need to know in case it's also a fire hazard. I'll take a look in there today, and depending on what I see, I'll call an electrician or a repairman."

"I'm in."

"I can do it. No need to tie you up."

He consumed the last slice of bacon with a pleased look. "Nope. I insist. You are hampered by the injury. Plus, while I'm no electrician, I'm pretty handy."

"I'll bet you are."

He grinned. "Can it wait until I've cleaned the kitchen?"

"I can . . . No, not yet. I mean I can manage . . ."

"It'll take me two minutes. It'll take you longer than that to get your jacket and shoes on."

"Is that a challenge?"

He started gathering up the dishes. "Maybe, but in a good way. I'll be happy to wait for you if you're slower."

****

We approached the garage cautiously. The lock was obviously in place on the sliding door.

"I keep both doors, front and back, locked unless I'm in here." I unlocked the door. The door on the alley was closed. The interior was dusty, and the car and all the stuff we'd stored in here filled it up. Cars had gotten bigger over the years, presumably. This old garage had not, and as one does when looking for something, things had been moved out here and left on the worktable and set in the narrow walkway.

"As you can see, I'm not often in here."

It was a close fit. There was no room for moving around inside, even if someone had been motivated to do so.

Sam and I stood at the open door. He stared. I was embarrassed, feeling as if I could see it through his eyes. *Neglect. Messy. Slovenly.* Which adjectives were swarming in his mind?

"That's your car? How long since anyone drove it?"

"Long."

"You'll need a mechanic to check it over. See if it's drivable."

"Or sell it."

"That too."

He was staring into the dusty murk, so I waited. After a long minute, he grunted and shook his head. "I'm trying to envision someone messing around in here, and it's hard to imagine what they would be trying to accomplish." He moved into the interior and stared at the concrete floor, then up at the ceiling.

"I'd check that overhead light fixture now, but with the car in the way . . ." He paused, then asked, "Where's the light switch?" But he didn't wait for an answer. "Here it is." He reached into the corner. The light came on.

His hand moved and the light went off. He gave it a few more tries.

"There's a switch at the other end too." I said, "From this end, the fixture appears to be working fine, so what did I see last night?"

He didn't say the obvious or repeat what he'd said before —that I must've been mistaken or half-asleep and dreaming. He said, "Who knows? Moisture, maybe insects could affect function."

"But probably not an intruder."

He looked at me. "That's good news, isn't it?"

I shrugged. "I suppose so." At least it meant I didn't need to call the police. "We should check the switch at that end too."

We did. We exited through the gate in the back fence. After I unlocked it, the garage door on the alley rolled up just fine. The light switch performed as expected.

"I see no indication that it's a wiring problem or that anyone was in here. My advice?"

"Go ahead."

"Get the car out of there, get it checked, and while it's out of the way, have an electrician check the wiring just in case. And while you're at it, have someone service this roll-up door too."

I grunted noncommittally.

He smiled. "Let's fetch the prescriptions the doctor wrote for you. I can probably pick them up myself if you'd rather stay here."

"Sam."

"Yes, ma'am?"

"You are very kind. But I'm going to have to figure this out for myself." I pointed to the bandage. "I'll be good. Careful, even. Please know how much I appreciate your help."

"My pleasure." He ignored the rest of what I'd said and

continued with, "Today, I am at your disposal until later this afternoon and then I have to go to work. Tell me what you need."

I shouldn't. I knew I shouldn't take advantage.

"Cat food and litter. Maybe a few groceries?"

He grinned. "That I can do."

Chapter Twelve

When Sam returned, I was tired and my fingers hurt. Sam read the prescription instructions out loud—one for pain meds and the other was an antibiotic.

"I'll get a glass of water. You can take the doses now, and I'll leave the bottles on the kitchen counter." And he did.

And I let him.

I said, "You don't have to leave right this minute unless you actually do need to. I admit I'm taking advantage of you."

With a glance, Sam took in the pillow and blanket I'd left on the floor in the wide opening between the foyer and living room.

"I hung out with Harvey and the quads while you were gone."

Without a word, he leaned back against the other end of the framed opening. With a slow, controlled movement, he eased down to the floor. "Mind if I join you?"

I laughed. I sat too. We stretched our long legs out in front of us; the tips of our toes would've been touching if we hadn't been sitting slightly aslant. Sam was wearing navy socks. His foot size made my own feet look almost petite. Not that it mattered.

We sat in that comfortable silence for a couple of minutes, and I wondered, *What does Harvey make of all this*? Perhaps Harvey's magic was working its way beyond her tiny family and encompassing the two of us.

Into the warm and fuzzy space, Sam said, "Don't get me wrong, I know Florence loved her house, and maybe you do too, but you're a different person than Florence. Don't you feel isolated or alone here?" And then he kind of laughed, saying, "Or did, right? But while Harvey and family are pretty cute, it's not the same, is it?"

My jaw felt frozen. Only defensive words came to mind. I reminded myself that I'd invited him to hang out and I was grateful he'd been so helpful.

"I stay busy."

He nodded, but he looked unconvinced. "I think you're more of a doer than Florence. She was a dreamer." He paused, then added, "Have I said too much?"

"I understand that you mean well, Sam. If you didn't, you would never have been so very kind and helpful. But I don't think . . . I mean, a lot happened in my family, and it's taken a while to get past it. Might take a while longer."

I'd kept my voice clear, calm, and steady. I looked down at my hands and then over at the nursery, feeling a little agitated and not sure where to take this conversation.

He said, "Okay. Makes sense."

But he left it there, which annoyed me.

"May I ask *you* a personal question?"

He nodded.

"None of my business, so you can refuse to answer, but you are so good with Harvey. Clearly, you have an affinity for animals. Why didn't you stay in that vet program?"

Shrugging, he said, "It's true. I'm good with animals. Not quite the touch that Don has, though." He sighed, but softly. "I don't mind saying it—I cared too much. I couldn't separate my feelings from the living, breathing ones and deal with the other side of that, too."

"Oh." I was so very sorry I'd asked.

"Analytics and managing risk were where I landed. A good vet, like a good doctor, can care but to do the job as it should be done, they must also be objective. That was hard for me."

"Thank you, Sam."

He met me eye for eye. "It's a blessing, Leigh. It's good to know where you belong. To be able to find joy in both the thing you're good at, as well as the thing you love." He nodded again. "It's all good."

We were silent for a few minutes and then I noticed his attention had shifted. He was looking across the living room toward the open doorway of the small side study.

Florence had called the tiny room her library. It wasn't large, but it was jam-packed with books of all sorts, except for an open spot directly in view. A painting was displayed there —a landscape of a rough hillside and a plain house. An old two-story farmhouse, but the lighting was kind and the blue sky above the field and buildings gave the scene a certain grace.

Florence could spend hours in there curled up in an over-stuffed corner chair, reading, journaling, daydreaming. I watched Sam staring at it, wishing I could read his mind.

Now he was watching me. He smiled, saying, "It does kind of look like a window, doesn't it?"

"Pardon?"

"Florence's painting." He smiled broader, but in a gentle, remembering kind of way. "When I was a teenager, she said she hung it there so that when she caught sight of it, even from the corner of her eye, it was like seeing through a window. A window to the past is how she phrased it."

Wanting to be polite, I nodded. "I can see that. If there was a window there, we'd only be seeing the brick wall of the next-door neighbor's house."

He waited. I wasn't sure for what.

I shrugged. "City life, right?"

He said, "The place in the painting is where she was born. Her family's place. Her father moved them into town when she was young and rented the house and farm out."

I had a recollection of Florence pointing out the painting and mentioning property out in the country. But it was when she was introducing me to her house soon after I arrived. I, myself, was in chaos, my whole life feeling fluid and volatile. Florence hadn't said much about the house and land in the painting, and that was the only time I could think of her mentioning it until her attorney had explained the will to me. More recently, her accountant had mentioned paying property taxes on the land and that the insurance costs were going up.

I glanced over at the painting, then back at him. I murmured something like, "She mentioned it."

He shook his head. "She loved the memories of it, but she also loved the city—the convenience, the close neighbors and her friends. Even so, she was lonely. She was glad you came to stay with her and continued to stay. I was sitting here listening to the cat sounds, remembering, and thinking Florence would love this." He laughed. "Can you imagine how excited she'd be about Harvey and the kittens?"

I nodded, my eyes stinging. "No doubt. It was a shock at first, you know? But they find their way into your heart quickly."

"Uh-oh," he said. "Don't tell me you're already worrying about letting them go?"

"Jerk." I looked down at my fingers, clasped and resting on my thighs. "Anyway, no, because I barely have them. I hardly even know *what* to think." We both knew I was denying the truth.

"Well, okay," he laughed. "When you *do* have those feelings, know that it is rational. And I'm sure it will feel equally rational to consider new homes by the time those helpless, adorable, cuddly furballs currently living in your guest bathroom are older and mobile and impossible to contain."

I nodded. "Thanks for your help yesterday and the day before."

His smile dimmed a bit. "Glad I could be of assistance."

"Seriously, Sam. Grateful doesn't cover it." I lifted my bandaged hand. "When this is better, I think I'll owe you a meal. I might even cook for you, if you're open to that."

He frowned. "*Can* you cook?"

"Where's the trust, Sam?" I laughed. "Where's the gratitude?"

****

Sam showed up every day for the next few days. I'd get a call or a text asking what I needed. He was careful, though, about respecting boundaries. Gradually, my defenses weakened and I began looking forward to that notification on my phone or the ring that might be from him. Florence's hairdresser came over and washed and trimmed my hair right there in the kitchen. Awkward? Maybe a little, but I felt pampered. The kittens were moving more too, and their meow-squeaks were, if not louder, certainly more demanding each time Harvey left the box to take a break. She never stayed away long, and it was during one of her mommy breaks about a week after they were born that I snuck a closer peek and discovered the gray baby had her eyes open.

Blue. Don had mentioned that all newborn kittens had blue eyes and that they'd change. I'd researched that online and found it to be true. Not finding mama, little gray tried to fix her unsteady gaze on me, her wobbly head almost seeming to bob in surprise at seeing me. I ran the back of my finger along the sleek, silky baby fur of her neck and back. She stretched her neck, raising her head, and then gently toppled over. Harvey returned. I backed away.

I had no idea whether the kittens were male or female.

Didn't matter. I was enjoying watching them, so tiny and helpless, growing and changing before my eyes, and their personalities were already showing. Well, I might be over-stating that. They were barely a week old. It would probably be more objective to say that the gray kitten seemed pushier and bolder. The ginger baby was more vocal. The other two, a calico and a light peach, would have to step up their game.

In my head, I heard a warning, like something my mother might've cautioned me about if I'd had the kind of childhood where it might have applied—*Don't get too attached. At some point, you'll have to let them go.*

It was like having Sam's voice in my head. And I remembered he'd said it was reasonable to get attached. Not foolish at all. It was simply human.

****

Almost two weeks since the kittens were born and almost a week and a half into my fingers healing, the results were good on both counts. My fingers still required bandages, but adhesive strips were sufficient. The bandages also served to remind me to be careful for a while yet.

Sam had been out of town for the past three days working for a client for whom he was doing risk assessment work, and I thought that was a good thing. His absence—and me being alone in the house except for the cats—had helped me refocus.

Aside from the cats, I lived alone. As far as I could see, I'd continue being on my own for the foreseeable future. Focusing on what needed to be done could be very satisfying. All of this —everything that had happened since the day the woman had thrust Harvey upon me, and into my life—had reenergized me. I'd been coasting with Florence but never moving forward. Hiding. And after losing her, that hadn't changed. I might even have been going backward. So yesterday, I'd made arrangements for a mechanic to help me with the car, to check out whether it was drivable.

There'd been no new problems with the light in the garage, at least not that I'd seen, and this morning I'd felt emboldened to walk to the store again. Symbolically reclaiming my life? Maybe. But it was more than that. Had it been so hard to move on with my life because I could never go back, and some part of me resisted that?

Had I truly enjoyed my life before the downfall? At the time, I'd thought I did. I'd been busy. I'd felt successful. Now I wondered what happiness truly felt like. Had I just been performing? Wanting to feel accomplished and worthwhile? Valued?

But if I couldn't go back . . . the problem was that I didn't know what going forward looked like.

With my tote bag hanging from my shoulder, I walked along the sidewalk attuned, as usual, to the cracks and roots beneath my shoes and the trees overhead. Everything around me looked brighter. I felt lighter. Sam was due back tomorrow evening. I intended to find something edible that would require minimal use of my fingers to cook. I'd surprise him with a meal.

I grabbed a few toiletry and grocery items for me and Harvey, including a soft brush thinking she might let me groom her a little, and a frozen entrée and bagged salad for Sam, then headed home, though I did pause in front of the brown stucco house. There were still no signs of life at the old woman's house . . . and I was okay with that.

Wherever they were, I hoped both women were doing well. Because Harvey et al. and I most certainly were.

****

Home again. As I stepped into the foyer, I set the tote bag on the area rug, slipped off my shoes, and heard kitten sounds. Harvey was probably taking a mommy break. I walked down the hallway and peeked into the nursery, and yes, Harvey wasn't there. The babies seemed fine. Just restless, except for little Flo, who was curled up and napping.

In the kitchen, I emptied the tote bag only half thinking about the task because Harvey wasn't in her litter box, she wasn't at the water and food dishes . . . Might she have wanted a bigger break from the babies? I called out, "Harvey? Where are you?"

A loud, long meow, an urgent one, came from the far side of the back door.

Without hesitation, I flipped the deadbolt and twisted the doorknob. Harvey rushed through the opening, slipping right past me, ignoring me, and heading straight to her little ones.

As for me? I stood there, hand still on the knob, stunned. Shocked. I couldn't move away from the door.

This made no sense.

I stared outside at the porch and the screen door. The porch door hook lock was hanging free again. The latch bolt had been pushed back.

The front door of the house had been locked when I left, right? Yes, surely. I knew I'd locked it behind me, and it was locked when I returned because I'd needed the key to come in.

I shook my head. Was I losing my mind?

As for the kitchen door, I hadn't opened it since yesterday. It was locked, for sure. Since the broken bulb adventure, I'd been especially careful. So someone . . .

The bits and pieces swarmed in my brain. I pressed my hands to the sides of my face, trying to calm down.

This made no sense.

Should I be checking inside the house for intruders?

But why? How did Harvey get out to the porch? Was an intruder still in the house? The deadbolts, front and back, required a key.

Whoever had opened the door and let Harvey out had almost certainly left that way . . . but hadn't come in that way because the screen door had been latched. I was sure of it.

My cell phone rang. I didn't recognize the number, but given the turn this day had taken, I answered it.

"Hello?"

"Leigh? Ms. Sonder? This is Don . . . the vet? Sam's friend?"

"Oh, of course. Sorry. I was distracted."

"Is this a good time to chat? I called Sam first to ask about Harvey and the kittens, and he suggested I call you directly. I hope that's okay?"

"Do you think there's a problem?" One more problem. I was getting that piled-on feeling.

"No, not at all. I had a few minutes free and remembered your cats and wanted to check on them. Any signs of trouble like problems feeding or listlessness or gunk in the eyes?"

I smiled despite myself. "Is that an official medical term—gunk in the eyes?"

He laughed softly. "It's descriptive."

"So far as I can tell, everyone is fine. Harvey takes regular, brief breaks, and the babies always seem to be eating or sleeping. They are growing before my eyes—and speaking of eyes, two, maybe three now, have their eyes open." I closed my own eyes. How tempting it was to lose myself in this conversation and pretend that nothing had happened.

I cleared my throat. "Actually, if you don't mind, and if you have a minute, could you hang on the phone with me while I walk through my house?"

Chapter Thirteen

"Pardon?"

I said, "I know this sounds ridiculous. I won't go into details, but I just got back home and somehow Harvey had gotten out . . . and I want to check upstairs in case . . . I'm so sorry. I can't believe I'm asking you to hold my hand over the phone while I reassure myself that no one else is here in the house."

"Maybe you should call the police?"

"Generally, yes. But cats slip out, right? I might've forgotten or slipped up and didn't notice her getting out when I was leaving earlier . . ." I dismissed the other stuff that argued against that. For now, I needed reassurance. "So, if you don't mind . . ."

"Okay. But if I hear anything alarming . . . or don't hear anything, for that matter, I'm calling the police. I've got your address here."

"I feel better already. I'm just jumpy. Hang in here with me, okay?"

And by golly, I did it. I went through the house, both the

main floor and upstairs, chatting with Don as I opened closet doors and peeked under the beds and behind the couch.

"It's a small, narrow house. Not many places to hide. I think I can safely say there's no one here but me and the cats. Do you think I'm unbalanced?"

"Not at all. But next time I hope you'll call the police if you are worried or if stuff gets weird."

Breathing a huge sigh, I said, "Stuff does get weird sometimes, doesn't it? Though, I wonder if the weirdness is in the eye of the beholder, or the mindset of the . . . Here I go again."

I heard a distant voice speaking to the doctor, summoning him back to work.

"I'd better go," he said.

"Thank you."

"My pleasure, Leigh. If I didn't have a patient waiting, I'd ask what you would've done if I hadn't called just at that time. Don't misunderstand. I'm glad you spoke out and that I could help, but when in doubt, and you're alone, be safe even if you might be mistaken. Trust your instincts and don't worry about the rest."

Don't worry about looking foolish. That's what he meant. But he didn't know my history. He didn't understand my concern about not being noticeable, especially to law enforcement or to anyone who might get curious about me and have the means to satisfy that curiosity. Privacy, that's what it was about for me. And hiding. Even now.

I was better? Yeah. But I still had a ways to go.

****

Yes, I knew I was alone here. But I was uneasy. How could I not be?

116

It was tempting to call Sam, but it would seem as if I was suggesting he come home...and what? Hold my hand?

I was here alone (excepting the cats) because I lived alone. I did sleep that night, but my rest was uneasy.

In the morning, in the daylight, I felt better. Plus, Sam was coming back to town later today and I would surely be seeing him.

****

Earlier than expected, he called to ask if I needed anything.

"I'm still an hour or so out," he said, "so I can stop anywhere."

"I don't need a thing."

"Oh."

He sounded a little disappointed. Or I thought he did. Quickly, I added, "Let's do supper," I said.

"Okay. Sure. When?"

"Today. This evening."

"Good with me. I'll drive straight to your house. Will that work?"

"Perfect."

I turned the oven on to preheat and did a quick tidying up of the house and myself. It was fun to have a friend over. Especially a friend like Sam.

He stopped at the nursery door first thing. "They look great. I can't believe how much the kittens have grown." He knelt to rub the top of Harvey's head. She closed her eyes and looked pleased.

"Maybe she missed you too."

He shifted his position to face me. "Too?"

I gave him a pretend frown. "Well, you missed her, right?" Before he could answer, I added, "And, of course, I missed you. How could I not? You make yourself almost indispensable. I believe I've thanked you a few times. Grateful, right?" I grinned.

He touched my hand. "Not much of a bandage left."

"Healing well. In large part, thanks to you and your father."

He stood, still holding my hand. I lingered there with him for a moment until he asked, "Where would you like to go to eat?"

"If *you* don't mind, let's stay here. I've kept it simple. I bought bagged salad and a frozen lasagna, so the real work is already done."

"We'll stay here to eat?"

"If you're okay with that. And if you won't try to take over and do all the work yourself?"

"Promise. What can I do to help?"

"Relax. The lasagna will be coming out of the oven in about twenty minutes."

"I'll pour the tea?"

"Perfect."

I wondered if he would mention Don calling him and then calling me. Had Don given him an update afterward? Like about hanging on the phone with me while I walked through my house? I didn't think he had, though, because surely Sam would've mentioned it by now. Instead, Sam had paused at the sink. The fridge was adjacent, so he'd gone over there to get the tea . . . but now he was standing and staring out of the window. I got a tiny chill up my spine.

"Sam?"

He turned, shaking his head. "Sorry. Caught sight of the garage." He grinned, holding the pitcher. "Here's the tea. Do you want lemon?"

Sam managed to transfer the hot lasagna from the oven to

the table. As we served up the salad and pasta, I volunteered, "Don called yesterday to ask about Harvey and the kittens." I smiled. "Very thoughtful of him."

Sam nodded, but he didn't speak. Instead, he took a bite of the lasagna.

"Glad he called." He paused and his tone changed. "Was it a problem?"

"No, of course not."

"But it sounds like it might be?" His words were questioning. Almost careful.

"Definitely not. Happily, Harvey and the kittens seem to be doing fine. I just wondered if he might have mentioned . . . Never mind."

"Please, Leigh. Just say it."

"I guess he didn't." I grimaced. "It's a little embarrassing. When he called, I'd just returned home from walking to the store and back. When I left, Harvey was with the kittens. When I returned home, Harvey was on the back porch and howling at the back door—the locked back door—desperate to get inside."

"You let her out?"

"No. That's the point. She was on the back porch. I left by way of the front door, so even if she slipped past me somehow when I left, how would she have gotten stuck on the back porch?"

"Was the screen door to the porch locked?"

"No." I shook my head. "Okay, so you're thinking she could've come around to the back and managed to push the screen door open?" With an exasperated sigh, I said, "I suppose that's possible, but unlikely."

Sam seemed focused on the lasagna, but he'd been listening, so I waited.

He said, "So what's the alternative, Leigh? Someone broke

in? No signs of a break-in, right? You suspect someone managed to get into the house during that one time that you were away and did so without leaving any sign of how they managed it, right?"

I nodded.

"For what purpose? To let Harvey out?"

"What? No, of course not." I stared at him, almost daring, perhaps begging him not to dismiss my concerns.

He sat back and took a slow sip of iced tea. I did the same, cultivating a bit of cool.

"I've thought it through, Sam." I kept my voice even, almost disinterested. Like solving a puzzle. "If someone came through the front door and locked it behind them, then exited through the kitchen door and out the porch door, that would explain why the porch door wasn't latched or hooked." I took a lazy sip of my tea and set the glass back down gently. "Of course, to do that, they'd surely need to have a key to lock and unlock the deadbolts."

I let that sit for a long moment, then said, "Change of subject. I have arranged for a mechanic to check the car, to see if it can be driven safely. At least, driven out of the garage. Your dad recommended him. He's coming over tomorrow afternoon, so I'll go out there in the morning and move some of the junk out of the way."

He gave me a long look and nodded. "Good. But what about the problem of someone in the house?"

I shrugged. "Seems like we exhausted the topic."

"Not necessarily. Something happened. Might be nothing more than a sneaky cat slipping out when you left and panicking when she realized she couldn't get back in. They can move swiftly, quietly, and through surprisingly narrow gaps. But I agree, it seems unlikely that you wouldn't notice. I just don't have a better explanation. With you here alone, as you are . . . maybe that's not the best choice for you."

"As you say, it's how it is now. Florence is gone."

"Maybe there are other options."

"I'm okay. I'm careful about locking doors. I've never been afraid here, and I don't want to start now. It's my home." I shrugged.

"Then consider an alarm system."

I nodded. "I'll look into that."

"If you get uneasy, you know my dad wouldn't mind having you over . . . or coming over himself if you need company, but I warn you—he'll expect to control the TV remote." He smiled, but his eyes stayed somber. He reached over and touched my hand, lifting the bandaged fingers, then said softly, "And it looks like I have to pay for my meal after all?"

Bemused, I just stared. Seeing my fingers on his hand, his fingers brushing mine, was almost hypnotic.

"Working for my supper?" he prompted, then he turned his hand, and my fingers were now resting on his open palm. "These can't go into dishwater. Too soon." He withdrew his hand, and for a long moment mine remained suspended over the tabletop, my fingers still extended. He sat back. "I'll get to work rinsing the dishes and loading them into the dishwasher."

And he did. And while the dishwasher was doing its job, Sam stayed awhile longer. We took a moment to admire the kittens without disturbing them, and then, together, and while there was still light enough to see outside, we took a walk around the exterior of the house. I was reminded of watching those TV shows with Florence, or discussing her most recent true crime book, as Sam and I ruled out evidence of shoeprints below the windows or indications of someone messing around in the yard. He questioned where I might be hiding spare keys outside. I showed him my hiding spot of choice, and he approved it. On the front porch, he moved the large flowerpots, leaning them back to see underneath.

"Florence kept a spare here. Don't see it now."

"Oh, you're right. I'd forgotten about it. She must've removed it a long time ago."

Sam tested the porch lights, front and back. Inside the house, Sam checked each window to be sure it was locked. He rattled the doors and their locks.

"Need a recommendation for an alarm service?"

"You think I'll put it off, don't you?"

"I think that everyone moves at a different pace, often for very different reasons."

"I appreciate your offer of help, yet again."

When we were done with the security tour, Sam took the container of leftover lasagna and salad from the fridge, and together we strolled down the street to deliver it to his dad as a belated thank-you for the pot pie.

Chapter Fourteen

The next day was remarkable on several counts. The weather was beautiful, for one thing, and being mindful of the mechanic coming later in the afternoon to assess my car situation, I went outside first thing that morning. I unlocked and pushed aside the sliding door of the garage. My task was to move some of the boxes and other junk out of the way so the car repair guy could get close enough to the car to assess what work was needed to get it safely running again. He was coming by after his day job to take a look. Samuel had recommended him, saying the mechanic was young but reliable. I could trust him to tell me what I needed to know.

The wagon was still here. It might be useful for moving some of the junk. I'd almost forgotten the mystery of the overhead light from more than a week and a half ago because so much had happened in between—both good and bad—from the broken bulb to Harvey being locked outside, though my fingers protected by adhesive bandages, still in the process of healing, often reminded me.

Another exciting event was a milestone for the kittens. As of this morning, all of them had their eyes fully open, and wow, that step seemed to have signaled a leap forward in their development. They were all over the place, but still within the box except for Baby Gray, who was the largest and promised to be the most adventurous of the litter. She had tried to pull up on the side of the box with her paw while mama was gone, had fallen over with limbs waving, and cried out. Without thought, I'd reached in and picked her up, holding her in the palm of one hand while rubbing her forehead gently with my finger, to console her. And then Harvey returned. With hardly a look at me, she reentered the box and gathered her children to her, then gave me a stare as if . . . My imagination, surely. But as if letting me know that I'd had my fun but it was time to return her baby to her and keep my paws off.

Which I did.

"Thank you, Harvey. Your babies are beautiful."

She put her head down, closed her eyes, and drifted off into a nap.

Ridiculously, my eyes stung. I needed fresh air. I left the foyer and went out to tackle the garage.

Much of what was stored here didn't need to be kept. Other things were keepers. The hard part was that almost all of it had belonged to Florence, and so I couldn't simply toss it. I had no idea what was in most of the boxes and bags. But once these things were gone and the workbench surface was visible again, I could make much better use of the space.

Florence had managed fine without ever driving a car, as I'd done okay for the past two years. Well, until recently. But I was due for a change.

Shortly before lunchtime, I closed the garage door and locked it. I planned to come back out here after lunch and finish up before the mechanic arrived.

When I went into the house, and as soon as I stepped through the kitchen door, I heard Harvey hissing and meowing.

She was standing in the doorway of the bathroom but facing toward the living room. I hurried over to her, but Harvey ignored me. I looked into the living room, and there sat Andrew in my gooseneck rocker. His elbows were on the armrests, but one hand was lifted, and on his palm was Baby Gray.

I didn't freeze and my mind didn't go blank. This was not a stranger, and he was not an unknown quantity when it came to peril. This was Andrew. He didn't belong here, true, but that was a question to ask later. For now, I walked straight toward him, my hands extended.

"Give her to me, Andrew. Carefully."

"Cats? Really, Leigh Ann?" He shrugged and smiled as he placed the mewing kitten in my hand. He muttered in a dismissive way, "It's just a cat."

His slightly amused demeanor . . . I didn't trust it. And I didn't appreciate the condescending tone, though perhaps he hadn't meant it to sound that way. I sensed he was annoyed but didn't want to anger me. I let it go for the moment and instead held Baby Gray close to my body, not too tightly, just snugly enough that she would feel safe. I walked immediately back to Harvey and knelt, settling her baby carefully in the nursery box next to its siblings.

Harvey stepped into the box and her attention shifted to smelling Baby Gray and licking her for all she was worth. I whispered, "I'll be back." Then I closed the door slowly and gently so that the motion was almost soundless.

I swung around to face Andrew. Keeping my voice low and calm for Harvey's sake and for my own, I met his eyes squarely. "That was cruel. We've had our differences, but I would not have expected this of you."

"This?"

"Breaking in. Making yourself at home uninvited. Startling me. Messing with my kittens."

"You are overreacting."

"Your opinion. But this is my house. You don't belong here and you weren't invited, so you don't get to offer your opinions unasked for."

"Life has been difficult," he said, as if stating the obvious —which he was.

I responded in a hard tone, "I know that as well as anyone."

Leaning forward and causing the rocker to squeak, he spread his hands, asking, "Aren't you going to ask how I happen to be inside your home? Why I'm here? For that matter, how did I know where to find you?"

He stood, but he didn't move toward me. I focused on keeping my face blank. I could guess that he'd learned my location from my mother, but I wouldn't play his game by filling in that blank for him.

"So tell me," I said.

"I found your spare key." He grinned. "You look a little blank. Was it your cousin's key? Might've been. It was badly weathered. My best suggestion, Leigh, is to change the locks here and start fresh. Always a good idea in a house that predates your arrival." He pulled the key from his pocket and held it up like a show-and-tell, then set it on the side table.

"What's your *why*, Andrew?"

"I was hoping to chat with you about your father . . . and all that stuff." He shook his head. "I know you don't want to talk about the past, but I need to. *Must* discuss it with you."

"You can go now."

"Leigh. Please."

"I'm not involved in any part of it. Never was. Even so, my

career, not to mention my life, was eviscerated publicly and expensively."

This time his hands moved slightly toward me, and he came half a step closer.

I held up my hand, palm toward him. "Stay where you are. You weren't invited here. You aren't welcome."

"You know I testified against your father to protect you. I made sure you were kept out of it—that mess—as much as possible." His shoulders slumped and he looked sad. "It was a terrible time for all of us."

I spoke clearly and distinctly. "Say whatever you will, I never had anything to do with my father's business or what you may or may not have done as his employee or associate. You know that."

"You urged me not to take a job with him. You said you had doubts, that he wasn't to be trusted. You said—"

I cut him off abruptly. Suddenly I was back in that awful time. Did Andrew deserve my suspicion? I pushed any guilty feelings right off the emotional table. This was about self-preservation. I spoke clearly—distinctly and firmly—in case this exchange was being recorded. "My father and I never got along. I never discussed his business practices with him and never engaged in his business activities. I had precious little engagement with him, even in a family way. Furthermore, Andrew, I remind you that you are not welcome here and are trespassing. Leave now or I'll call the police."

"Calm down, Leigh. Believe it or not, even with all that has happened, I care about you and want to help you, as I did before. It was why I cooperated with the prosecutor." He shook his head. "I can see you aren't aware of this, and I'm sure you don't want to hear it, but you . . . you need to know about recent developments."

"Stop."

He shook his head slowly. "I can't. Please listen. Your father's new attorneys found some irregularities in how the case was handled, and there's some level of negotiation going on about resentencing . . . or more. I don't have the details. Just a whisper from a friend in the know. A heads-up." He nodded, adding, "That's why I'm here. I'm doing the same for you."

My cool demeanor failed me, but my lack of trust and the horror I felt at the idea of all this being resurrected . . . stunned me into silence.

Andrew said, "I wanted to tell you. Not over the phone, of course. I thought it better to come here discreetly, and as you've asked, I'll leave, no problem."

He stopped speaking but didn't move. If he thought I would weaken, he was hugely mistaken.

I found words, and if my voice shook, I couldn't help it and didn't care. "When you talk to my father again, you tell him not to contact me. Not to send his attorneys to talk to me. And not to send you again. I have nothing to say about any of this. I was never involved in it, and I'll stay out of any resulting chaos."

Andrew shrugged and looked down at his shoes. A lock of his dark hair fell forward. When he looked up, he combed the hair back with his fingers, but he didn't meet my eyes. "I haven't spoken to your dad or his attorneys." He put his hands in his pockets and grimaced. "The folks who put him away aren't happy about this."

"Don't, Andrew. Go, please."

"They want me to find out if you know of any documents, information, whatever . . . anything that you might have remembered recently or might have stumbled upon since the case concluded. They want to keep him in prison." His voice dropped. "You need to know. That's why I came today." He paused, then asked, "Have you remembered anything or found any documents that might be pertinent? They might not seem important to you but might to them . . . the authorities." His voice sounded calm and reassuring as he said, "I can help. I want to help. I'll be the go-between and keep the feds off your back. I spoke for you before. You can trust me, Leigh."

Trust? I shook my head. "I have nothing, no documents of any kind, related to my father. As for knowledge, I never had any knowledge of my father's dealings. I can't make myself any clearer than that."

Andrew moved past me into the foyer and turned toward the door. "The . . . authorities? That's who told me where to find you. I told them no, that I wouldn't approach you because enough damage had already been done to you . . . to your life. But I owed you this because—if for no other reason—because of what we meant to each other." He pulled a slip of paper from his pocket and placed it on the foyer table. "My number. It's not my usual phone. Call me if you need me. If there's anything I can do. Our engagement ended, and I understand what I represent to you and the memories that are attached to me in your mind, but you loved me not so long ago. Remember that. If you think of anything, you should let me know. I'll help you, Leigh."

I thought of Sam, both Senior and Junior, and of Marla too. They were my friends. Not Andrew. Even the neighbors I wasn't cozy with, to whom I waved in passing, were more trustworthy than Andrew.

As if he could read my mind, he added, "Remember, I may not be the only one the feds put pressure on for information. You know how they tend to draw in friends and family. Keep that in mind, Leigh."

With a parting nod, he moved toward the door, then paused on the threshold to ask, "Is it true, Leigh Ann? That you rarely leave the house and haven't driven since you arrived here? What? Two years ago?" He frowned and appeared concerned.

"No," I said. "It isn't true."

"So you still have our car? Maybe there's a touch of sentimentality in you after all."

I refused to respond and held the door wide. This time he complied.

To all appearances, Andrew moved casually as he descended the steps, but whether he was truly relaxed or not, he moved quickly, and when he reached the sidewalk, he was soon out of sight.

I closed the door behind him and slid down the length of it until I hit the floor. My legs couldn't hold me. Drawing my knees up close to my chest, I pressed my face down against them. My hands were shaking. I couldn't go back. Not to that time.

Noises came from the bathroom. Harvey likely wanted out.

I couldn't function yet. I was stuck here in this spot. When Andrew had shown me the key—Florence's key—I'd known that it was he who'd been in my home, who'd let Harvey out. Not intentionally let her out, surely, but he'd been here. He'd let himself in that day with the old key he'd found. He hadn't come to warn me because I hadn't been here. Whatever he'd wanted and had hoped to find—apparently, he hadn't. So he'd come back today, this time to surprise me and to confront me in person.

He might say that he wasn't here to trick me or compromise me, but I didn't believe him. Andrew didn't want to hurt me generally—I couldn't even imagine that—but he was under pressure. Truly, I didn't believe he would've come here the other day, or today, without that pressure. And that pressure might drive him to do things he wouldn't otherwise do.

I couldn't trust him.

Not a surprise.

And according to him, *certain* people were interested in me. Again.

I realized I was rocking back and forth, having regressed into this pathetic lump of fear . . . For just this moment I couldn't control it, so for this moment I was going to embrace it.

And within that permission bloomed the understanding that I'd been watched—was *being* watched, if I could believe Andrew.

From near or far? For how long?

It had never really occurred to me that I was hiding from the federal government. After all, I filed tax returns. I had taken ownership of this house. I paid property taxes. Going by a different last name was mostly about staying out of the public eye while the scandal died down. But *they*—the authorities—were still interested in me . . . probably since my father and his attorneys had started contesting . . . what? The trial? The evidence? I had no idea. I wasn't going to let myself fixate on that. To show interest might make me look . . .

I stopped that thought process before I spun totally out of control.

Harvey needed attention. I stood and limped along the foyer, feeling very old. I opened the bathroom door and allowed her to exit. She glared at me as if I'd forfeited all the trust I'd worked to earn.

"I'm sorry, Harvey. That was unfortunate for all of us. But I'm innocent. I have nothing to offer to either help or to hurt my father."

Harvey wanted out of the bathroom, but she wasn't budging. Not while I was standing here.

I understood. She didn't trust me not to close the door again. I pushed it wide open and stepped back.

"No worries, Harvey. The door will stay open unless you close it yourself."

She looked at me, and with one more meowing complaint, she brushed past me, tail held high and slapping my leg with it as she went.

I stayed in the doorway, staring down at the sleeping kittens. They were curled into one big, multicolored kitten fur ball. Only their colors distinguished them, one from the other. But I wasn't really seeing them. I knelt, leaning against the doorframe to hide my face, to disguise my posture.

Was it paranoid to think that a listening or recording device had been hidden here? Perhaps when Andrew had first come in uninvited and I wasn't here? Had others used his key? I tried to remember what I'd said and done over the past few days . . . But despite the farce of broken bulbs and garage lights and even the cat family now living here, I couldn't think of anything that could be twisted to implicate me, much less make me seem competent enough to hide evidence and obstruct justice, or whatever they'd call it.

But I knew—paranoid or not—anything was possible.

Could I use the listening devices, if any were planted here, to my advantage to show my innocence?

I didn't think I could keep up that kind of subterfuge without losing my mind.

I pressed my forehead against the doorframe. My head ached.

Maybe I could go away for a few days, somewhere I could let my guard down, where I wouldn't be imagining I was being listened to or watched.

Except for my cat family. I couldn't leave them here on their own.

What about fighting back, either discreetly or openly?

Probably not. After all, no one had officially knocked on my door . . . though that could come.

And Sam? By letting him be my friend, was I bringing him into a mess?

I would have to explain this to him somehow. Not here, though. Someplace where I could be sure we'd be safe from being overheard.

Harvey was back. But instead of returning to the bathroom, she headed over to the rocker and began sniffing it from top to bottom, following the scent from there to the door like a bloodhound.

"Did he frighten you, Harvey? Me too. He shouldn't have messed with the babies."

Was someone somewhere listening to me?

I added, "Don't worry, Harvey. We're innocent of any wrongdoing. Of even *knowing* about the wrongdoing. Surely that must count for something . . . even in today's world."

A slight noise came from the porch, like a scuffling noise, followed by low, muffled words only a heartbeat before someone knocked. As I stared in disbelief, they knocked again, this time more loudly—as if they meant business.

Chapter Fifteen

I forced myself to move. Crossing the short distance to the front door felt like I was descending a chasm straight into doom. My feet dragged, heavy as if encased in concrete blocks. As I reached for the doorknob, I drew in a deep breath and held it as I flipped the deadbolt, bracing my body against whatever was about to happen, and then I twisted the knob—never thinking of looking out the window first because there was a sense of inevitability about this. Of defeat.

But there he stood. Sam. It was Sam.

It's Sam—I heard the words, like a grateful cry, echo in my head. I saw his dark, ruffled hair and brown eyes, looking exactly like the last time I'd seen him, and my relief was so overwhelming that I totally forgot that only a short time before I'd sworn not to pull him into my mess of a life.

His eyes widened—I must've looked crazed—and then my knees gave way, surprising us both. Sam grabbed me, catching me as I fell against him.

He put his arms around me, supporting me as I gathered myself, then guided me to the rocker . . . I stopped him there, shaking my head. I tried to redirect us away from where

Andrew had just been sitting and instead to guide us over to the sofa. But he didn't let me go right away, and impulsively I leaned against him, putting my face in the crook of his neck, and whispered ever so softly in his ear, hoping that my actions looked more like a nuzzling kind of kiss or caress than words being spoken. "Sam, something happened. Please don't say much. Please suggest we go for a walk."

His posture stiffened, and he looked down at me.

Had he heard me? Had he understood?

Gently, Sam eased me down to sit on the sofa. He asked, "Are you okay? Lightheaded or ill?"

"I'm fine. Sorry." Very softly, I added, "Didn't mean to scare you."

Keeping his eyes on my face, he said, "That was quite a welcome, and very pleasant, but let's not do it quite that way again, okay? You worried me."

"Agreed."

"You're pale. Do you feel okay?"

"Fine."

"Maybe you need fresh air?" He grinned in that soft, friendly way of his. "I was going to invite you out to lunch . . . so how about that? If you're up to it?"

My sigh of relief was audible. He'd understood.

"Yes. I'd love to." I squeezed his hand. "Fresh air and a walk will be perfect."

****

"What was that about?" he asked. "Not that I'm complaining. You can put your arms around me and whisper in my ear anytime you like, but—"

I interrupted. "I'm sorry about that. There's an explanation . . . but I don't know how to tell it in a sensible way."

"So it wasn't my irresistible charm that caused you to swoon when you saw me?"

Swoon? Not far wrong. He was trying to make me smile. I tried for his sake, and mine.

We'd walked the few blocks to what I considered the heart of the Museum District, though adhering strictly to maps that wasn't quite true. Here, where the Virginia Museum of Fine Arts fronted on the Boulevard—Arthur Ashe Boulevard—were wide-open spaces, green lawns, and graceful old trees with spreading branches that offered welcoming shade. There were other museums nearby, and steady traffic moved along lanes of this old, major artery through the city. There was really nowhere for anyone to pause to listen, even in a car or van, without prior planning. They could certainly be easily seen.

As we walked along the sidewalk in front of the museum, I squeezed Sam's arm, unintentionally, as I assured myself that no one could possibly know ahead of time that we'd be here at this time. Here, we were in plain sight of any passersby, but we also had privacy.

"Are you going to talk to me?"

I nodded. "I think I've done you wrong, Sam."

He stopped, surprised. "How so?"

"By allowing you to help me. You know about what happened in my family, right? With my father?"

"Some. It would be hard not to."

"Florence told?"

"Not on purpose. But she was very proud of you when your modeling career was going well, and prouder still when you were the face of the PR firm and a driving force in it. Your face seemed to be everywhere for a while." He made a low, amused *humph*. "I traveled to the Northeast on business a few years back and saw it on the side of a bus, in fact—you smiling at me and every other person along the road."

He shrugged. "Florence had showed me your picture in a magazine before my trip. That's how I recognized you back then before we actually met."

"I see."

"I repeat. She was proud of you."

I nodded. "Until it fell apart."

He continued, "That was later. Your picture was in the newspapers, online, and on the TV screen when your father's . . . *business* . . . blew up and it all hit the fan."

I bowed my head, looking down at the ground, all but wringing my poor fingers back into needing new stitches or maybe a splint. Sam took my hand and gently tugged me away from the sidewalk, and we crossed the lawn to one of those huge trees and stopped in the shade.

"It wasn't even about me, Sam. But they were always there with cameras and cell phones raised and pointing at me, shouting at me."

"Your father was the story, but your face got more clicks online and more print sales because..." He broke off with a shrug and finished, "'It's not fair, I agree, but being attractive *and* a familiar face can drive media engagement."

"I used a different last name when I came to stay with Florence, hoping to be anonymous. But you knew, so others probably did too. I guess it didn't work very well."

"Or maybe it did? Just not on our block. Everyone who knew sort of kept it among themselves within the family of neighbors, so to speak." He tightened his arm in mine, returning my squeeze. "Most of them have lived on this block for decades. Together. And they all loved Florence. They wouldn't have hurt her for the world. And that courtesy extended to you."

Not far away from where we stood, the imposing doors of the massive building were closed to keep the cold in and the hot out. Beyond the walkway, and a distance from us, a group of children were engaged in some sort of activity with a teacher or caregiver. The low sound of their voices, the squirrel chatter, and the birdsong overhead were a gentle blessing.

I leaned back against the tree trunk, closing my eyes to listen. Sam followed suit, his shoulder against mine, waiting silently until I spoke.

"Thank you for your patience and for listening," I said. "I never wanted to return to the past, much less have it intrude like . . . like one of those monsters that won't die. I want to move forward. To find a better way, a way free of chaos. But it seems the past isn't done with me."

"In what way?"

Just that quickly, my nerves were back, rushing up to crush me as my heart rate quickened and my lungs tightened in my chest. I coughed, trying to interrupt the physiology that wanted to overwhelm my rationality. When I could speak, I said, "So today I had a visitor. He left only a few minutes before you arrived." I tightened my arm around Sam's as if he might shake me off. "Did Florence ever mention my fiancé? Ex, of course."

"Yes. Back when she and Dad were trying to get us together. She didn't say much, except that we'd both gone through breakups." He laughed, but there wasn't much mirth in the sound. "They meant well, I know."

"We weren't ready."

"Agreed." With a gentle motion, he took my hand in his.

"I'm glad you've been my friend."

"Agreed, again. But that sounds a bit past tense."

I nodded, not looking at him. "Because it is. At least for now. I don't want to pull you into this."

"What does that mean?"

"I haven't had much time to think this through, but if

someone is putting pressure on Andrew, then they may do the same to you."

He scoffed.

"Or on me through you."

This time, he stayed silent.

"Don't dismiss the possibility so quickly. You've been coming over to the house almost every day. You should stay away from me until this is over."

"Over?"

"Sooner or later, it will be. I wasn't involved with what my father did, except for being my parents' daughter." I shrugged. "But I understand why some people have trouble accepting that." I paused, then added, "And now, apparently, per Andrew, there's more going on about my father's case and conviction. I don't know what, only that his sentence may be amended . . . or . . . I don't know. Andrew suggested that the authorities suspect I may have remembered information or found documents after the conviction that may be pertinent now."

"Have you?"

That startled me.

"No. Nothing. How would I? I never knew anything. Dad and I didn't get along. Did I have doubts about his honesty? Yes. Did I know he was defrauding people? No."

"I believe you."

"I've been hiding out here for . . . what feels like forever." I breathed deeply. "Innocence is no defense if someone with power or some federal or regulatory agency targets you. I admit I'm scared. I don't think . . . Sam, I can't survive this again, and I refuse to risk taking anyone down with me. Certainly not someone who's been as kind to me as you have."

"Wow. Leigh, surely that's . . . It sounds . . ."

"I know how it sounds. That's why we're speaking here.

Away from my home. The least word can be misinterpreted, in error or on purpose, depending."

"Your home . . . you think someone is eavesdropping?"

"Maybe. Could even be cameras, I suppose."

"Leigh . . ."

"How can I live this way? Not knowing?"

"Is Andrew on the level?"

We waited silently as a family passed closer to us to reach the entrance of the museum. We watched them enter, and the doors closed behind them.

Sam asked, "Could he be gaslighting you for some reason?"

I shrugged, thinking. "I suppose, but why would he?"

"Do you have any confirmation, of any kind, that what Andrew warned you about is truly happening?"

"No, I don't, but why would he make it up?" I stopped, then began again. "The intruder who let Harvey out? Yes, that must've been Andrew. He used the key Florence kept hidden under the planter. It wasn't there when we were checking for spare keys. Why? Because he already had it."

"He had that key? Are you sure?"

"Yes. He had it with him today. He showed me. He held it right up in front of me—a form of intimidation, probably—and then left it on the table beside the rocker . . . which is where he was sitting when I entered the house and found him there. I'd been outside getting ready to clear some junk out of the garage. When I came back in . . . well, you get the picture." I stopped abruptly.

I was hunching forward again. Forcing myself to stand straight, I finished with, "I don't know what to do, Sam, but I know I don't want to drag you into it, so you shouldn't come over for the time being. I also know that I can't even run away to a hotel or anywhere else because of Harvey and the kittens, so if you have any suggestions, please share."

Sam tightened his arm around mine. He said carefully, "First off, we'll thank Harvey for keeping you here. *If* someone *is* watching you, then running away will make them more curious or even outright convinced they're right to be suspicious."

"I understand what you're saying, but I'm having trouble with this. I don't want to go back to where I was after everything with Dad and the authorities, the questioning, and the trial. It was an ugly place, emotionally and physically."

"I'm sure it was stressful."

I felt talked down to. He wasn't getting it. I faced him, keeping my voice low because I wouldn't risk my words carrying, and the low-voiced, harsh words came across almost like a hiss.

"You don't know. You *can't* know, Sam. When it comes to financial crimes and Ponzi schemes, many federal agencies have a stake in those. *Many.* It feels like they come at you from all directions. They *did* access my phone records, they came into my apartment, *my home*, and *took* my electronic devices. They searched every nook, cranny, and drawer and stole my privacy and devastated my peace of mind. I couldn't sleep. The least noise frightened me. *Were they at my door again? If I didn't answer the door quickly enough, what would they do?* I was alone, Sam. When I had to go in for questioning over and over . . . each time I feared they wouldn't let me leave. And that questioning? They were very clear about what would happen to me if I didn't cooperate. Innocence?" I shook my head and laughed, but it rang of incipient hysteria.

"Innocence. There's no such concept when these investigations get rolling—at least that's what I learned. You've heard that old saying that to a carpenter with a hammer, everything looks like a nail? I know the truth of that. They taught me well."

Sam stared at my face, then slid his arms around me and pulled me close. We breathed for a moment, and then he released me. I pressed my fingers to my eyes. They were wet.

"Bear with me here, okay, Leigh? Let me ask this. When they came to search, they had search warrants, right? And no one actually busted down your door, right?"

I pushed at him. "They did, yes, and no, they didn't. But how was I to know, and, Sam, legal or not, I can't explain adequately how totally invasive it is, how it breaks you down to your lowest level—that helpless feeling of having no control —of being at the mercy of strangers with power, whether their interest is justified or not."

He spoke softly. "Okay. Thank you for explaining. I imagine I'd feel similarly if I was ever in that position." He paused, then added, "And I mean that sincerely, even though I know words don't measure up to what you went through. Let's put our brains together and figure it out. Stop talking about protecting me. I'm in. You aren't alone. That said, I need to digest this for a little while."

The museum doors opened, and a young couple came out.

Sam smiled politely as they passed. He turned to me, a less doubting expression on his face. "Have you been in there?"

"What? The museum?"

"Let's take a walk through the exhibits. Let's see something different. Maybe it'll refresh our brains. Our spirits too."

"When I had bad days after I moved in with Florence, she would say, 'Let's reset the day. A do-over is due.'" I smiled, wishing I could feel it inside. "I came here a few times with her." I shook my head. "I don't remember much of what we saw."

He released my arm and took my hand. "Let's go inside and claim our do-over for this day."

"What about Harvey?"

"She'll be fine. You said Andrew left the house key with you?"

"Yes."

"We won't stay too long—only as long as you like." As we walked up the steps, he added, "Let's call it a breathing break before we do some serious brainstorming."

****

He was right. I needed breathing time. Thinking time. What was I going to do about this?

Immediately inside the main door was a security guard at a desk—or maybe he was only a greeter and provider of information and directions. At this point, I wasn't sure about anything. But he smiled, and Sam greeted him and led me to our right, toward the sound of children's voices. I had an impression of a resting area for small children and caregivers to relax, some classroom-like rooms where kids were creating things, and then we turned the corner to where the elevators were and then the atrium area. I did remember this. The height of it, the light and the space. Select items were displayed in cases. We stopped at the elevators, and Sam did the choosing when it came to the floor we went to and the exhibits. Thank goodness.

The paintings, both old and modern, were interesting, but the Fabergé eggs were my favorites. Same as when I'd been here with Florence. I tried to focus on refreshing my poor, tired, frenetic brain by taking in the beauty of old masters and modern art.

We didn't discuss the invisible elephant in the room with

us. We held hands and strolled through more collections, and I tried not to think but only to see what was around us. Maybe it helped. At least a little.

"Now," Sam said. "Let's go back to the atrium and visit the café." He squeezed my hand gently. "Ready to put thoughts into words?"

I sighed, wanting to say, *No, I'm not ready*. But I nodded.

The café was at the far end of the atrium, along the window wall. There were tables on the patio outside, as well as inside. I stopped near the gift shop, asking, "What do you think? About my situation?" The idea of a café with food and chatter made me feel sick.

"Not here, Leigh. Multistory and lots of glass and stone and metal—every sound carries." He drew me toward the café. "Please, come with me. Looks quiet in here. Let's have a seat, grab something to drink, and do that brainstorming."

I nodded.

He ordered coffee. I chose tea. Sam also brought two slices of pizza back to the table. This table was off by itself with no one at the nearby tables. We settled, and Sam said, "I hope you're not picky," as he slid the plate of pizza closer to me.

"I'm not. But I can't eat now. Too much going on."

"And what have you eaten today?"

I stayed silent.

"Then you are putting yourself at a disadvantage. The brain and body need fuel. Even . . ." He gestured at the pizza slices. "Chew on this while I think out loud?"

"But here, Sam? Is this a good place to . . . you know?"

"The perfect place. No one is close. The other people here are also chatting with friends. Keep your voice soft, but don't whisper. Whispering will always draw attention." He smiled with encouragement.

Accepting the pizza, and wanting to be cooperative, I bit into it tentatively.

He shook his head. "Innocent . . . I'm hesitant to say the word. I don't want to hit a tender spot, but it's the best word for this. If you're innocent of whatever wrong they thought you might have engaged in, then don't worry. It's not a magic bullet, I know. Saying *Don't worry* doesn't fix the potential issue. I acknowledge that.

"At the same time, don't be careless about what you're saying because someone *could be* listening." He leveled his gaze at me. "If I thought I was being watched, especially in my home, it would freak me out too. I'm not sure how to advise handling that, *but* I do think you should contact an attorney."

The breath I drew in was loud and ragged.

"I'm not saying that because you're guilty, or even because I think you'll need one, but it's a good precaution. A just-in-case action that's better to tackle now before you actually need to."

"I had one before. Mom insisted. She recommended him. He was helpful, yes. Also expensive. He's up in New York, though. Not down here."

"Is it a money issue? If so, I can help. I'm not wealthy, but I have some funds set aside."

"No. I'm good for now. I owned a big part of that PR firm." I shook my head. "It galls me to think money has to be spent defending myself from something I didn't do."

"I understand." Sam nodded. "Then set up a phone meeting with him. Give him a concise rundown of what's happening. If the distance is a problem for him, ask for recommendations. See what he has to say. It might give you some peace of mind." He added, "Money well spent."

I shuddered, remembering how it had been when I'd first

contacted Leland Graves, but I had to agree. "That's a good idea."

"Maybe call him away from your home. Inconvenient, but—"

I leaned toward him. "Inconvenient or not, phones aren't really private anymore, regardless of where you use them."

Sam offered, "What about my dad? He still has a landline. You can call the attorney from his house."

"No," I said. "I won't risk involving your father." I shook my head. Feeling stronger now, I said, "Nope, I'll call my attorney from my own phone and in my own home. I'll watch what I say, but hiding isn't . . . It didn't work for me before and doesn't seem to be working for me now. I have no reason to hide except to protect myself from harassment and having my life wrecked all over again, and if that's not working—the hiding—then I need a new plan."

"Are you sure?" He sounded doubtful.

"No. Yes." I shrugged. "But I do have a favor to ask."

"Name it."

"*If*—and I think . . . I *hope* it's a *big* if—if they take me into custody for whatever reason . . . or if I have to leave my house for a while for any reason, will you take care of Harvey and her family?"

Chapter Sixteen

Sam's eyes opened wider as his brows grew closer in a frown. "I can't believe that will happen. As for Harvey, take her and the kittens off your worry list. If anything does happen, including illness or whatever, Dad and I will make sure the cats are okay until you return."

Despite the chaos in and around me, Sam's promise uplifted me.

With a grateful smile, I said, "Knowing they've got somewhere safe to go helps more than I can say."

"Speaking of 'saying,' what will you say to your attorney?"

I shook my head. "Not sure, but I'll figure it out."

"So let's brainstorm it here." He looked around. Lunch hour was well past, and aside from a young couple hunched together over an open laptop on the far side of the room, we were alone.

"Okay," I said, shrugging. "I'm thinking that I'll call Leland and ask him to look into whether some sort of review or challenge is going on with my father's case, or with his sentence."

"He'll ask what's happened to cause you to wonder."

"I'm sure he will. I'll tell him Andrew let himself into my house and told me about the review and warned me I was being watched." My heart was speeding up again, and I tried to slow my breathing.

Sam could see I was struggling. He waited. I nodded, then tried again. "I'll say that Andrew found out where I was living and showed up uninvited and suggested that I was being watched."

"That sounds good."

"I feel like I should say that I might also be being *listened* to."

"He represented you before. I think the words *being watched* will tell him the rest. If he wants more . . . well, that will give him a heads-up. He might ask you to come see him in person—that's possible. But I'd let him take the lead, I think." He shrugged and shifted his cup on the tabletop. "Trust your instincts. Your rational instincts . . . even your gut instincts—not your stressed and anxious instincts. Keep it simple." He took another sip of coffee, then asked, "He did a good job for you before?"

"Yes, I believe so." I took in another deep breath and held it before releasing it slowly.

Sam grinned. "You're doing fine. And remember, you truly don't know that *anyone* other than Andrew is watching you, much less that they're listening in on you."

"True. Andrew could be gaslighting me for an unknown reason, I know that, but maybe new attorneys or federal agencies *are* taking another look at Dad's case. It's possible."

"Possible, yes. But would that necessarily involve close surveillance of you?"

That had a reasonable ring to it. Close surveillance? The authorities hadn't talked to me in more than two years. While my worries could be right on, Sam could also be right. That perked me up a little. If I only had Andrew to deal with . . . and not my father and prosecutors . . . And why *would* they use Andrew to . . . to do what? To find out if I knew more? That made no sense.

Why wouldn't they just ask me themselves first, even if they believed I might not cooperate?

I said, "Andrew said the feds were putting pressure on him because of what was happening in my father's case . . . but maybe it's not only about my father. Maybe they are also interested in Andrew? Suppose he's not being pressured to ask me but is actually pressuring me on his own, hoping I'll give up something that *he* can use as leverage for himself?"

Sam started to speak, but I interrupted him by reaching over to where his hand rested on the table and taking it in my own.

"I think I'm clear on this now, Sam. I'll say enough but not too much. I don't want to send Leland down rabbit trails out of fear. I'll be direct, and then if Leland wants more info from me, he'll ask." I slapped my hands on the table, gently, but even so it wobbled. I pressed my hands flat against it to steady it. Luckily, the cups weren't too full, so nothing spilled. I even managed a smile. "And if he wants, yes, I'll take that trip to New York, and you can babysit Harvey and the kittens."

Sam picked up his coffee cup and lifted it, holding it, waiting for me to do likewise. We tapped our mugs together as in a toast. I hadn't felt this good in a while.

I even finished the last bites of the pizza slice.

As we walked back to Hanover Avenue, I felt so much lighter, like a ton of bricks had been lifted from me. I'd linked my arm through Sam's, and he seemed pleased.

Brainstorming, as Sam had called it—or maybe it was just sharing worries with a friend—had helped me to see the problem with a more objective view. That said, this lighter

149

feeling wouldn't last, but when I got racked up again I'd try to remember it. To that end, I shifted my arm without unlinking it from Sam's so I could reach his hand and give it a squeeze.

Could it be that Andrew was only fishing? That his intent was only to help himself? Maybe the feds weren't trying to prevent Dad's case from coming undone. Maybe Andrew, himself, was in trouble and they weren't watching me at all. Andrew might well have found my current address through business and tax records.

I was still mystified as to why he thought he could leverage me in any way. He knew, of all people, that I was innocent. Unless he'd hoped I would say or do something to make me look guilty and he could thereby hope to shift any investigation back to me, taking the heat off himself?

"That was quite a sigh," Sam said.

"Yes. Unfortunately, I was feeling good and dropped my guard, and now the worry is rolling back in."

"Tell it to go away. Tell it to come back later when you have more info."

I laughed. "I'll try."

"If you want me nearby . . . I can hang around."

"Thanks, and I may wish I'd taken you up on the offer, but I can do this."

He grimaced. "I'm reluctant to say this, but it feels necessary. Leigh, if Andrew is feeling sufficiently threatened in some way, enough that he'd do what he's done, then is he dangerous?"

"No. I can't imagine Andrew threatening me with physical violence." I remembered Baby Gray in his hand and Harvey being shut out on the porch. But that had been inadvertent, I was sure, and as for the kitten, Andrew hadn't hurt her, and now that I was past that first fright at seeing him in my home, I was sure the Andrew I'd had feelings for, had wanted to marry, wouldn't. And yet, I felt a sudden huge relief that we *hadn't* married.

Sam and I were now standing on the sidewalk in front of my house. Marla was on her porch watering a fern. She waved. I waved back with a smile. It felt good to be recognized and greeted.

On some strange impulse borne of I knew not what, I leaned against Sam and pressed a quick kiss onto his cheek, then released his arm and ran up the steps to the door, stopping there like a shy, embarrassed teenager.

I called out a soft *Thank you*, offering the words with a grateful smile as I gave him a small wave and let myself into the house.

$$****$$

Even before the front door had fully latched behind me, I was scanning the hallway and living room for signs of intrusion. I did a quick circuit of the first floor, testing the back door to ensure it was locked, and then glanced out the kitchen window to verify that the screen porch door was also locked. I'd search upstairs after checking on Harvey, but for now, I could relax at least enough to slip off my shoes.

Harvey and the kittens were fine. I knelt beside them for a minute, stroking Harvey's forehead. She not only allowed it, but she closed her eyes as if soaking in the feels. I took courage from that and touched each of the kittens. They all had their eyes open now and had picked up weight, losing that squishy mouse look. And they were finding their way around the box—not easily and often ended up bumping their noses into the cardboard sides—but they didn't give up. Soon they'd notice the low-cut area in the side of the box and discover it was easier to scale—and likely tumble over it, onto the floor—

but they'd be unhurt. Surprised and maybe a bit alarmed, and they'd be learning. They were so new that everything they did taught them a new lesson in navigating life.

And if they overreached their abilities, if they cried and needed comfort or rescue, Harvey would be there. I'd already witnessed what an attentive mom she was.

Daggone it. I was tearing up.

I had the soft brush I'd picked up at the grocery store in case Harvey would allow me to groom her thick, dull coat of fur. I wondered if she might allow it now? Soon, maybe.

Thus far, I'd been silent, both in movement and in sound, aside from the occasional soft squeak of a floor plank as I moved. I had no sense of an intruder here now, or of having been here. Even so, I carried my phone with me up the stairs, with 911 predialed and ready to complete the call if anything alarmed me up there.

Nothing was amiss upstairs. All was well.

I sat on the side of my bed, staring at my phone.

Rerunning my conversation with Sam through my head, recalling our brainstorming, I made sure I was clear about what I would say to Leland. More than likely, I'd have to leave a message with his assistant and wait for a call back. So for the message, I'd be very brief. I'd keep it simple.

I hit Dial. Ann answered. I hadn't spoken to her in two years, and she wouldn't recognize the last name, Sonder. I'd have to be me, myself. She answered and identified the law office. "How may I direct your call?"

"Hi, this is Leigh Ann Eden."

"Hello, Ms. Eden. What can I do for you?"

"I'd like to speak with Leland."

"He's out of the office today, but if it's urgent, I can reach him."

"No need. Tomorrow will be fine."

"Anything more I should add to the message, Ms. Eden?"

"No. He has my number. It's the same."

"Are you well? It's been a while."

Her tone was a touch more personal now that the business part was done.

"I'm well enough. You?"

"I'm quite well."

"Good to hear."

"Yes, ma'am. I'll give Leland your message."

We disconnected. I drew in a breath and continued to sit quietly and think a bit longer. Sam was right. I should live my life while I had it to live. If anyone wanted to listen in uninvited, then more power to them. Never mind them. I was innocent of anything they were interested in.

If, in fact, anyone *was* listening.

I thought Sam was probably right. That level of surveillance for someone like me who'd already been investigated and dismissed seemed unlikely.

But then . . . what was Andrew's angle?

My phone rang and I jumped, grabbing the call, my heart already racing.

It wasn't Leland.

It was the mechanic. I'd completely forgotten he was coming. I remembered as he said, "Ma'am? I'm out back? Here to check your car?"

Chapter Seventeen

"Mason, ma'am. Bill Mason. You're expecting me?"

"Yes, of course. I'll be right out. Just a sec."

"No worries, ma'am."

As I emerged from the back door, still trying to get my second foot in its shoe, I said, "Sorry. It's been that kind of day." And that was surely the truth.

"Yes, ma'am. I understand."

As we crossed the backyard, I said, "Let's take a look, shall we? I was clearing out stuff from the garage earlier but was interrupted and didn't get the job finished. Maybe you can start looking over the car while I move more junk out of the way."

"Yes, ma'am. And I'll lend a hand with moving stuff. Happy to."

Judging by his appearance and easy movements, Bill Mason had to be in his early twenties. He had messy blond hair, blue jeans and a T-shirt, a comfortable, sweet southern accent, and he seemed perfectly at ease, as if he was exactly the person he was born to be.

I said, "Bill, please call me Leigh."

"Yes, ma'am. It's *Mason* for me, if you don't mind."

I couldn't help smiling. "Got it," I said, adding, "There are doors front and back. I'll unlock them and we can open them up. It will give you better light and fresher air."

I opened the sliding door first, then went through the gate into the alley and unlocked that door. As I pushed it up, I saw Mason moving in the front of the garage, with the car between us. He called over, "Mind if I move these boxes out?"

"Go for it, and thanks."

****

When I thought about it later that evening, it struck me how so much could change within just a few hours. And change more than once. Good, not good, good again, then tanked again. Like a frickin' rollercoaster. But after such a day, I was grateful to be utterly exhausted—physically and emotionally. Hopefully exhausted enough to sleep well.

Those nights of interrupted sleep when Harvey had first arrived had stopped after that third night, and I wanted to keep it that way.

Mason and I both worked to clear the space in the garage that surrounded the car. As he began checking the car itself, my phone rang.

"I have to take this call, Mason."

"Yes, ma'am. I'll keep on."

"Yell if you need me." I stepped away with the phone pressed to my ear, saying, "Hi, Leland. Thanks for returning my call so quickly."

"What's up? Are you okay?"

I heard the wind in the background. I guessed he was out on the lake. I was surprised I remembered that he liked to go fishing out there with his son and grandson. He might be doing that right now. Life went on.

"Sorry to interrupt you," I said.

"Not at all."

"I had a visit from Andrew."

"Your former fiancé?"

"The same. He surprised me in my home. I walked in and found him. No overt threat, but he said questions were being raised about Dad's conviction or about the evidence. He was vague-ish about exactly what, and he suggested that people connected to the case were unhappy about it and were watching me."

"You haven't heard from anyone else? No contact otherwise?"

"No and no."

"Would you like me to look into it?"

"Yes, please."

The conversation continued for another minute, and when we hung up, I felt like I could breathe again. At least for a while, until I heard back from him. During our chat, I'd walked around the side of the house and was now standing on the front porch steps. I went the rest of the way up to the porch and sat in a wicker chair, thinking–not thinking. Did some wishing too, but other than for peace and to be left alone by authorities and people with agendas and more power than me, I didn't know what to hope for.

Meanwhile, out back and out of my sight, Mason had continued doing whatever. The front door to the house was locked and I must've left my keys in the garage, so I made myself move.

Mason was outside the garage squirting some kind of cleaner on his hands and scrubbing at them with a rag. He gave me a quick rundown of what he'd done and his current thoughts on the state of the car.

"The battery is dead and corroded. My charging cables

won't reach, and frankly, I think the battery is too far gone, anyway. I'll bring one tomorrow to see if we can get the motor to turn over. I'm hoping we can back the car out into the alley and bring the tow truck over. We'll tow it to the garage where I can go over it properly." He dropped the rag into a pail full of stuff. "The garage and the alley make it awkward, but we'll get it done."

"The car has been in there for two years, and it was tricky getting it in there."

"I'm betting the garage on the opposite side of the alley wasn't there at that time or it would've been even tighter." He shrugged. "No worries, though. We'll work it out. And while I'm thinking of it, the panel on the side of the garage, the one that's just sort of wedged in? That thing isn't going to keep much of anything out, including the weather. You might want to get that fixed."

"Loose panel?"

"Yes, ma'am. Over by the bush?" He gestured toward it.

He was ready to go and I didn't want to hold him up, so I dropped that subject and asked, "Tell me, Mason, should I just call the car a loss and donate it to whoever will tow it out of here?"

He smiled, but it was more like a squinty expression. Cute, though. "No, ma'am. Might be worth spending a little money on it for parts to see first, unless you *want* to be rid of it. In that case, I know some folks who'll pay you for the parts."

"They'll pay me?"

"Not much, but it would more than cover the cost of the towing. I'll have a better idea of what it'll cost to make the car roadworthy after it's in the shop."

I nodded. "Okay, then. Let's see what tomorrow brings. I'll wait to hear from you."

"Yes, ma'am."

He left. His long-legged walk had the bounce of someone with plans. Good plans. For the evening. Probably with friends. Maybe a girlfriend.

Those felt like good wishes. Simple wishes.

Except for Mason, it might not seem so simple. He'd have his own worries, right?

And because I was exhausted, I was going to treat myself to some time with Harvey and the babies. And then baby myself a little too. Maybe a movie, popcorn included, or a bubble bath or something. And tomorrow? Tomorrow, I'd call a locksmith to get the locks changed.

Andrew might be wrong about a lot of things, but he'd been right about that.

****

I woke again in the middle of the night. A simple waking, no cat howling or nightmares, yet given recent events, rolling over and resuming sleep was impractical without checking things out first.

Two weeks ago, I'd thought something similar, hadn't I? I touched my fingers.

Didn't matter. I still had to look.

A quick walk through the house to check on things, a longer pause at the kitchen window—which is when I remembered what Mason had said about the loose panel in the side of the garage, but for sure, I wasn't going to check on that tonight. Tomorrow morning would be time enough.

A quiet visit with Harvey and her family reassured me that all was well, and I returned to my bedroom. As much as I wanted to fall into bed and into dreamland, I knew what I had to do even if the actions were largely symbolic.

Not only did I lock my bedroom door, but I also pushed the

dresser in front of it. No light shades over my eyes, no noise plugs in my ears. If someone tried to force the door open, it would wake me, no question. And it might buy me a minute in which to act, and my phone was right beside my pillow, ready to dial.

****

The next day started peacefully. I'd slept without my mask and daylight found me as the sun rose, which, along with the street noise, woke me pretty much with the dawn. I lay abed for a few minutes contemplating the dresser blocking my bedroom door, remembering I'd planned to call around to alarm companies and remembering also that Mason would be bringing a fresh car battery today, and I wondered if, after all this time, the car fob battery was still charged. Likely not.

So I rolled out of bed, rolled the dresser aside, and then went downstairs for caffeine. Armed with a hot, aromatic mug of caffeine, I'd go back upstairs and grab a quick shower before the rest of the day *rolled* in, in earnest.

As I hit the bottom step and turned to walk through the foyer, I found Baby Gray in the open bathroom doorway. She was up and swaying on unsteady legs, her head lifted but bobbing a little as she gazed at me with big blue eyes wide as tiny saucers. She seemed to stare at me, surprised to see me.

Could she see me from this distance?

I moved forward slowly and dropped to my knees. Beyond her, I saw Harvey and the rest. The babies were growing so fast that the nursery was becoming more like a cat bedroom now. Maybe more like a cat condo or efficiency. In a soft, coaxing voice, I said, "Harvey, what's up? Looks like a certain little one is escaping."

159

Harvey opened her eyes, slow and lazy looking, and meowed.

I picked up Baby Gray, her front legs between my fingers, and her full belly warm in the palm of my hand. I pressed her side to my cheek and felt her heart beating through the soft fur. She squeaked a meow. Moving her nose to touch mine, I whispered, "Time for you to return to mama." Harvey received her without fanfare, but still with a tender paw hugging her baby close to her.

Suddenly, I understood with sharp clarity what this meant to me. I may have guessed it was a need to belong, to be needed, that drew me to them, to their sweet world, but it was more than that. In their mews, their baby paws and rumbly purrs, they gave out endorphins or serotonin or dopamine or oxytocin—or some combination thereof—like joyful hearts bubbling up in riotous profusion on a social media page, but warm and breathing. Even just watching them . . . instinctive or not, I was seeing what I'd wanted in a mother, a family, albeit in a very basic way. Security, safety, everything I'd wanted to feel as a child, even as a grown child. To fit in. To know that I'd fit in no matter what.

I had fit this family into my life. Perhaps into the gaps of my life?

And my heart had become theirs.

It's just a cat. I heard Andrew's voice saying those words. And he was right.

When my mother had said, *Life isn't fair,* and when my father said I was too soft . . . *You're a born victim, Leigh Ann. You've got to toughen up, girl*—maybe they were right too.

But this . . . *this* was the *right* I wanted. This I *chose.*

It caused a true physical pain inside me as I tore myself away. Yet it was also the sweetest pain because they weren't going anywhere. They'd be here when I returned. Each time I returned.

A smart person would add, "For now." And maybe that was okay too, because sometimes *for now* was the best we had.

"I'll get you fresh food and water, Harvey." That sweet pain whooshed through me again, and I welcomed it, the moisture welling in my eyes. And I loved it.

Tasks attended to and with that cup of coffee now in hand, I was all set to return up the stairs to grab a shower—and there was Baby Gray again in the hallway.

No wonder Harvey hadn't been upset. She'd probably been chasing Gray into this hallway all night. Poor mama kitty.

Inside the nursery, Orange Fluff was just that instant toppling over the low cut-out area of the cardboard.

Oh dear.

"Harvey, I see the problem."

There was no way that I could risk these babies getting caught or stuck under something or . . .

It struck me again—I'd never been responsible for anyone but myself. No one had ever depended upon me for their happiness, much less survival.

For now, it wouldn't take much to block the door enough to keep them in and allow Harvey an easy in and out. I did a quick mental survey of available options. Pillows? Books?

In the end, I went with books. I took them from Florence's bookshelves—her Agatha Christies, the cozies, the true crimes, and Dr. Whos—and lined them up in stacks of two and three across the bathroom doorway. Not high, just enough to deter adventuring kittens but an easy crossing for their mama. Good enough for now. The kittens might be determined and have strength of purpose, but they lacked the physical strength to push those books aside. I double-checked to make sure the

toilet lid was down—surely unnecessary, but I did it anyway—
and tucked the babies back in with Harvey.

"Shower time. Y'all be good."

Feeling for all the world as if I had no more trouble in *my*
world than errant kittens, I ran up the stairs and started the
water running in that shower. Yes, I knew there were still problems coming my way, but for this *now*, this actual moment in
my life, I'd take Sam's advice and tell the worries and fears
they had to wait until I had more information because, for *now*,
I had other, better things, to attend to, like calling that locksmith. No time like the present to move forward. And fate may
have agreed with me because I was offered an afternoon slot.

****

After my shower and my coffee, I walked out to the
garage, intending to check out the loose panel that Mason had
mentioned.

I found the panel he was talking about near the back fence.
A bush obscured the space where the panel was attached to the
side of the garage. I squeezed back into the space and saw
readily that this was almost like an access panel, and it was
definitely loose and even a bit askew. That could've been due
to Mason checking it out, as could be the shuffled dirt and
broken twigs on the ground. On the other side of this panel was
an open area below where the light switch was. Some items
had been stored there, and I couldn't have said whether the
items there had been disturbed or not.

But the space covered by that panel? It was about two-foot
square, plenty roomy for someone to have used as a means to
entry. And the bush would've provided excellent cover in low
light.

****

Mason returned about noon with the battery, saying, "I'll give it a check. If it works, I'll come back with Tommy and his tow truck, probably tomorrow."

And it did work. We checked the key fob and it was still dead, so we replaced that battery, and voilà—the motor started, the headlights lit up, and we were back in business, so to speak.

Mason said, "If you don't mind, I'm gonna go ahead and clear out more stuff."

"Do you need more room to maneuver the car out into the alley tomorrow?"

"Wouldn't hurt. But I'll get it done. Won't take me but a minute. I see there's some stuff in the car too. No need to take that to the shop. I'll set it all on the porch, maybe? You can go through it all when it's convenient."

"Thank you so much." I added, "I'm expecting the locksmith any minute now. Do you mind doing all that without me?"

"No, ma'am. I'll finish up," Mason said. "You go ahead. I'll leave the keys on the porch when I'm done. As for the tow truck, I'll let you know as soon as I confirm with Tommy. I'm hoping for tomorrow sometime."

"Sounds great. Thanks, Mason."

"Yes, ma'am."

Later, when I saw he was gone, I went to retrieve the keys. He'd left them all, garage key, spare car key, and key fob, on the small table on the porch. Not visible from the yard, but hard to miss as I came out of the house.

I paused and cast a slightly despairing look at the array of items Mason had brought in here. Much of it was stuff I'd left in the car, items that I'd told myself I'd fetch from the car if I needed them and then had never thought of again.

A lot was junk like old magazines and a worn pair of sneakers with balled socks still stuck in the toes. *Yuck*. There was also a stack of papers interspersed with tattered-looking folders. Old junk mail. Why had I brought any of it with me? Because I'd left my New York apartment in a hurry and hadn't taken the time to go through it. I'd assumed I'd have the time, and the will, to do it later.

But I hadn't and I knew why. It was because of what it represented. Each old bill, crumpled flyer, or any other item from that time was inextricably linked in my mind to the trauma. I wouldn't risk bringing the dark days and weeks back, so I'd ignored things like this that had the power to revive the awfulness. Even if it was mostly trash. But some of it wasn't. Like those folders.

My suitcases had come inside with me the day I arrived here. The bottom layer of stuff in my trunk and back floorboards had been tossed in when I left New York, never to be disturbed again.

Until today. I sighed.

I'd been in a bad way back then. This was, in a small way, evidence of that.

The papers looked dog-eared and disordered, but at first glance, I didn't see signs of rodent or insect nibbling.

Anything that had been timely back then was no longer worth keeping, but I should go through these papers and other odds and ends before tossing them wholesale into the trash bin. But not tonight. Tonight, I'd bring them inside in case of rain or wind and stash the pile somewhere in the house. I laughed because with all the present distractions, the stack would probably live quietly undisturbed for a few more years.

Chapter Eighteen

"Ma'am?"

I heard Mason calling and stepped out to the porch. He'd arrived early to get here ahead of the tow truck, which we were expecting soon.

"Do you need me?"

"Yes, ma'am. Actually, I was giving the car a last once-over, and when I checked the spare tire I found this in there with it."

He was holding up a piece of paper. No, it was a plastic sleeve with paper in it.

Puzzled, I accepted it from him. "In with the spare tire?"

"In the compartment where the spare is stored." He squinted like he was puzzling over something. "No extra space in there, and it was shut tight. This was sort of fitted over the side of the spare and tucked in alongside. You can see how it's a little rumpled. Figured I'd just pass it on to you and you can decide what to do with it."

This was too odd. I shivered.

"Anything else in there?"

"Not that I can see."

"Okay, then. Thank you." I nodded, not wanting it. Because . . . Because why? Because if it was something related to the tire or the car, Mason wouldn't have thought twice, or if it had looked ordinary, he might've left this on the porch as he'd done with the other items he'd found. But he sensed this was odd, just as I did. And in my life? Odd didn't usually augur well as good tidings.

And the quick glimpse I'd gotten through the plastic sleeve? I hadn't wanted to stare at it, with Mason there. But it gave me pause, and I stopped.

"Hey, Mason?"

"Yes?"

"Could you ask your friend to hold off towing? I know he's already on his way, and I'm sorry for the inconvenience. Please tell him I'll pay for the wasted trip."

He gave me a long look, which slipped briefly down to the plastic sleeve for a second, before he said, "Sure thing. Should I lock the garage and leave the keys on the porch again?"

"Is the spare tire cover back in place?"

He nodded.

"Then lock the car too, okay?" Still standing there, I added, "Mason? One more thing, if you don't mind?"

"What's that?"

"Before you lock up, would you mind unhooking the wires to the battery?"

He looked at me, staring. I kept my gaze straight and solemn.

"I know this all seems odd, Mason, but it would be best not to speak of it to anyone for now. Just tell your tow truck friend that I've had second thoughts and will be back in touch. Can you do that?"

"Will do, ma'am."

Mason returned to the garage, his phone already in his

hand, notifying his friend to turn the tow truck around. As for me, crossing the yard back to the house, I tried to walk casually, as if nothing unusual or concerning was happening, but as soon as I reached the kitchen, I dropped the plastic bag on the table. I'd touched only the top corner—and I'd gripped it with my fingernails which had probably looked even odder to Mason, but I couldn't worry about that. I didn't want my prints on this at all. Every instinct I had said these papers had teeth, sharp ones, that I wanted to stay clear of.

I locked the back door and rummaged in the pantry for the latex gloves that Florence had kept in there. Over time, the box had worked its way to the back of the shelf, where odds and ends were shoved and forgotten. I wasn't fooling myself that residue from latex gloves wouldn't show up in a forensic examination, but, for sure, I didn't want my fingerprints on any of it.

Florence had manila folders in the bottom drawer of the desk. A few unused ones were left. Then I took her old tablet and made sure the Bluetooth was switched off and the Wi-Fi was disconnected. I removed the SIM card too. The operating system hadn't been updated in ages, so those online resources might not sync up anyway, but I wasn't taking a chance with it. This tablet would take photos, and they'd be more secure on this old device than on my phone.

I refused to tell myself that I was overreacting.

This was it. This was why Andrew had been here.

I didn't know what this meant or what to do about it, but caution was called for.

Back in the kitchen, I removed the tablecloth from the table, and with the gloves on my hands, I carefully flexed the plastic to slide the paper out. Papers. Three very thin pieces of paper. And not pristine. They'd been handled before having been put into that like-new plastic sleeve.

Columns of numbers . . . some names and some initials. Even some handwritten notations.

As I read through the list, a sharp chill sliced through me.

What was this? I didn't know, but I had suspicions.

When I was finished, I finagled the pages back into the sleeve in the same order as I'd found them. I tucked them into Florence's manila folder and then went to find a safe place to stash them until I knew what to do—or not to do—about it.

****

Sam was coming over this afternoon when he was able to get clear of work. For now, it was only me, Harvey and the kittens, and that sleeve of papers that terrified me. I borrowed a kitten and sat in the rocker and stroked Calliope Calico's silky back. Harvey didn't seem to mind.

I tried to think. What would I tell Sam when he got here? I wanted to be clear and specific without including details that could bring him into the people of interest circle if the authorities became involved.

The kitten dozed and so did I. I fell asleep thinking that Calliope Calico, while a very cute name, was entirely too long, formal and complicated for this sweetie. I woke, surprised and touched that Harvey wasn't showing concern that I'd kept her baby so long.

Sam arrived. I greeted him. I pressed my hand to his cheek and said softly, "Let's go out." He took a long look into my eyes and said, "Lead the way."

We walked. No specific direction. Random. Down Hanover, turn this way, walk, turn that way. When we stopped, I turned slightly away from Sam, hoping I'd choose the right words and speak them calmly and that he wouldn't hear my fear. I couldn't bear to see doubt or suspicion on his face—even though I could hardly blame him if those thoughts passed through his mind when I told him . . . about the documents. Seemed like all I brought into this relationship was chaos and doubt.

"Sam." I stayed where I was, my back to him, but now leaning against him. How had that happened? "Sam, I've found something—" How to say it?

But Sam, himself, moved, putting his hands on my arms and moving still closer. "I've found something too, something that's become precious to me. Someone."

"Sam," I said.

"Leigh, you look frightened. Others may not be able to read that through your careful control, but I can." He tightened his grip reassuringly. "There will always be things happening, good and bad, things that muddy our choices."

I touched his hand and squeezed it. "I agree," I said. "But—"

"But? A dangerous word."

I nodded. It was a strange sensation, nodding like that while we were so close and his arms were around me. "It is . . . and yet."

"Okay, I give up. What is it you want to tell me?"

"Sam, what you said is nicer than nice. But you might want to rethink how precious all this is *after* I tell you what I have to tell you."

Now I shook my head. Or tried, but then I just stopped.

I scanned the street. We were alone. None of the nearby cars had visible occupants. But then I thought of something else.

His phone was in his pocket. I reached in to grab it, startling him. I put my finger to my lips to shush him. Then I took my own phone and put both of them just inside a low brick wall, out of view. I whispered, "We won't go far. We'll keep an eye on them. They'll be fine."

He frowned but said nothing as I pulled him a short distance down the block.

"I never thought of the phone risk. Better to be safe than sorry, right?"

Sam looked annoyed.

"Please," I said in a low voice. "Just listen. I found documents."

"What are you talking about?"

"From the time when . . . well, you know what time."

"I don't understand."

His voice had a vague noncommittal tone. I hoped it was because he was listening and not thinking that I'd lied or was imagining or overreacting.

I drew in a clearly audible breath, expelled it slowly, and said, "Mason found them. He didn't understand what he'd found. He called me out there and gave me the papers. I'd never seen them before, and now I have to figure out what to do with them."

"What are they, specifically?"

I didn't want to say. Instead of explaining that they appeared to be account information and names, I said, "Not sure. But I think they relate to, you know . . . Back then."

"Want me to take a look?"

"Thanks, but for your protection, I'll say no. I'm going to drive up to see Leland. I'll ask him to examine them and see . . . well, see if they are what I think they are."

"And you'd rather not tell me what you think *they* are?"

I shook my head. "After Leland gives me his take on the situation, I'll share, but only if it won't come back to hurt you. I won't give investigators any reason to drag you into this." I hugged him and stepped away. "I went through this with

Andrew. I know the situation is different now and you aren't Andrew. Andrew was involved. You aren't. I want you to have deniability." I took his hand in mine. "My father damaged a lot of people. I refuse to add anyone else to that list."

"I'll go with you."

I smiled, even though I wasn't really feeling it. "Thanks, but I need you to watch Harvey and the kittens while I'm away. I expect to be gone one night, maybe two. But on the off chance that something goes wrong, it might be longer."

He put his arms around me again and pulled me in close. For a few minutes we stood there without moving, heedless of anyone who might pass by or otherwise notice.

"One thing occurs to me, Leigh." He spoke near my ear, still holding on to me.

"What?"

"How'd the documents get there? In your car? It's not likely they found their way there by chance."

"You mean they were put there *on purpose*? Yes, I'm sure that's the case."

He nodded, and as he moved, his cheeks felt rough against my hair.

"I know." I sighed. "The stuff in the car, including papers and old magazines and whatnot, was put there by me when I was hurrying out of the New York apartment. I never emptied the car after arriving at Florence's house, so these documents must've been there since then. As for who put them there, it could've been either my father or Andrew, but my father didn't have a key to my car, as far as I know. It has to be Andrew who put them . . . hid them there." I'd left out certain details deliberately. Like the spare tire compartment. I'd already told him too much. I couldn't bear it if he got pulled into this.

I drew in a long breath and prepared to step away as Sam

said, "And then two years later he came back to retrieve them?"

Sam and I stared at each other.

I said, "Seems like."

He nodded. "Seems like."

Slowly, carefully, I said, "He might return while I'm gone. Maybe you should take Harvey and the kittens to your place? Or would your dad . . . No, don't ask your father." I was remembering what he'd said about Marla having too many cats around to suit him when I first brought Harvey home. "Leave him out of it, okay?"

Still eye to eye, Sam touched my cheek, saying, "No worries. I've got this. Just leave me a house key and I'll take care of this end of things. You go see Leland."

"Thanks. One more thing. I need a car. Could you give me a ride over to the car rental place?"

Sam grinned. "You need me."

"More and more," I said without inflection. It was a simple fact.

"We can stop for food while we're out finding a car to rent."

I took an envelope from my pocket with Sam's name written on it. "This is for you. You'll need it while I'm gone." Inside it was a shiny new house key. "The locks were all changed yesterday."

"You moved quick."

"And paid a premium price for the quick service, but it's done and it's good."

He accepted the envelope and put it in his pocket, but when I turned to walk toward home, he called out, "Not so fast. I believe you're forgetting something?" He pointed toward that low brick wall.

I dashed over and grabbed our phones. I handed Sam's

phone to him, then paused with a smile. "Never hurts to take precautions. You're the risk guy, right? So you get it."

"I get it."

"Thanks for your help, Sam." I smiled. "And while I'm away, please take good care of the kids."

****

I got an early start the next day. Sam would come to the house later. I told Harvey and the kittens to be good while I was gone. And enjoyed saying it even if it sounded silly.

Leland didn't know I was coming up because I hadn't wanted to share that on the phone. But here I was, driving up Interstate 95, passing through Fredericksburg, and his name was lighting up the phone screen.

"Hello! Leland?"

"It's me," he said. "Can you talk?"

A car zipped around me, reminding me of when I lost the can of tuna, except that this time I was also driving fast on a busy interstate and having what might quickly become a stressful conversation. I saw the blue rest area sign ahead.

"If you can hold on for a moment, yes. I'd like to get off the road. I can call you back if that's better?"

"No problem. I'll hold."

What were the odds? I was never comfortable with coincidences, like Leland calling me just as I was driving north to pay him a surprise visit.

I should've called him from home. I could've just come up with an excuse—like I was coming up there anyway and wanted to drop by his office. But this impromptu trip had seemed a good solution to a tricky situation.

We'd be talking on the phone after all, but it would have to do. I pulled into the parking area away from the other vehicles, thinking that every minute it took me to get off the interstate and to a quiet, safe place to concentrate was costing me. But as Sam had said at the museum, *money well spent*. I hoped.

"Sorry, Leland. Believe it or not, I'm on my way to Connecticut. I hoped to stop in to see you on my way through New York . . . hoping that you'd have good news for me."

How had that sounded? Like carefully crafted lies. At best, misdirection. I hated the feeling of paranoia that crept into everything I did recently.

"You would've missed me."

Oh. I asked, "Are you at the lake? I remember how you enjoy that."

"Not this time. In the DC area. This trip is mostly business. I'm about to be pulled into a meeting, but first I wanted to give you an update on that concern we discussed."

My stomach literally clenched. How was that even possible? "And?"

"All good. There is some level of discussion around the case and the sentencing, but nothing that involves other parties. I can't be one hundred percent certain, of course, but I can be relatively certain that there's no formal action or official interest in your direction at this time."

"He deliberately misled me."

"Maybe. But why?"

I almost blurted out what I knew but bit my lip instead. After a moment spent recovering from my near blunder, I said, "I don't know, Leland, but I appreciate your efforts."

"I'm glad the news is good. I'll be in touch if anything does come up."

"As a matter of fact, Leland, if you're passing anywhere in the vicinity of Richmond, I'd love to treat you to dinner."

There was a longish moment of silence, and then he said, "That's tempting. It would be good to catch up. I'm not sure when I'll be leaving DC, but I'll give you a call. Maybe we can meet somewhere in the middle before I head north?"

"Please do. I know of an excellent Greek restaurant partway along. Let me know when, and I'll get you the name and address."

"Sounds great. Thanks. You know you can always call me."

"Thank you, Leland. Travel safely."

We disconnected and I leaned back, collapsing into the shape of the seat as my muscles went weak and I felt without substance, much like a human puddle. I'd perspired so excessively despite my perfectly effective antiperspirant and body powder that I needed a change of clothing. This was not the image I'd cultivated for so many years. Which thought, oddly enough, gave me a chuckle because I'd abandoned that veneer when I became the second neighborhood cat lady, hadn't I? I thought of Harvey and the kittens, and of Sam babysitting them, and how much all of that meant to me.

The air began to refill my lungs. My body seemed to be recovering its normal mass.

Relieved? Yes, of course, I was relieved not to be a person of interest in whatever was going on with my father's case. No guarantees about the future, of course, but for now, I was good. Andrew had been gaslighting me for his own reasons, and I'd fallen for it. What was the phrase? I'd fallen for Andrew's manipulation hook, line, and sinker.

He wanted the documents. He'd tried to find them in the car but couldn't access it properly because of the stuff in the garage, and likely because his own key fob—which he'd kept and I hadn't given a thought to—hadn't worked either, so he'd come after me. He'd messed with me. He'd put my cats at risk. So, no, he couldn't have those documents, regardless of what I ultimately chose to do with them.

My reluctance to mention them over the phone showed that I wasn't wholly convinced that there was no substance behind what Andrew had said. Nor was I free of this paranoia. But maybe sometimes paranoia was no more than the brain's instinctive drive for self-preservation and it might be worth listening to. If I gave the docs to Leland . . . everything could change.

Did I think, *If I gave* . . . ? If?

Yes, if I officially acknowledged having those documents, my life could be thrust back into what I feared most. What would the authorities make of them? Because those were account numbers. Overseas or offshore, maybe, whichever the term was. I could say I didn't know, but in my heart, I did. And the names that were written in the margins of the sheets . . . most I didn't recognize, but one of them was mine.

As far as the authorities were concerned, they didn't know this document existed, right? If they *had* known, they would surely have asked me about it during their interviews with me when the investigation was ongoing.

Or maybe they *had* known and this information may have already been dismissed as not pertinent? Maybe they wouldn't even care.

Except the papers had been hidden in my car sometime before I left New York. And if Andrew was after them . . . then it didn't argue in favor of the documents being meaningless.

My palms were wet again. I discovered this when I grasped the steering wheel. I wiped them dry on my slacks.

Shifting the car into drive, I followed the route that would lead me back onto the interstate and the southbound lanes. I'd wasted time and gas by being so secretive, but I consoled myself that it was not as big a waste as making the drive all the way up to New York only to find Leland wasn't even in the region, much less the office.

Heading south and homeward again, I was glad. I thought of Sam and my feline family. I was conflicted about the documents, but light at heart with what felt like a reprieve and space to breathe.

Until I heard from Leland again, I would put the documents in a safe place—not in the spare tire well of a car trunk or under a flowerpot on the porch. Almost unbelievably, I laughed out loud. I would enjoy this reprieve as a gift.

The only question was whether I should call Sam and tell him my plans had changed or should I surprise him? Maybe I would invite him out to dinner as a thank-you for his willingness to help. And yes, I'd also invite him because I wanted to spend time with him.

If this was indeed a reprieve, I chose to make the most of it.

Chapter Nineteen

After a stop at the bank and a visit to the safe-deposit box I'd shared with Florence, I drove home. I pulled up to the curb and parked the rental car, thinking that maybe when Sam and I went out to dinner we could also handle the car return . . . or maybe I'd keep the car for a few days. I'd ask Sam what he thought about that.

It was fun to have someone to discuss things with. I'd lost that when Florence died.

Sam's car was also parked at the curb, and the front door of the house was ajar. I grabbed my overnight bag from the back floorboard and all but skipped up the sidewalk and the steps to the porch, but as I neared the door, I heard voices. They came clearly through the screen. Sam's and someone else's—likely a woman. I couldn't make out words, but the tone was contentious.

I opened the door and stepped into the foyer.

****

Mother's eyes were already showing a hint of red and were

watery. She pressed a tissue lightly to her lashes.

"Cats," she said in disgust. "Why?"

"If I'd known you were planning to visit, I would've advised you to come prepared with a good allergy medication."

"I thought to surprise you."

"You did."

Sam seemed stressed. Meeting my mother could have that effect. And he was surprised to see me walk in. "Leigh," he said, sounding relieved. "I was about to call you when—"

Mother interrupted, ignoring Sam. "He said you were out of town."

"I was. I'm back sooner than expected."

"I thought you didn't go anywhere."

I frowned but tried to soften it with a slight smile. "Mother. Why are you here? Did you fly up?"

"Of course. Too long a drive for me." She glared at me, the whites of her eyes decidedly beige-ish. "A quick visit. You're my daughter. I haven't seen you in a while. I'm allowed to visit, aren't I?"

I shook my head slowly. This was too much mystery, and I wasn't in the mood to interrogate or to be interrogated.

"Why are you here?"

She continued to glare, but she shifted her eyes toward Sam without moving her head, so the movement was like a question to me.

"Allow me to introduce you. Mother, this is Sam. He's my friend. Sam, this is my mother, Lydia Eden." I gave them each a stern glance. "Mother, if you'd rather chat with me privately, then you'll have to wait while I walk outside with Sam because I need to speak with him. Make yourself at home. There's iced tea in the fridge." I looked past her to Sam. "How'd it go? The cats are okay?"

He scratched his jaw, puzzled. "All good."

"I'll walk you to your car."

"Okay."

As we stepped out, I pulled the front door closed behind us, trying to gain a smidgen of privacy.

"I hope you know that I'd rather visit with you than with my mother. You were doing me a favor, and now I'm returning that favor by letting you escape. I only wish I could take off with you. Maybe by the time I go back inside, she'll be leaving."

"She's your mom."

"Do I sound harsh?" I shrugged. "Not interested in the criticism. Anyone's. She didn't want me at her house. That's how I ended up here with Florence."

"Oh."

"That's right." I paused with a groan to show my frustration, then shook it off. "So that's the bad news, I guess?" I nodded toward the house. "The good news is that Leland called as I was driving through Fredericksburg. Turns out he's traveling. At the moment, he's in DC for business and tied up. No time to meet. I didn't want to get into things out there on I-95 and over the phone, so I suggested we meet up if he's traveling anywhere near Richmond. He agreed. We kept the conversation light. *But* the important thing—and the good news—is that he says no one involved with Dad's case is interested in me at all." I shrugged. "For what that's worth. After all, he would've had to keep the touch light else risk rousing curiosity and thereby drawing interest."

Sam leaned against the car, his hands in his pockets while looking down at his shoes, seemingly deep in thought.

"What are you thinking, Sam? Am I mistaken about it being good news?"

He shook his head. "Not as far as it goes, no. Mostly, I'm wondering why your mother is here. A surprise visit? Is it connected to what's going on?" He shrugged. "If she isn't visiting just to see her daughter, then the timing seems . . . too coincidental."

"I wouldn't be surprised. For sure, it's annoying. I'd planned to invite you out for dinner as a celebration of Leland's good news." I shrugged and leaned toward him. "Before I knew Mother was here, I'd decided this was like a reprieve, at least until I hear from Leland again. I want to relax and enjoy it. I need to practice having fun." I stared up at the house, pretty darn sure that Mother was peering through the sheers at us.

Sam breathed out with an audible sigh. "Sounds good to me." He shrugged. "Why not bring her with us? She needs to eat too, right?" He grinned. "She's curious about me being here. Let's make her guess about us and keep whatever she has on her mind bottled up inside."

"Oh my. I think you may have a slight cruel streak."

"Not cruel. Just disappointed."

I laughed, looking up at the blue sky and the trees and rooftops and all the stuff that formed a city neighborhood. I took his hand. "Thank you for being willing to take care of the cats, and if the need arises again, I hope you'll still be willing. I do not include my mother in that request." I returned his grin with my own, but it was quickly gone as I asked, "Did she say anything about why she was here?"

"She wanted to know where you were and seemed annoyed that you weren't here."

"Oh well, that's just her usual demeanor."

He laughed. "In that case, I'll take a rain check on the dining out."

"Yeah, and I'd like to take a rain check on the cooking. She has a reason for being here. I'll take her out for a meal, she can tell me why she's visiting, and then she can return to Florida.

That's where she wants to be. Not here with me." I squeezed his hand.

Sam crossed his arms and shrugged. "You know, I like the idea that you aren't going to be alone here tonight and for however long she's staying."

Was he kidding? I thought not. "There's that, I guess." I paused, then asked, "Did anything happen while I was gone?"

"No," he assured me. "You were gone for, what? Five hours at most? What about the documents? They're somewhere safe, right?"

I hesitated. Sam frowned. He said, "I ask because you still don't have a working security system. Kudos on changing the locks, but it's not enough, Leigh."

Slowly, I said, "I have an appointment with an alarm company. Florence never turned hers on, and I can't work it. Don't even know the codes. It's old. I'm going to get it updated."

He looked curious, then his expression went blank. Blank because I'd ignored the first question and answered only the second.

"I'm keeping you out of this, Sam . . . or trying to. I'm not doing as good a job of that as I should. For now, I'd better get back in the house and make sure my mother hasn't tossed the cats out the back door."

"Here." He reached into his pocket and offered me the house key I'd left with him.

Acting on impulse, I took his hand in mine and closed his fingers around the key and held them there. "Keep it." I added, "For now, anyway."

"You're sure, Leigh?"

"I may yet need your help." I smiled, but he didn't return my smile. I looked aside, not wanting to meet his eyes, feeling that I'd misjudged my timing, perhaps had overstepped the mark, but needing to express myself. I continued, "I've grown accustomed to being grateful to you, Sam. But if I'm ever a burden, please be honest with me." I was about to add that his friendship had become an important part of my life—using the word *friendship* would help ease the awkwardness, I was certain—but he reached behind me, pressing his hand in the small of my back, and stole the words right away from me. I hardly breathed. He was going to pull me close. He was leaning toward me, his eyes focused on my face, my lips.

And then he stopped. A dead stop. I couldn't read his expression.

I froze at that moment, thinking I should start breathing again.

Sam said, "I should go." He dropped his hand from my back and stepped away. "Call me if you need me."

****

A swirl of embarrassment mixed with desire, attachment, hope, and regret nearly kept me in place right there even after he'd gotten into his car and driven away.

What had happened? Could I have read our relationship, or his receptiveness to something more, so very wrong?

Of course I could have. When had I ever had a successful personal relationship? That girl whose face had decorated the sides of buses, who'd waved fans away with a distant look and the smile of a duchess . . . That girl had been as fake as the carefully composed expression on her face. How could I possibly ever expect to find and nurture a healthy relationship with anyone, much less a guy I hardly knew? That's right—hardly knew. *Hah.* If we didn't count that first date a year ago, I'd actually known Harvey for a day longer than Sam.

No wonder I'd misjudged.

Not even my parents had wanted me around much. They'd preferred their own interests to the company of their daughter.

I turned to face the house. *Okay, Mother. I see that curtain swishing back into place.* Only heaven knew what meaning she read in what had passed between Sam and me. And only heaven knew why she was here.

In her own way, she was as calculating as my father.

Maybe I'd sensed that personality type in Andrew when we met. Maybe I'd subconsciously stuck with what I knew.

That couldn't apply to Sam, could it?

No. Sam wasn't that kind of person. And maybe that's why, despite seeming so open and eager to help, he'd recognized the kind of person I was—someone who was taking advantage of him? Maybe this apple hadn't fallen far from her parents' orchard.

Well, that was a strange allusion. It conjured a crappy image of abandoned apples rotting in a field being buzzed by yellow jackets just looking for unwary souls to sting.

Well, I could sting. And I was in the mood to do it.

Groaning, I shook my head. No self-pity or getting even was allowed.

I grasped the railing and climbed the steps up to the porch and prepared to converse with my mother.

And given my mood, I almost felt sorry for her.

****

My mother was standing in the wide opening between the foyer and the living room. Her expression was almost unreadable except that it was obvious she was distressed.

"I thought you were *never* coming back."

I shrugged, holding my hands wide, my palms up. "I said I would." I stopped there, not inclined to be helpful.

"This animal crawled out into the hallway, and now it just cries." She waved her arms. "Am I supposed to do something about it?"

The book barrier was in place, but two were slightly askew and had allowed the escape—sort of an escape by accident.

"It's mewing. It's what kittens do. It's adventuring as it gets better at walking. Again, it's what kittens do."

Mother fixed her blue eyes on me. "Then why doesn't its mother come and get it?" She was now waving her hands despite keeping her arms close to her sides. She was genuinely agitated.

A grim smile formed on my face, but a smile nevertheless.

"Have you met Harvey, Mother?"

She gasped. "Harvey? Is someone else here? I thought you lived alone. Are there *two* men here with you?"

I rolled my eyes and didn't care if she saw me doing it as I walked past her down the hallway. I paused to pick up Orange Fluff. My face close to his, I said, "So we have two adventurers now." I opened the bathroom door wide and gestured to Mother to join me.

She eyed me suspiciously as I cradled the kitten, holding it against me.

"There are cats in there, and you know I'm allergic." She came forward anyway.

"That is Harvey. Sam didn't introduce you to her? How long had you been here when I arrived home?"

"Not long, though it was very disconcerting for the door to be answered by a man when you weren't even here and I thought you were living alone. How long have you and he been seeing each other? Long enough that he's moved in with you? Where did he go? When will he be back? I came to spend time with you, not to . . . not to . . . ."

"Calm down, Mother, please." I turned to Harvey, speaking

in a low-key, more soothing tone. "Harvey, this is my mother. Mother, this is Harvey and her babies."

I held Orange Fluff out toward her, but Mother demurred, refusing to take him, saying, "You're taunting me."

"Nope. I'm introducing you to your fur grandbabies." I returned Orange Fluff to the box. Not that he'd likely stay there for long now that he'd learned how to fall out of the box and had gravity to help him. "And that is Baby Gray, and that's Calliope Calico also known as Callie. And this last-but-not-least cutie"—I lifted the runt of the litter, a creamy peach beauty—"I named her Flo. She's the smallest but has a mighty heart." I pressed a kiss to the top of her head and returned her to the box from which she'd yet to escape. I smiled at Mother, saying, "That's the family. Please be sure to leave the bath-room door open so Harvey can access the litter box and food and water dishes." I paused, then added, "And watch your step. One never knows what might show up in the hallway when one has cats."

I touched her arm gently to soften my words. "As far as allergies go, I'm sorry this will be unpleasant. I can offer you an over-the-counter antihistamine, but otherwise, you're on your own. The cats don't go upstairs, so you can take refuge there if you need to before you leave. Which will be when?"

Much of the distaste that had been obvious on her face suddenly vanished. She pressed a hand to her midsection. She'd complained about a nervous stomach for years. She said, "I need to speak with you."

"Okay, but I should warn you that while I believe it's unlikely, it is possible that listening devices have been installed here."

I expected to shock her and for her to say something mock-ing, but instead she said, "Oh, sugar. They don't even need devices. Don't you watch TV? They've likely got a van parked nearby picking up every last noise that happens here—if they are listening."

Wow. *Huh.* Maybe I came by my willingness to believe what Andrew had said honestly. Maybe it was bred in my DNA. And then it hit me . . .

"Has Andrew been talking to you too?"

Her expression went blank.

"Hey, Mom, why don't we go get supper? Get some fresh air while we're at it?"

A quick nod, and she said, "Let me change to my walking shoes. I expect to be here tonight only. Do you have a bedroom I can use, or shall I go to a hotel?"

"Top of the stairs and turn right. It's the room at the back."

"Thank you. I'll only be a moment."

I stood as she walked past me, picked up her small bag and purse, and then went directly to the stairs and up. I stood there because I didn't know what else to do. Mother and I were functioning in unknown territory.

My whole life was feeling like *unknown* territory. I wanted to talk to Sam. But now it felt awkward.

My life was a mess.

But even a mess could be cleaned up.

And with that upbeat (sort of) thought, I went upstairs too, to freshen up, but first I checked the hallway to make sure no kittens were making a break for independence. They were far from ready for that level of adventure.

Mother was faster than me. As I descended the stairs and saw her waiting by the front door, I noted she was wearing a solid pair of walking shoes. Good.

I said, "The weather is lovely and there's plenty of daylight left. Let's take a stroll through the neighborhood to Cary Street. We'll have lots of restaurants to choose from there."

As soon as we were clear of the house and had both

scanned the street for suspicious vans, I said, "Okay, Mom. You first. You flew up here?"

She nodded but kept looking down, watching for breaks in the sidewalk and other tripping hazards.

"How'd you get here from the airport?"

"I should've called first. I don't know why I didn't. Anyway, I hired a car at the airport to drive me here."

"I would've picked you up, you know."

"And then you weren't here."

"Because I didn't know."

She shrugged. "Actually, I'm glad you're getting out again. Driving, even."

We'd already walked a block and a half. We were conversing, yes, but slowly, as if picking our way carefully, not just because of the vagaries of the aging sidewalk but also because of us, who we were. *How* we were.

Into the silence, she said, "Andrew did call."

I waited, looking down as Mother was, but not at the cracks. Instead, I noted the shadow patterns of the tree boughs overhead . . . single leaves, clumps of leaves, with bright sunshine shapes differentiating them. I *felt* separate. Joined, yes, but tenuously, and so very isolated.

We paused on the corner to wait for the Walk light to come on.

"He said your father was going to be released. Something screwy about the evidence and the handling of it."

We crossed the street. When we reached the other side, I stopped to face her. "How can that be?"

"I don't know." She faced me squarely. "I don't *want* to know, but I wanted *you* to know."

Shaking my head, I said, "I don't believe it. There could be a deal, maybe, but nothing that would involve us."

"I hope you're right. I don't need all of this to flare up

again. You don't either. You're finally getting out." She turned away, pressing the back of her hand to her lashes.

I let the gesture go unremarked. I'd never seen her get weepy over anything. I didn't know what this meant.

"This is Cary Street," I said.

Lots of people, lots of cars, and restaurants and shops lined both sides of the road. The eateries and shopping options had changed over the years, but many had been around for a very long time. Everyone in or near Richmond knew Cary Street.

"Just down that way, Mother. A restaurant we'll both enjoy. Can Can. It's a French restaurant but offers a wide variety. I've eaten there before. You'll like it."

She nodded, but with a jerky movement, and started walking ahead of me. I gave her a split-second head start so she could recompose herself, I understood that. When I caught up, I touched her arm to stop her.

"Slow down and breathe."

She glanced at me. I glimpsed her reddened eyes before she looked back at the street.

"Why do you call me that?"

"What? *Mother*?"

"Everyone else . . . my friends . . . their children call them Mom. Was I so very awful?"

I frowned but I also laughed. "I don't know. It always just seemed to . . . fit."

"To fit me? Or to fit us?"

Her tone, her expression, it all read as genuine. I felt no manipulation.

I said, "I'm not sure. I'll give it some thought."

"Well, if we're going to eat, let's go." She grabbed my hand briefly and smiled. "Maybe we'll think all the better for it. You never did eat enough, Leigh Ann."

Chapter Twenty

After we placed our orders and were alone at the table, she said, "He called."

I understood she was referring to Andrew.

She continued, "I already told you what he said. I don't know why or what it means or what it will mean to you and me, but it unnerves me. You've been doing better. It's been a long road for us. If this will drag us back into your father's orbit, his life, his bad decisions . . ." She stopped, shaking her head.

I put my hand on hers. "Let's not borrow trouble, Mom."

She looked at me, almost shyly.

"Did you follow up with anyone after he called?" I asked.

"No," she said, shaking her head vigorously. "I came here. I got on a plane without stopping to think." She pushed her utensils around almost absentmindedly, straightening them on her napkin. "I should've called first, I know."

"You're repeating yourself, so this must've really thrown you. It did me too, when Andrew showed up at the house uninvited. But I'm pretty sure he's trying to unsettle us for his own purposes, which—I don't know exactly what those purposes are, but I—" I did a quick change of tense, saying, "I'll contact Leland and see what he can find out."

Making it sound like I hadn't already done exactly that was a lie, yes, but trust had never been a habit between me and my parents. I found it difficult to slide into it now. I was glad when the food arrived because it gave me the natural opportunity to look away from her and pick up my utensils and all that. Calling her *Mom* felt awkward too, but in a strange way she was working toward earning that name by flying up here to talk to me and by acknowledging her awareness of the rift between us, of her concern—though not necessarily *just* for me —and thus acting impulsively because of it.

"After the plane was airborne, I began to worry that me even just being here with you would somehow contribute to . . . unwanted attention. I don't want to bring that on either of us. But how could I call and share any of this over the phone?"

"I understand."

She shook her head, bit her lip, then shook her head again.

We tried to eat but only went through the motions. Finally, sitting back and pushing the salad away, my mother said, "You think you understand, but you don't *know*, can't *truly* know. Because if he does get out, I won't allow him near me or my home. I'll get a restraining order and a guard dog, if necessary." She drew in a deep breath, released it, and said, "When you were growing up, you didn't like me to speak against him."

"He didn't speak ill of you. Despite his flaws, he never did that. He never put me in the middle between the two of you and your issues."

She looked almost angry now. "You don't know because as a child you weren't his focus. But this time, there will be precious little to distract him because he's run out of assets—

except for you." She looked at me directly. "And I can't be there for you. I am sorry. I can't do that."

Her eyes, her face . . . the lines had never seemed deeper. I believed her and felt a stir of pity.

"Maybe he's changed," I suggested softly.

She shook her head. "Andrew is calling and dropping by, right?"

"Okay. I don't know if Andrew is acting on his own or scheming with Dad. Does it matter? I know this much—we aren't children, Mother . . . Mom. We aren't helpless. I won't take pleasure in it, but I'll have no problem doing whatever is necessary to keep both Dad and Andrew away."

"They might not like your friend . . . your new live-in boyfriend?"

I smiled, but there was nothing genial about it. "The man you met when you arrived at my house is a friend, and he has nothing to do with any of this." I gave her a steady look. "And if anyone tries to involve him, they'll have to go through me."

Her eyes widened and her glare turned to surprise and a smile. "Okay, then. Just remember what I said. If there is a problem, it won't be coming from me." She clasped her hands together on the tabletop. "And your father will know not to expect help from me, so he'll visit you. You should be prepared."

"If he gets out."

"If."

I needed to call Leland again. This was getting entirely too screwy.

"Thanks for the heads-up, Mom. I do believe you mean well."

Was that a flash of hurt in her eyes?

I stood. "Why don't we head home? It's getting on into evening. One of Florence's favorite shows is coming on in thirty minutes." I offered her a quick smile. "I'll make us some popcorn for dessert."

She stood too, nodding, and gave me a ghost of a smile in return. She extended her hand, and I took it in mine. We walked to the door.

So it wasn't perfect, but it was something. A consolation of sorts.

It struck me that a consolation prize is still a prize, right? So we walked home in silence, but a comfortable one for most of the way.

"Mom, did Andrew actually tell you that Dad was getting out early?"

She stopped for a moment, thinking. Finally, she said, "No. He suggested and implied."

"I felt like he was gaslighting me. Like he was using the suggestion as a means to another end."

She shrugged and made a soft *humph* noise. "I can see how it might seem that way."

"Just speculating here, but since I didn't jump into whatever reaction he was hoping for, might he have gone harder with you guessing you'd warn me, that it would make this feel even more urgent?"

She stopped and looked at me straight on. "Possibly. But what reaction or action is he trying to push you into? Because if that's his goal, it would have to be something that would benefit him."

"He said the feds were pushing him to find out if I had information I hadn't yet shared." I had my hands in my slacks pockets and couldn't help crossing my fingers—discreetly.

"Well, that's ridiculous. Anything you might have had or might have known, you would've shared with them eons ago. It took them long enough to accept that you knew nothing."

Her tone was sounding a lot like Sam's when he'd argued

that close surveillance like eavesdropping seemed unlikely. Yeah, more and more I was thinking this was all about Andrew and those documents in the spare tire space.

We were nearing the house now, so I said, "I'm going to live my life. If they want anything from me, they can ask me directly." I said it bravely, more boldly than I felt it, but I'd said it several times now over the last few days and was almost believing it.

"You know, Leigh Ann, it's really a pretty house that Florence has here. That *you* have here." Mother shot me a sweet smile. "I'm glad it's yours. This time of day when the last of the sunlight hits the rows of houses, the avenue looks timeless."

"I agree."

"It's not as large as the other houses, but it's a perfect size for you, and a walkable, pleasant location."

"I miss Florence."

"You two got along quite well, didn't you?"

"We did. I appreciate what she did for me, but mostly, I'm grateful I had the chance to get to know her before we lost her."

"Well," Mother said, in her own special way, "I'm glad too. At least something good came out of the mess your father made."

As soon as we entered the house, I said, "I have to check on the cats, clean up their area and such. It will only take me a few minutes."

"If you don't mind, I'll take a look around?"

"Please do."

She wandered off and I focused my attention on Harvey's food and water, and all the kitty stuff. When Harvey hopped out to take her mommy break, the little mouths she'd left behind called out for her, but in no time they'd stopped their meowing and were more interested in climbing over each other. It was a little crazy—like kitten bumper cars. I lifted them out onto a fresh towel on the floor, then removed the soiled towels and added fresh ones, including the one I'd situated them on, and they were already moving again in a fun sort of scoot and walk as the towel beneath their paws rumpled and tripped them. I laughed softly and picked each of them up gently and returned them to the box. Next up, the task was to rebuild the low wall to keep them from wandering into the hallway again and possibly getting stepped on.

I shuddered at the thought.

Calling out so Mother would hear me from wherever she'd gotten to, I said, "I'll be right back, Mo . . . Mom. Get yourself something to drink or snack on. Snacks are in the pantry." I ran upstairs to make sure the guest room was all set.

Her bag was already there. No one had stayed in the back room since Florence had passed. During those last months, she'd insisted we exchange rooms. She'd always enjoyed the larger front bedroom with the street view, and when she'd suggested we switch, that she'd take the quieter room at the back of the house, I'd resisted. She'd convinced me she was sincere, and I gave in. "I find I prefer the quiet now, Leigh Ann. I can open the window here, away from the street noise, and enjoy the fresh breeze and birdsong."

Cherishing the signs of life, she called it. She'd sit there and watch the world, or she'd sit with her Bible or devotional book open in her hands. And she never complained.

When I returned downstairs, I went to the kitchen and found Mother out back on the screened porch. The day was passing into twilight. I flipped the switch to turn on the porch light . . . and of course remembered the pain of cutting my fingers and Sam Sr. taking me to the hospital for stitches, then Sam Jr. bringing me home and fixing me breakfast. How quickly we'd grown close, and then in an unexpected moment he'd cooled. Maybe I'd read him wrong.

"Leigh?" Mother was standing in the doorway. She asked, "Everything okay?"

"Sorry, I was staring. I was thinking of something else altogether."

"I hope I didn't create problems for you by coming uninvited?"

"No, not at all."

"Good," she said. "I was thinking too. This house is cute from the front and has potential. You should do something with the back, though. Maybe create a mini English garden or such? And do something with that garage or whatever it is."

"The yard is a small area. Not sure it's worth the effort," I said, trying not to sound dismissive. "The garage, though, does need help. It isn't very practical. I have some ideas for that."

She shrugged. "Oh well. If you don't mind, I may share some ideas with you. Of course, it's your decision, but you know I have a knack for this sort of thing."

Did she? I was surprised to hear her say that. Maybe she did. Maybe if she'd made herself a part of my life for the past decades I would've known.

She was saying other words—something about her friend's pool house—but her voice trailed off as she walked through the dining room to the living room, thereby avoiding the open bathroom door and the cats.

Just as well, I thought.

****

Mother chose the show that evening. She'd already settled on one—some home renovation show—such that when I joined her, I didn't bother suggesting we see what else was on.

I don't think she was paying all that much attention either, though she tried to look engrossed. I let it go. We hadn't spent this much time together in . . . honestly, I couldn't begin to say how long.

Plus, I missed Sam. I fidgeted in my chair. What was Sam doing this evening? I wanted to talk to him.

I pretended to watch the show with my mother as the time ticked away. Sooner than expected, she said, "Sorry, dear. It was a very early day for me and stressful too. I hope you don't mind, but I'd like to go to bed."

And I breathed—as if I'd been holding my breath for hours, waiting for my mother to leave so that I could resume living my life? Or was it because I so badly needed to reach out to Sam?

"Of course. I understand," I said. "I think everything you need is in the room and bathroom. Just yell if I've missed anything." My phone already in my hand, I added, "I'll check on the cats and the locks and such before coming up."

We settled on what time we'd need to leave the house in the morning to make her flight, and then I told her good night.

"Good night, Leigh Ann," she responded. Then she placed her hands gently on my shoulders. Her good night kiss was no more than the usual touching of our cheeks before she released me and climbed the stairs.

I watched her go. She didn't look back. She moved . . . old. Like a much older person than her usual self. Once she was out of sight, I heard the telltale squeaks of certain floor planks as she walked along the hallway upstairs.

Suddenly I felt alone, struck by an unexpected loneliness. I looked at my phone and chose to put it on the foyer table. I wouldn't call Sam. Not with this mood upon me. I was feeling a little too needy tonight.

The cats were fine. All were sleeping. I checked the book

barricade, then dishes and litter, then double-checked the outdoor lights and locks. Stronger now, I reclaimed my phone from the foyer table and went up to read in bed. Hopefully, I'd drop off to sleep quickly.

During the night, I woke, as one does, for no obvious reason. No nightmares tonight. Just a slow awareness of being awake. Checking my phone, I saw that it was almost one a.m. But then I heard a soft creaking noise from downstairs and threw the covers back. I had to check. There was no way I could go back to sleep without first assuring myself that all was secure.

Creeping down the stairs as quietly as possible, I paused halfway to listen and stare into the dark foyer and living room. The usual night-light was on but weak, but features and forms began to reveal themselves.

What was I seeing?

Keeping one hand on the railing, I eased silently down to sit on the step. My forehead against the spindles, I watched, not wanting to disturb the scene before me—a scene that defied all logic.

The night-light in the foyer, the moonlight filtering from the kitchen window and up the hallway, and the city lights from the street contributed too—they all seemed to serve the sole purpose of highlighting my mother, who'd fallen asleep in the rocker with Harvey curled on her lap. Mom's hand was resting on Harvey's back.

The feelings that swarmed in and around and over me were so mixed, I was stunned. This was a scene spawned from a strange world. An upside-down land where things-gone-wrong magically felt inexplicably right. Not like random bad luck, but with an outcome that might be welcome. I stared at the tableau, trying to read its meaning like a map of a foreign—perhaps alien—land.

As I stared, the headlights of a passing car caught in the windows and moved across the walls of the living room like a lighthouse strobe.

Mother may have had trouble sleeping. It was unlikely that she'd come down here in the dark to play with the cats. Maybe she'd thought to watch more television.

Harvey may not have waited for an invitation. Cats took advantage of opportunity—or not. Cats were contrary.

Mother may not have consciously put her hand on the cat, as if in welcome or encouragement to stay, but as a reflex. Cats could move stealthily. Or not. Again, they were contrary, inspired by their own mysterious motives.

Not just cats. Most of that could also apply to my mother.

Harvey would probably slip off my mother's lap and return to the kittens very soon. If not, Mom would probably wake up and return to bed herself.

As I was about to do.

Quietly, I stood and climbed the stairs, careful not to hit the squeaky bits on my way back to bed. None of the living creatures down here needed me just now.

For whatever reason, and for however briefly it might last, my mother was snug in that warm, good vibes healing bubble with Harvey. I prayed she was benefiting from it as I had. Maybe some of those heart-healing feelings would last and encourage her. I hoped, too, that it would be worth the itchy eyes and sniffles she'd surely suffer tonight and on her trip home tomorrow.

****

In the morning, I carried her small suitcase down the stairs and out to the car, and we began the drive to the airport.

"That antihistamine helped a great deal," Mom said and

199

then sneezed again. Her nose was red and irritated due to repeated contact with a tissue. "When I get home, I'll speak to Dr. Hoyt and see if there's something more targeted that he can prescribe in case I come back to visit again."

"I hope you will. Call ahead and I'll pick you up at the airport." It was easy to say because I knew she wasn't likely to make this trip again . . . but she might. And I might not mind. There were sights in Richmond she'd enjoy seeing.

We were nearing the airport. There were so many things I'd wanted to say since we'd gotten into the car, but I'd called back most of them. I had to find the right balance. I wanted to end this visit on the right note. This time between us had been different. It felt like an opportunity for us to find a better way forward.

"I'm glad the meds helped some," I said. "Thanks for dealing with the effects as best you could. Until Harvey came into my life, I didn't realize how lonely I was . . . had been since Florence died. Luckily, I'm not allergic."

"You take after your father in that regard." Her voice and tone were sharp, and she ended the sentence abruptly.

With a quick glance sideways, I saw her shake her head. Maybe she was wishing she could call those words back. I decided to let the remark go uncontested. We were almost at the airport anyway. No point in starting something—especially when the allergy bit was likely true.

The airport sign was just ahead at the next intersection. The flight tower was clearly visible from here.

Keeping her gaze directed forward, my mother said, "What about your friend Sam?"

Shaking my head, I said, "Exactly as you said, he's my friend." I tapped the steering wheel with my fingers in a rapid triple tap. "Same with his father who lives a couple of doors down, and Marla across the street, and so on."

"It's good to know your neighbors."

I smiled at her. "You and I can agree on something, at least."

"We agree on more than one something."

Nodding, I said, "Yes, I think we do."

"In fact," she said, pulling out her phone and keying in the four-digit code, "take a look at this." She practically shoved the phone in my face.

It was a photo of Harvey in the nursery box with her babies. Two were asleep, curled together, and two were roaming—checking out the sides of the box and probably searching for that cut-down area.

I smiled at Mom. "Seriously?"

"Well," she said. "It's not their fault I'm allergic." She took a long look at the photo, pressing her fingers against it to make the photo zoom. "I have to admit that they are cute. The gals are going to *love* these photos." She put the phone back into her purse, shaking her head. "I can't imagine what you'll do when they get older."

"Let's just roll with the good for now. The same applies to the Dad stuff."

"We can agree on that too, though it's easier said than done."

I nodded, turning into the departures lane. "We can indeed agree on that."

Chapter Twenty-One

Mother and I had parted at the airport with a hug and a cheek press, which left me feeling upbeat. Back home again, I dived into my usual morning chores, which now included a growing list of cat-related tasks like changing the towels in the cardboard box and refreshing the litter and making sure the book barrier was still doing its job. As I went about the tasks, my mother was very much on my mind, including the things she'd said about my father and Andrew, and even the photo she'd taken of Harvey and the kittens.

When I went upstairs to gather the sheets from the guest room for washing, I had another moment. Mother had forgotten her pashmina. In my limited experience, she took one or the other of them most everywhere with her. She tended to be on the cold side—no knock on her personality intended. This one was blue and silky. She'd left it draped over the back of Florence's chair.

Mother couldn't have known about Florence's chair, that it was where she'd lived her last weeks, here by this window.

Suddenly spent, I sat on the side of the bed, my fingers

wrapped in the shawl and with the coverlet jumbled beneath me.

Those last weeks of her life . . . I could see her still. She'd always been petite, but robust even so, and with a dynamic energy that gave her a youthful aura. She became frail. Thin. The fragile bones of her hand showed right through the flesh as she held a piece of paper or maybe a card, seeming to simply stare at it.

I'd stood in the open doorway—she didn't like the room to be closed—and asked softly, "Can I get you anything?"

Florence shook her head but didn't speak.

I took that as an invitation and walked into the room. I sat on the edge of the bed as I was doing now, more than six months later, and I asked her what she was holding.

"A postcard, Leigh."

"It looks old."

She nodded. "I'm old."

I didn't know what to say to that. By rights, she should've gotten a lot older before reaching this state of frailty, with death hovering around her like a wispy cloud. There were times I was afraid to touch her for fear I'd hurt her—she seemed just that fragile.

"A boyfriend," she said. "Sort of. An almost sweetheart."

"Oh?"

"Long ago. A boy I met when I was small, back before we moved to the city. His father worked for my daddy on the farm and he'd bring his children along sometimes." She moved the postcard between her fingers and looked at the picture side. "France."

"He went there?"

She sighed. "Eventually. His family moved onto the farm as tenants when we left. He'd come into the city from time to time and stop by to visit. My parents didn't approve."

"I'm sorry."

"Just how it was. No profession, no property, no prospects." She shrugged. "He was supposed to go to college. His family wanted it. I thought he did too." She laid the postcard on the blanket covering her lap. "Instead, he came here one day. He surprised me and said he was going to travel . . . no money, no nothing . . . and asked me to go with him."

I touched her arm so lightly, so gently.

"No, I didn't go. I was my parents' only child and a daughter." She reached over and pressed her free hand to mine. "That's my regret. My biggest regret. Really the only one worth mentioning."

"That you didn't go with him?"

"That I never asked my parents. I didn't . . . *do anything* except tell him *no*." She shrugged. "If I'd gone, I might've regretted that choice, but I never even considered it, though I wanted to go. Badly wanted to. I remember that day so clearly, more clearly than I remember the faces of my parents."

She faced the window and stared. "We stood out there away from the house and he asked and I said no, and all the while some blasted bird was singing like a crazed loon in that tree out there." She paused to release my hand and pressed her own to her eyes. When she took her hand away, she said, "It was a smaller tree then, for sure."

After a couple of long minutes of sitting in silence, neither of us moving, I asked, "What about him? Did he go? Where did he end up?"

"He went. All sorts of places. He sent this." She tapped the postcard with her finger. "Last one he sent. Never came home. Someone said he took sick over there and passed."

"Wow, Florence. I'm so sorry."

"Don't waste pity on me. I made my choice." She looked at

me fully for the first time since I'd entered the room. "Don't do as I did—waste your years listening to every daggone bird call trying to figure out which one was out there that day."

I smiled softly.

"I think it was like a siren bird." She chuckled, but it was a low, hardly heard sound. "Not like a siren-siren, but like one of those mermaids who lure men at sea astray, perhaps to their doom." She whispered, this time sounding heartbreakingly sad, "Or maybe an angel bird offering me a gift that I refused."

"Leigh," she said, "I heard it that day, but I was afraid. I didn't go. I didn't even consider it beyond my first impulse to say yes." She paused again to breathe before finishing with, "That's my regret. That I didn't even try."

My eyes were burning then and now. Then, I'd pressed my fingers to my lashes to brush away the tears lest she see them. Now, I simply let them fall. One dropped onto Mother's shawl. But that day with Florence, I'd knelt on the floor beside her chair and had tucked her shawl and blanket in around her properly.

"Thank you," I said, "for being here for me."

"My pleasure," she said, ending with a cough.

"I'll be right back with fresh water. Maybe you should take a nap?"

"I should've listened to that call. My heart wanted to go, but I never went beyond the world I knew—" She broke off abruptly, coughing again.

I wasn't for sure that I'd heard that last bit correctly because her voice had gone so raspy. But it didn't matter. I knew what she meant.

Later, after she'd died and I was going through her things, I found that postcard. After a moment or two to consider, I took it downstairs to that painting and tucked it into the frame.

Sometime later I taped it, in an envelope, to the paper on the back. It seemed to belong with that picture.

The young man's name was Alfred. He'd written a short message saying he missed her and that he had toured the Louvre and wished she had been there with him. He'd signed it, *Forever yours, Alfred.*

****

The world often seemed determined to intrude into my safe place, usually bringing worry with it. I peeked out the front window and saw Sam. He caught me looking at him and waved. I let the lace sheer fall back into place, remembering how we'd parted the day before. I'd overstepped. He'd gone cold. Now what? I opened the door.

"Good morning, Leigh."

"Good morning, Sam."

"Your mom still here?"

"I took her to the airport."

"Then you're free today?"

Was that a grin? Maybe an embarrassed one. Sam and I seemed to be in very different emotional places.

He added, "I texted asking if I could drop by. When I didn't hear back, I came anyway."

"I didn't see the text," I said. But he continued standing there looking at me expectantly, so I asked, "Would you like to come in?" There was no welcome in my tone, but I was a bit chagrined to hear a hint of hope in it.

"Actually"—he grinned again—"I'd like to know if you can come out to play?" He paused, then continued, "Before you say no, consider the weather. It's a gorgeous day. Also, you wanted to enjoy these days of reprieve while you wait to hear from you-know-who, right?"

Reprieve days. Yes, I'd said that.

I stepped back, opening the door wider.

His grin gone, he walked past me with an odd expression, almost sheepish, and then stopped to check on the cats. "Wow. New skills. Overnight, even."

I stood beside him to see what he was going on about. Harvey wasn't currently in sight, and the kids were all out of the box walking on little kitten legs, sometimes plopping over, at times stopping abruptly midstep to take an impromptu *kitten* nap. The book barrier was in place, intended to keep them from straying into trouble.

A furry body brushed against my leg.

I looked down as Harvey gave my other pants leg equal treatment, twining herself around my slacks and leaving a coating of fur, and then she stepped delicately across the barrier of books to check on her babies.

Somehow, I was now leaning against Sam—just barely. Our arms were touching.

Keeping his focus on the kitten box, he said, "I left abruptly yesterday."

"Seemed like."

"Sorry about that."

"Guess I threw you with the key thing?"

"Yes, sort of. But it was on me. Not you."

I tensed. I could feel that tension in my body and my face. Sam read it by looking at me. He said, "Let me explain?"

I shrugged but moved to put space between us. Keeping my expression as noncommittal as possible, I faced him directly.

Sam said, "I realized that you'd given me the key for your convenience, like, for instance, if you needed a friend to step in and take care of the cats—as I've promised to do and still promise to do. But in that moment . . . my mind went in a different direction. I thought . . . Well, I realized I've taken advantage of you, in a time when you were vulnerable. I've always considered myself a decent guy, not an opportunist or someone who'd mislead a friend."

"Mislead? You've been a huge help to me and a valued friend too, as you said. Other than inconvenience . . . or the emotional reward of doing good deeds . . . what do you get out of it? If you misled me . . . then to what purpose?"

We hadn't moved, and I continued to stand there, arms crossed, watching his face as a flush tinged his cheeks.

"What's going on, Sam? I don't understand. Yes, you've been good to me. Remember gratitude? I'm still grateful and not inclined to take offense. I do owe you."

"You don't owe me. I wanted to help because . . . Well, I wanted to help, but mostly I wanted to be with you. Around you."

"You mean you enjoyed my company?"

He frowned. "Well, yes, but . . . I don't know how to say this. Don't take offense. I realized how easily I was slipping into a . . . a feeling of intimacy with you. But the key you gave me was for convenience. I know you don't trust me, not altogether. So I then realized that that feeling of . . . intimacy . . . not just attraction . . . but of something more, might be one-sided. Maybe my instinct for self-preservation kicked in."

"I did wonder if you had ulterior motives—might even be snooping for dirt about the family infamy—but we'd gone out before, and your dad . . . Well, if you weren't on the up-and-up, I don't think he'd cover for you and keep that quiet from me."

"So I have my dad to thank for you deciding to take a chance on trusting me?" His tone sounded amused, and a little offended too.

I shrugged. "Not exactly. Mostly, every time I doubted

you, I just couldn't keep that suspicion, as being pertinent to you, in my head. Like a fact that didn't fit . . . it just kept slipping away. I don't know how I would've managed without you, Sam, especially during those days right after my fingers were cut, and then giving me an outlet, like a safe place to vent and someone to talk things through with after Andrew showed up."

Watching his dark brown eyes—it was as if I could see his thoughts churning, and I waited patiently, hoping he'd tell me what those thoughts were.

"I asked if you'd come out with me today—a play date, if you will. I've got the day off. You have the reprieve." He shrugged. "Plus, I have a good deed to do, and I'd love some company for the drive there and back."

"To where?"

"To show you the kind of thing I do when I'm doing what I enjoy—not the day job. I'll explain on the way, if you'll come along for the ride." He added, "We should learn more about each other."

"Okay," I said.

His face lit up.

"I need to clean the cat hair off my slacks first."

"And can you change to hiking shoes? Just something for a walk. No mountain climbing, I promise."

His expression had been poised somewhere between serious and sincere, and now it went to solemn as he touched my arm. "Trust me?"

"I'll be ready in five. Have a visit with Harvey and her crew while I'm getting ready?"

"Will do."

A pair of sneakers was as close as I could come to hiking shoes. Since I was changing my footwear, I also exchanged my furry slacks for a pair of jeans. I rarely wore jeans. I'd purchased them and the sneakers for yard work—which I seldom did. I was, and always had been, a city gal.

I refrained from asking until we were clear of town, but then I couldn't help myself. I asked, "Where are we going, Sam?"

He grimaced and said, "So, remember the painting in the library?"

Chapter Twenty-Two

Sam had asked, "Remember the painting in the library?"

Of course I remembered the painting. I walked past it many times every day, and just that morning I'd been thinking of Florence and recalling her words about Alfred—not to mention what she'd said about sirens or angel bird calls.

I groaned. "This is about Florence's country property? Sam, I don't need to be anyone's *good deed*. You know my plate is full right now. I can't take on anything new. For now, that property is fine as it is. It isn't going anywhere until I sell it, and likely, that's exactly what will happen when I am ready to figure it out."

"But you've never seen it, and I haven't been out to the farm in years."

Interstate 64 ran nearly straight, due west toward Charlottesville, and was lined for many forested miles on both sides with occasional breaks in the trees offering glimpses of pastures, farms, and old churches. It all passed in a scenic blur as Sam drove us west to the property that Florence's family had left when she was young, that she had inherited, and had passed on to me—without telling me what she wanted done with it. For me, for now, I chose to let Florence's accountant continue to pay the property taxes and insurance until I had the focus and energy to deal with it.

Sam said he hadn't seen it in years—thus he *had* seen it.

"When did you go out there?"

"Florence asked me to take her. I brought her twice, but that was years ago." He cast a sidelong glance at me. "Back then, the property was rented out for farming and tenants. It's been empty for a while now. But that's not—*you're not*—the good deed."

"Then why are we going there today?"

"Because the day is beautiful and the property is out that way. Why not take a look at it after I handle my errand?"

"What *is* out here? Woods and fields? I don't mean to sound callous, but it isn't for me. I'm a city girl."

"Do you intend to return to New York? Or is Richmond city enough for you?"

"*No* to New York. That life is over for me. As for what I'll do or where? I don't know. I can't make plans like that until I know I'll be free to pursue them."

"Then this is a good time for gathering info and enjoying a day of distraction."

Sam took the exit. The big green interstate sign read *Mineral* and *522.*

I couldn't help wondering how important this property had truly been to Florence. She'd never asked me to drive her here. Hadn't even hinted at it. But maybe my car being parked in the garage with stuff piled around it had told its own tale. She knew I didn't want to drive anywhere. Really didn't want to go *out* anywhere at all.

But if she'd asked, I would've taken her.

"Was that a sigh? Did I do a terrible thing pushing you to do this?"

"Sorry. I was just thinking."

"Don't stress. After I take care of my errand, if you truly do not want to visit Florence's property, I'll take you back to Richmond."

I didn't answer. I was watching the scenery and noticing houses. Most of them were older homes of various sizes and conditions, a few pastures and barns, and new houses too—beautiful ones—and new housing developments. The curving, winding road was very different from the interstate, and here, some of the parcels of rolling land looked denuded. I'd heard of timber being harvested for sale, and I presumed that was what had happened to the acreage where it didn't look like it had been cleared for farming or pasture. But there were still large forested areas, and as we turned off the main route, those far outnumbered the open spaces.

The back roads and forests blended together in my mind. I couldn't have said whether we were going north, south, east, or west.

"There are a lot of trees out here."

Sam grunted, a doubtful sound, then said, "Not as many as there used to be."

He leaned forward as if he could see around the next curve if he stared hard enough, and then he slowed the car. "Here it is," he said, just as the sign, black metal on a large wooden board, came into view.

"Why are you stopping?"

"We're here."

"Here?" I looked through the car windows. "All I see are trees."

"We turn here."

It was a dirt and gravel road with ditches on both sides, and it was dark, very shady due to the tall trees that arched overhead as if they were straining to touch boughs.

Panic doubled down on me in a sudden rush. I pressed my lips together, refusing to give it voice. I'd already spent too much of this trip complaining and whining. I might understand where it came from, but Sam couldn't possibly get it.

After a deep, cleansing breath, I said, "Sam, I know you meant well, and I'm happy to go along for the errand part, but as for the rest…" I pressed my hand to my forehead.

"If you're worried about missing a call from your attorney, you should have cell service out here. Anything else isn't worth ruining your day over."

In reflex, I checked my phone. The service looked good. I bit my lip, trying to stop myself from saying more things I might regret.

"The sign said Cub Creek Stable?"

"That's the place."

"I don't ride."

He laughed and mimicked lifting a nonexistent cowboy hat from his head, nodding as he said, "Well, ma'am, you'll be reassured to know that horseback riding is *not* on the agenda today." He shook his head, dropping the drawl. "You really *don't* trust me, do you?"

I pressed my lips together and shook my head. "Not that. I don't trust people . . . No, that's not true. It's *surprises* I don't trust. And people keeping secrets. And what people mean behind what they're saying out loud." I reached up and grasped the panic handle above the window. "What if someone is driving toward us?"

"There are wider areas for passing. We're going slow. If we meet another vehicle, one of us will back up or pull over and allow the other to pass."

"This road needs to be improved. Widened." I took a breath. "As for the heart of the matter—trust—I have trusted you more than I've ever trusted anyone, so it's not that I don't trust you, but some people have a strange idea of what surprises might mean to other people. Some weird expectation of the surprise being a delight—when it really only serves to satisfy the giver. I learned not to trust surprises a long time ago."

"And the rest? Secrets and openness?"

"Maybe later. I'm not used to this sort of conversation." I reached over and touched his arm. "Except with you. I'm getting more and more used to that."

He pulled up in front of a small log building where there were spaces to park. The sign on the front of the building repeated the name on the sign by the road, Cub Creek Stable. I saw a fence beyond it—a paddock—and a larger building on the far side of this smaller one. It all looked fresh and new, including the tall trees surrounding the large open area. The tops of those trees seemed to be reaching up to touch the bold, blue sky above. A breeze, high above us, rustled the uppermost branches, creating a distant rushing noise. Around us, closer to us, the birdsong and creek sounds called a welcome.

"I'll keep that in mind," Sam said.

"What?" I asked, startled. My attention had been snared by the surroundings.

"Surprises. You don't care for them. I'll remember. Secrets and other concerns are on the agenda for later." He unsnapped his seat belt, saying, "Mind giving me a hand?"

"Might as well be useful," I said. "Whoa. Check that. I'd be happy to help."

He gave me a look.

"Did you catch that? The *whoa*? *Stable* . . ." I groaned. "Well, if I have to explain it, then it's not funny."

His face stern, Sam said, "No, ma'am. Not funny at all. We'd best giddyup and get this job done."

I laughed. I liked laughing. *I should do it more,* I told myself.

He opened the back door of the vehicle. "Can you carry this bag?" he asked as he reached into the back and then offered me a massively large flowered vinyl tote, even bigger than my reliable grocery tote.

"Okay," I said, accepting it from him. "What's this?"

"Blankets. Horse blankets. It's bulky but light."

"It is."

He hefted a box containing a jumble of items. "Tack. Horse-riding gear."

On closer inspection, I saw that the items were neatly laid in the box. It was the assortment that gave it the jumbled look.

"Were these yours? I didn't know you enjoyed horseback riding."

He shrugged. "I have, though not recently. But no, this wasn't mine. A woman who's given up keeping horses wanted to donate the gear to someone who could make use of it. I suggested Cub Creek Stable."

"Why?" I asked. "I thought you did risk consulting for businesses. Do you also deal in used horse gear?"

"*Like new* and *gently used*, you mean." He gestured at the bag of blankets. "And those are freshly washed."

"Well then, I'm greatly relieved. The right words make all the difference." Yeah, I sounded snarky.

He grinned, saying, "Don't they?" He closed the back of his vehicle. "I'm glad to see your wit is back, alive and well."

"Sarcasm, more like. I'm not going to apologize."

He gave me a quick glance, saying, "You really are uncomfortable about this."

I sniffed and looked away. Surprises messed with my mood. And secrets and ulterior motives too. Those things led to intrusion, curiosity, lies, and regrets. I gave myself credit for *not* saying all that out loud. Instead, I said, "Not so much now. Back on that road . . . But I'm okay now."

A woman with long blonde hair exited the building. As we left the vehicle, the woman recognized Sam, greeting him with a smile. She raised her hand in a wave and called out, "Hello. I hear you have a box of tack for us?" Her eyes strayed my way.

Sam said, "Kris, this is Leigh Sonder, a friend of mine."

He'd startled me when he said *Sonder*. Except for legal and medical matters, it was the surname I'd chosen to use—my hiding name—and Sam knew that. But coming from him—in his voice—the name felt jarring somehow.

Kris smiled. "Pleased to meet you, Leigh, and thanks for helping Sam bring the gear."

I offered her the tote. "Not much help, I'd say." I gave her a quick smile, saying, "You have a beautiful place out here."

"Why don't we walk over to the barn? We can leave the donations there and I'll give you a short tour. We're still getting this enterprise up and going."

She looked into Sam's box. "Nice."

"Mrs. Landon said she hopes it will be useful for the program, and generally, of course."

Kris said to Sam, "Given our shoestring budget, I'm sure it will be. Kind of her to think of us—which I'm sure I have you to thank for that, and thank you too, for bringing it all the way out here."

****

The barn was small, with a central walkway and three stalls on each side.

"We'll extend the stable out when we can. *When we need them*," she amended, but stopped short as another woman walked toward us from the far end. Also blonde, she was leading a brown horse.

Kris said, "My sister, Jen."

Jen nodded to us as she led the animal into a stall.

The whole place smelled like new wood. Fresh straw covered the floor of the stalls. The sliding doors at each end of the building were open, and the breeze carried its own freshness inside to mingle with the scents currently here. A bench was outside one of the stalls, and Kris set the blankets there; Sam did likewise with the box of gear. I was taking it all in and ridiculously thinking of Harvey's box in the half bath and the litter box in the kitchen. There was no true comparison, of course.

"Leigh?" Sam nudged my arm. He gestured toward Kris.

She laughed softly. "Sorry, I was running on. I asked if you ride?"

I shook my head, hopefully looking amused. "No."

"Would you like to?" She grinned.

Her smile was infectious.

"Thanks, but no. I tried once, long ago, during a stint at a boarding school. Didn't last long."

"Well, if you change your mind, you know where to come."

I nodded. "I do."

****

We paused at the fence. The horse in the paddock ambled over to where we stood. I wasn't comfortable with horses. Sam reached out and rubbed the animal's face between her eyes, and as she stretched her head forward, he scratched between her ears.

"Hazel," Kris said. "She's very gentle and good-tempered."

Thinking of the kittens, I wanted to reach out but hesitated. Sam glanced at my hands. My fingers gripped the fence board except for the braver fingers that moved, wanting to touch the blaze on the horse's face.

Sam lifted an eyebrow in a silent question. I shook my head and looked away.

Kris was speaking again, "The owner of Wildflower House sold us this property when we lost our lease on our prior location. Clearing the land, the fencing, even for the road . . . it's costly and takes time. We have a lot left to do."

Without thinking, I said, "And in the meantime, the clients and customers find other sources for the services they want."

She grimaced. "True. It will take time and money, but at least no one can evict us. We've got a grant that's been approved, so we'll put that toward the facility. We need to be able to board horses to bring in recurring income, and get lessons in full swing, and . . ." She pressed her hands to her cheeks and laughed. "And the list goes on and on." She touched Sam's arm. "Thanks to the time and generosity of people like Sam, we are making progress."

I nodded, cutting off my next remarks. They didn't need my interference. I knew nothing about caring for horses or managing a stable. "We're in the way, holding you up. Thanks for showing us around."

"Not at all. Gotta get the word out. Plus, this is my favorite subject. My sister and I have overcome obstacles before."

She left us soon after, and when she was gone, Hazel moseyed off too since we weren't offering snacks. But Sam stayed put. He said, "Let's go down to the creek? There's a path along Cub Creek."

"A path to where?" I cringed inside, wishing the words back.

He was silent for a moment before saying, "We can leave and go back to town now if that's what you want."

I nodded, then said quietly, "I don't know why I'm so anxious about this."

"Because you don't like surprises?"

"Maybe." I looked away. "Sam—"

A cool nose touched my arm. Startled, I stopped. Hazel was back.

Sam whispered, "No expectations, Leigh. Just do what you're comfortable with."

I wouldn't meet his eyes, but still I smiled, suddenly feeling contrary. Apparently, I had that in common with cats and my mother. I touched Hazel's white blaze, and nothing terrible or embarrassing happened. I moved my fingers over and ran them lightly along the curve of her jaw. She closed her eyes. I took my hand away and reached for Sam's resting on the fence near me.

"Let's take a walk, Sam."

Chapter Twenty-Three

When Kris left us, Sam and I were standing at the far end of the paddock, near the creek. Cub Creek was a narrow watercourse with banks of rock, roots, and moss. The water was dark due to whatever mineral content the earth offered here, but a sandy-looking bottom showed through where the water was shallow. The larger rocks thrusting up from the water looked old. I wasn't sure why I felt that. Maybe it was because of their lined, craggy faces.

Sam wasn't speaking. I looked right and left. To the left, the way was choked by undergrowth, including large sticker bushes, but the other . . . While it wasn't cleared for walking, it was less choked with wild growth. More open space was visible beyond, following the course of the creek.

"Walk where?" I asked.

"Leigh?"

"Sorry. It's very different from a city sidewalk." I stared at the lesser growth to our right. "Is that a path over there?"

"Sure is."

"Is it trespassing? Going onto private property, I mean?"

He nodded. "It's private property, but they won't consider it trespassing. It's cleared on purpose—for *this* purpose."

I gestured in the other direction. "Then why does it stop here?"

"That's a longer story. Let's walk, and I'll tell you what I know about it."

He offered me his hand to trek through the thin undergrowth between us and the path. Actually, there wasn't much growth to worry about, but I kept his hand anyway until some of the narrower parts of the path made it difficult to stay side by side.

We walked upstream. The woods were thick alongside the path, and the same was true on the other side of the creek. The shade was lovely, and the sunlight picked its way through the overhead leaves as it did with the trees that lined the city sidewalks, but here it also lit up the movements of the creek as the water flowed around rocks making small waterfalls, even flickering with bits of light in the shallower areas when the sun hit it just right.

Sam said, "It's probably the mica. This whole area is situated on a mica schist. Yes, I had to look that up the first time I heard the word. It means veins of mica in the ground." He shrugged. "Lots of quartz too."

"Cool."

As we walked, the forest began to fall away on both sides. The creek widened here, and the banks were neat with a domesticated look. A wide, well-manicured slope led up to a mansion, perhaps late Victorian, or so I guessed in my limited knowledge of architecture. The term *mansion* was relative, but this was a very large, roomy place with decorative woodwork and turrets. Someone had lovingly restored it. Even from down here at the base of the slope, I could see colorful flowers and even a statue up near the house.

"The man who bought it and restored it intended for it to be a bed-and-breakfast, but the building and grounds are mostly used as an event space, like for weddings. And a home too." He paused in front of a bench. "Need a rest?"

"I'm good. That wooden bridge over the creek is sweet."

Sam took my hand. "Mind?"

I squeezed his in my own. "Not even a little."

We walked to the bridge, stopping halfway across it. Leaning against the railing side by side, we faced to look back at the way we'd just come.

"Can I say something, Leigh? Without you getting angry?"

"Depends on what you say." I meant it as a quip, but we both knew it was true. "I'm out of my element here, Sam. I don't mean to be negative or sharp. It just comes out that way."

"Protection?"

I shrugged.

Sam said, "This trip wasn't about an agenda or trying to make you decide and choose or anything else. This was about a day out together. It was about . . . okay, a tiny agenda. I wanted you to think beyond the four walls of your house. What worked for Florence won't necessarily work for you. You are a doer. You are a different person with a different background and living in a different age.

"Sometimes people need something to look beyond—beyond the immediate troubles—to help keep the worries a manageable size. Trouble is part of life. Don't let life pass you by while you're focusing on the trouble part."

"Okay. Great. Easy words. But the things I fear . . . they are real. What don't you get about going to prison? About financial ruin and people hating you?"

He nodded. "I understand and I don't discount those or the trauma from living through the troubles with your father. But

223

don't feel threatened, not with me. This trip, this drive in the country today, isn't about decisions. If nothing else, it's a walk in the woods together while I fulfill a commitment." He paused. "What you do or don't do with this property is up to you. I have no opinion on that. You don't need to feel pressure.

"Leigh, you know that hiding won't keep the bad away. Better to have a wider view, a look at the horizon and everything in between so you're prepared when you need to be but can enjoy life when that's possible, because in my experience, it's usually the things you *don't* see coming that are the worst."

We stood in silence for a long moment before he said, "That's it. No more preaching from me. Anytime you need me, Leigh, call me, text me, find me. I'll have your back, I promise."

Staring straight ahead, I said, "Since we're already out here, let's go see Florence's property."

From the corner of my eye, I saw him grin. His grin lifted my heart.

"We can do that," he said. "We'll walk back up to the stable and then drive over to the property because, unfortunately, the stable is where the path ends."

"I guessed that already. You aren't as subtle as you give yourself credit for, Sam, but you *are* quite charming."

Sam flushed ever so slightly. His hand brushed my cheek and then found my back and stayed there. I moved toward him, lifting my face until my lips touched his.

And I realized the birds were singing here too.

****

Florence's painting depicted a wide landscape view of a farmhouse, a white clapboard two-story surrounded by open fields and framed by forest. The fields were in use, some plowed, another with something leafy and green growing in rows. The painting, and even the scene before me, had a Grandma Moses quality with the elements blocked and clearly delineated, but with unexpected movement shaping the land-scape features.

She'd told me about the old farm, and I hadn't expressed much interest because I was consumed by my own fears and busy protecting my wounds from further injury. After all, fate had proven that bad things could happen regardless of reason.

If I had expressed more interest, perhaps she would've told me more.

If I had expressed interest, then I might have better understood why she chose to bequeath it to me in her will instead of learning of it by surprise after she passed. My best guess was that she simply didn't have anyone else to leave it to.

I did know that the property had come to her from her father's side. Not my side of the family. But like me, she was an only child. She had cousins on her father's side, but they lived elsewhere and she didn't know them well. If any of them had gone out of their way to be in touch, I imagined that Florence would've offered the land to them . . . but maybe not. I'd never know.

Because I'd been consumed with myself above all else.

I could've come out here with her. I could've offered.

But that was in the past. Today was fresh with new possi-bilities.

The rental car was still in my possession. I had driven. I'd ventured out into the larger world and my world hadn't imploded. Media hadn't chased me down. Nothing bad had happened as a result. In fact, having the car meant that I'd been able to drive to meet Leland (even though that trip had ended an hour up the interstate) and I'd taken my mother to the

GRACE GREENE

airport. Little things. But sometimes the little things were the critical underpinnings of everything big.

I was healing. Whether by time, because of Florence's help, or whatever, I was getting better and stronger, and it had taken a can of tuna (sort of) to shake my shell and crack it enough for me to start pecking my way out.

And I was going to try to remember all this when setbacks occurred. As they surely would.

He drove us up the slope, the old fields now fallow and overgrown on each side. He stopped and parked where the ruts were too deep, the washed-out potholes too risky, and opportunistic saplings slapped the car.

The house was much like it was in the painting, but shabby and neglected. Forgotten.

He said, "Looks a lot worse than when I brought Florence out here. Of course, back then a family was still living here, farming." But then he reached over and squeezed my hand.

"You don't know this about me. I'm sure Florence would never have told you." He cleared his throat. "My teenage years were rough—personally rough like it is for a lot of kids. I got lucky, maybe. More likely, it was a combination of my dad not putting up with much, but talking to me, guiding me; the prayers of my parents, their friends, and many others; and Florence, who trusted me with my new driver's license, still fresh from the presses, in my pocket, to drive her out here. I was glad to be driving and glad to be out of the house. Florence and I got along. But I was pretty much estranged from everyone back then. Not just one big chip on my shoulder —but one on each shoulder, and maybe even tied to my back and ankles. I was angry at the world in those days."

As he was speaking, he'd opened the car door for me, encouraging me to get out. I was leery of the insects and reptiles lurking in the tall weeds. He kept a hand on my elbow as we picked our way up the old driveway. We stopped short of the house and stood, facing the gentle slope up to the crest of the hill where the house sat. He'd moved close behind me. Standing only a few inches away, I could feel his words . . . his breath on my hair as he spoke. He put his hand on my shoulder.

"One day, just after I'd finished the latest shouting match with my dad and I was feeling angry and wretched and worthless, she stopped me as I was walking past her house. She called to me from the porch. 'Sam Jr., I need your assistance. I understand you have earned your driver's license, and your father says you're a good driver.'"

He laughed, but softly. "That surprised me, Leigh. Seemed to me back then that Dad was always giving me a hard time. But I was even more surprised when she asked me to drive her out to the country. She wanted to see the place where she was born and had spent her early childhood. She had a *yearning* to see it, she said."

As Sam and I stood there, still and close, Sam said, "I hesitated. I couldn't really put it into words at the time, but I sensed it meant a change for me. Too many things in my life had fallen apart, and I was just trying to keep what I had, and it took all my energy. For me, I think being angry was a cover for fear—fear of losing everything that mattered, including myself. But I agreed. We drove out here and stood somewhere near this spot, and then she got down to brass tacks. She wanted my undivided attention.

"She told me that each day was important. To live each day in a mindful way because it would be gone and wouldn't come back. No do-overs for past days or messed-up days. But this is the thing—each day is important because it builds the path to the future. You're standing *here* in the *now*, but—and she pointed her finger at the fallow field over there before tracing the crest of it. That, she said, is the future. That's tomorrow and tomorrow. She tugged on my shirtsleeve—that tiny woman yanked on my sleeve—and said, '*Live* the moment, but don't focus on it.' Focus on that wide-open future and the options between here and there for reaching it in the way you want. She turned to me and said, very lovingly, very kindly, 'Don't mess it up, Sam. Your life depends on this.'

"I was pretty stupid back then, I admit, but even then, I knew she was talking from her own experience, about herself, even though she never actually said that."

Sam went silent. His hand had moved down my arm. I was comfortable standing there . . . content? Maybe. I could be annoyed that he was preaching this message to me, but why bother? If he was trying to manipulate me, then what did he get out of it? Not money. Not cooperation. This certainly wasn't a sure recipe for seduction.

He was sharing a message from Florence. One he thought I'd want to hear.

"And did you?" I asked.

"Did I?"

"Mind your days to build a better future?"

He nodded, but we were standing so close that his cheek brushed my hair, and I leaned back a fraction into his space.

"That horse gear?"

"Yes?" I said.

"Melanie Landon lost her husband. She had no use for that tack, but it meant something to her, and she knows I talk to everyone. I knew the two gals at Cub Creek Stable and asked if they could use it. They could." He paused. "Someone told me about an elderly couple who needed a ramp. I know a guy out here in Louisa who owns a landscaping business who can do outside construction like that and someone else who donated the lumber. I facilitate finding and moving donated groceries to food banks in town. Small stuff. I'm not bragging. It's just one person here and one person there, but over the years, it has given me a satisfaction that nothing else has. I do my job. I like my work. But I always keep my ears open for needs that I might be able to help solve."

"And I'm your project?" Did he hear the warning in my voice?

He laughed.

"No, Leigh. When it comes to you, I'm being completely selfish. I want to spend time with you, and I'd like you to feel the same. If you're distracted by other troubles, then there isn't room for more—*for me*—in your life." He stopped and this time pressed his lips to my hair before stepping away. "I'm not here to preach or give unwanted advice, and telling you that story was maybe the scariest chance I've ever taken." He paused and then added, "You might've heard how fast my heart was beating."

"I did."

"I appreciate you not blasting me for it."

"Thanks, Sam, for bringing me out here. Thanks for letting me hear Florence's voice."

"My pleasure, Leigh."

Chapter Twenty-Four

Leland called a few days later. He apologized for the delay and we arranged to meet at the rest area, the same one where I'd parked when we'd spoken before, but this time we were meeting in person.

"I didn't want to discuss this over the phone, Leland." I nodded, trying to reassure myself that I'd made the right decision to discuss it *at all*. I said, "Something was found—not by me, but by a mechanic who was getting ready to work on my car, a car I haven't driven since I arrived in Richmond. The mechanic gave me all the odds and ends he found in the vehicle, including the document I'm concerned about. It was found in the spare tire space in my trunk. It may or may not be connected to Andrew's visit and his gaslighting of me. But he wants these papers badly—I think this because he even called Mother to get her to pressure me. At least, that's my guess about his intent."

"Do you have them with you?"

I shook my head. We were sitting away from the cars and trucks, and the restroom facilities, at a picnic table. The shade was welcome, as was the privacy.

"You probably think I'm being overcautious. Andrew did a job on me, it seems."

"Caution is good. What makes you think this document is related to Andrew and not your father?"

Shrugging uncomfortably, I said softly, "Both. Relates to both of them, I think."

He nodded, but I couldn't read his expression.

"The document is safely tucked away. I took photos of it on my tablet. It's an old tablet that belonged to my cousin. It isn't connected to Wi-Fi, internet, or Bluetooth." I selected the images and passed the tablet to him. "There are three pages in all, but I took some close-ups, so there are extra images."

He swiped through, image by image, pausing to look at each and choosing to enlarge some of them while I waited silently. Finally, he set the tablet on the table and returned his reading glasses to their case.

"You saw my name there."

"Yes. Those look like they may be account numbers, and the notations in the margins look interesting, but obscure."

"I thought the same. I know nothing about any of it or whether this could possibly relate to money laundering, or what do they call it? Offshore accounts? And I have no idea why my name is there." I spread my hands. "I don't know why, and I don't like it."

"And if these . . ." He waved his hand over the closed tablet. "If the documents hadn't been found? Perhaps were never seen or shared?" He kept his gaze fixed on minc. "I'm not suggesting any particular action, but I want to be sure you've thought this through and understand the possible repercussions."

We sat, letting the question—and the potential within the question—sit there and breathe with us as an ant walked across the table plank, making his way toward the tablet. Leland brushed him away but didn't squish him. I appreciated that.

Slowly, I said, "Except, Leland, someone *does* know about it. Maybe I've watched too many thrillers or crime shows—we can blame Florence for that—but whoever stashed those pages in such an inconvenient spot knows. Presumably, Andrew or my father, but Andrew would've had the most opportunity. And if the documents still have importance to them, then they —or others—may come looking for them too, as Andrew did. Perhaps on their behalf."

I paused to let the potential of that risk sink in before I continued, saying, "Andrew had access to the car before I left New York. As far as I know, he still has a key fob, but the other night when someone was messing in the garage, the car wasn't accessible because the garage is tiny and was jammed with stuff. Also, the car and fob batteries were dead.

"But someone *was* in the garage, and then Andrew let himself into my house and gave me warnings." I shook my head firmly. "As of now, after the mechanic's visit, the batteries work. The car is still in the garage and more accessible than it was before." I spoke as clearly and directly as I could, saying, "I don't want this hanging over my head, Leland."

I stopped to draw in a slow, deep breath before continuing. This next part was the most important. "Leland, If the document is nothing, great. If it is . . . if these are account numbers, and if they connect to my father's or Andrew's misdeeds, then maybe there's a way to get some of the money back that he stole—to return it to his victims."

I grimaced and looked away. "That sounds naïve and foolish, I know, but if there's any chance . . ." I nodded. "If there's any chance that some of the monies can be found and returned, then that's what I want to happen. As for me, I'd like to avoid trouble—I don't want to relive how it was when the agencies were investigating my father and anyone associated with him, but keeping the pages hidden doesn't guarantee peace. I'll pass them on to the authorities—like a goodwill gesture. That feels like the least-worst choice. But I'd rather pass them on with a witness like you present, and with a statement prepared ahead of time, written and witnessed, setting out the basic facts of how it was found."

Leland nodded. "That won't limit them if they choose to take this further."

"I understand."

"It's up to you, Leigh."

"Can you help me craft that statement?" I paused to manage my nerves, then added, "And arrange a meeting to transfer the document to the right people?"

"Will do. Please make sure the car stays in-place and secure. I suspect the authorities will want a look at it. May even wish to take it."

"They'll have my blessing to do so. I'd like to have it, and anything associated with this whole mess, far away and out of my life."

****

I was exhausted and still had to drive home. Leland and I had stayed at the table for a while as we considered the best words and phrasings for the statement. Leland seemed engaged yet unemotional, but for me, it was as if I was fighting myself. I'd built up layers of protection as a defense against scary knowns and unknowns out in the world—had been working on perfecting those protections all my life. Trying to get around them now was like being trapped in a punching bag and having to punch my out while avoiding the blows the bag was intended to block. It was very hard emotionally. My body hurt as if the blows were real.

When I arrived home, Sam was waiting. He was seated in a wicker chair on the front porch, and I joined him there, dropping my purse on the porch floor, kicking off my shoes and all but collapsing into the companion chair.

"Sam, I don't know what will come of this. I think this is the right thing to do about . . . you know. But there are no guarantees . . ." I shrugged.

I reached across and took his hand. "Leland and I will meet with the other interested parties. I hope you'll keep yourself available to fill in for me here in case I can't return home as quickly as I'd like." That last word almost didn't make it out as my voice broke. I stopped and looked away.

Sam squeezed my hand, then stood and pulled me up with him, releasing my hand to slide his arms around me. I rested my head on his shoulder.

"Thank you, Sam, for being my friend."

He made a sound—something like *hmmmph*—then said, "It is my honor to be your friend, but I hope I'm more than that."

I smiled and lifted my face to look him in the eyes. "Yes, Sam. Much more. In fact, I am amazed by your patience and your willingness to go through this with me."

"Don't be amazed. I'm here because I want to be."

****

After Sam left and I was alone again, I asked myself, "Now what?" *Waiting*, that was my answer. It was in Leland's hands now. He would contact me when he had my statement ready for me to sign and the meeting had been arranged. For my part, I could only wait.

I walked through the house, looking for anything that suggested an intruder had entered while I was gone—and feeling so very relieved when I found none. Had I watched too many of those crime shows with Florence? Funny, though, how it seemed they'd toughened me up in some strange way, because now I found myself better able to consider the unlikely as a real possibility. Was that good or bad? I wasn't sure, but I was glad of the new locks. An alarm system installation was scheduled. Florence had had one, but she'd rarely used it. I'd tried but couldn't figure it out. It was time for an updated security system.

It was as if I was waking up after a long time in hiding.

The cats were fine and not missing me. I walked out back for a look around, pausing for a longer look at the bushes along the garage and fence. Satisfied, I unlocked the garage door and pushed it aside. The car stared back at me, or seemed to. When Macon had found the sleeve with the documents in it, I'd called an immediate halt to the repair work and tow truck. Nothing had changed in here since then.

So far, so good, but I'd breathe much more easily when the document was out of my custody and beyond my reach. As for the vehicle, they were welcome to it if they wanted it.

****

The next day Leland called.

"It's arranged," he said. "Tomorrow morning, early."

"So quickly."

"A good thing."

"Agreed."

"I'll pick you up." He named a time.

After we disconnected, I texted Sam: *I need fresh air. I'm taking a drive.*

The message was only a tiny bit cryptic. It was enough info that he wouldn't worry if he didn't find me at home.

I wanted birdsong and blue sky. I wanted a wide horizon and the shelter of a forest, and I wanted it alone—to do this of my own volition instead of being *brought* to it. I needed to untwist my mind and unravel my thoughts and emotions. While the property might be a few miles away, it was certainly not out of reach for an impulsive drive in the country.

And I still had the rental car. I was paying for it. Might as well use it.

I changed into my sneakers and jeans and took a bottle of water with me.

A wider horizon? Maybe a place with a view—open and wide enough to see the future . . . at least a glimpse of a future open with possibilities . . . with the present surely and firmly around me—solid ground under my feet.

I loved the city too, but Sam was maybe right. If I didn't restrict myself by fear or anxiety, if I could trust myself, I could choose more.

****

I had decided that after the garage was finally empty, I'd go shopping for a small vehicle, one that would be easier for me to navigate in the city. However, as I turned off the main road and onto the dirt track on Florence's property, it occurred to me that a larger car might be more practical, depending on what I chose to do and where to do it. I was lucky to have choices. I hoped it would stay that way. Meanwhile, I'd make decisions based on that hope and not on luck or fear.

Today Florence's property was a sunny, peaceful place. In the tall weeds and wildflowers, the butterflies and bees were busy, clearly not expecting me, and I tried not to disturb them. The house, a two-story wood clapboard, was in bad shape. I didn't go inside in case the roof decided to fall. I'd get the house inspected and assessed. It might be best to have it pulled down and hauled away.

For now, I sat on a large rock near the well, trying to imagine Florence here as a child. She'd been young when her parents moved their family into town. And yet she set such store by this place, and the painting had hung prominently in her home for who knew how many years?

What had she said about Alfred? That her parents disapproved of him for their daughter because his family rented the land to farm? They'd wanted a husband for their daughter who had more to offer—a man with prospects, with a profession and economic security.

When I'd tucked that postcard from France into the corner of the frame, I'd noticed the artist's initials . . . AWS.

I went to the Louvre yesterday. Wish you were there with me to see it. Forever yours, Alfred

That's what he'd written.

If I'd understood Florence correctly, Alfred had moved here with his parents when her family moved to Richmond. It seemed obvious now that she'd kept the painting front and center in her home because of her memory of him. Or sadly, as a reminder of her regret.

I had to believe that AWS was Alfred's initials and that Alfred had painted the landscape of this place where he and Florence had met as children.

Sighing, I stood and brushed off a tiny bug that was crawling up my arm.

Down near Cub Creek, the understory growth was too thick to find my way through without scratches or worse. The creek path ended back at the stable because clearing this growth would have to be done by the property owner. Me for now.

I walked along the treeline, enjoying the shade, and spied a break in the woods that looked inviting. An old path? Was I up for a stroll in the forest?

It was a nice walk, not like city-sidewalk walking, but lovely with the birds overhead and the squirrels ignoring me and going about their day. And then, as I descended a low, sloping ridge, I saw a clearing beyond. It was the stable that the sisters were trying to turn into a worthwhile, yet profitable business.

I stood just within the tree line. The place was neat and nicely situated. The paddock was fair-sized, but the buildings needed expansion, in my opinion. The problem was that you couldn't expand the business without the infrastructure in place to support it. Clients needed to see the vision for the business—and they couldn't see into your head unless you helped them. That's what marketing and PR was all about.

They needed a wider, better road too.

And capital.

Hazel moved into view. I had nothing to offer her, but I felt drawn and so I went. I stopped near the fence. I liked this place. No particular reason that I could pin that feeling on. The draw of potential, here but unrealized . . . It had always called to me.

"Leigh, right?"

It was the sister . . . Kris.

"Yes. Hi. I happened to be walking along the trail." I

gestured back toward the woods. "The trail ended here. I hope you don't mind me hanging around for a few minutes."

"No, not at all." She was pleasant, but I heard the unspoken question in her voice.

"My cousin owned the adjoining land. I was visiting and saw a path . . ." I smiled. "And followed it."

"I'm glad you did. It's quiet here right now. Can I offer you more water? Might even have a soda in the fridge, if you prefer."

I raised my water bottle. "I'm good." I grimaced, wishing I could hold back the question, but knowing I couldn't, so I might as well go for it. "What are your plans here?"

"*Umm.* Well, like I said—"

I broke in. "I'd like to hear it again from you? Mind?"

She hesitated before saying, "Well, the usual stable . . . you know, boarding, lessons . . . We had a decent business at our old location, but it's harder than I thought to make the move and to recoup the clients we lost during the transition."

Hazel nudged my arm. I reached up and touched her blaze again. "Sorry, girl, I don't have any treats for you."

"Hazel was a rescue. We can't afford to take in rescues unless we have paying customers. We can't offer riding therapy services at an affordable rate if we can't pay our bills."

"Got it. I see it."

"I wish I did." Kris sounded discouraged. She leaned against the fence and scratched under Hazel's jaw. "I thought we'd grow more easily. It's not like we're new to this business."

Was I going to do this? I couldn't believe I was opening my mouth. I knew I should wait until I was totally in the clear. And yet the words came out anyway. "Let me introduce myself again. Leigh Ann Eden. I don't know if you have someone to

assist you with marketing and public relations, but I have experience in that area."

She frowned. "We can't afford that kind of help."

I nodded. "Understood. I'm willing to offer my expertise
for free if I believe I can help you and if you'd like me to try."
I saw her face change and light up. I cautioned her, "I know
something about selling services and raising capital, but my
life hasn't been trouble-free, so let me tell you a little about
myself, and my recent history, before you agree to talk
further."

"Sure, of course." She brushed some hair back from her
face. "Why don't we go into the office and talk? I'll give Jen a
call to come join us. Maybe you'll change your mind about
that soda?"

****

I walked back along the trail, returning to the field and the
old house, but I didn't get far before the tears started. Good
tears? Double yes. I seemed to be having crying episodes a lot
lately, yet I couldn't remember hardly ever crying all the years
before now. Maybe that's what happened when the façade was
breaking. Like a dam? Like a release of too many fears and
pain held back for too long.

I emerged from the woods, half-blinded by the sunlight
hitting my tear-filled eyes. I stumbled over something because
I wasn't capable of seeing at that moment—and hands touched
me, gentle hands steadied me.

"Leigh. Are you all right?"

I fell right into him and wrapped my arms around him.
"Sam, yes, I'm good."

"Are you sure?" He lifted my chin, wanting to see my face.

"Yes, I promise. Sam, I think maybe I've never been better."

"Despite tomorrow's plans?"

"Regardless, Sam. I think the word is *regardless*."

He told me later that he'd read my text and hadn't hesitated. He knew I was most likely coming out here and that there was no need for concern, but he'd felt that draw to come here, to be here with me.

"I know it's not over, and yes, stuff can happen when least expected, but truly, Sam, I think it's going to be okay."

Chapter Twenty-Five

I was ready when Leland's shiny black car pulled up midmorning. The house was locked up tight, and I had to trust that no one would mess with the cats.

Leland forewarned me that he expected the exchange to be seamless. He had no reason to believe it wouldn't go well. He was telling me this ahead of the meeting because he wanted me to breathe, get some color in my face, and not faint midway through. I wanted to laugh at his concern, but I couldn't because it was a valid one.

While we were still at the house, I read and signed the statement Leland had drawn up per my instructions. His driver notarized it.

One of the agents who met us at the bank was familiar to me. That encouraged me. He knew what had gone before. None of that should need to be revisited. I nodded, as did he, but we didn't exchange spoken greetings. Honestly, my mouth was so dry I could hardly swallow, much less speak.

He and Leland spoke to the bank officer with me along, and she agreed that they could accompany me into the private room to open the safe-deposit box. The other agent stayed just outside the door of the room. Before opening the box, Leland handed the agent with us the statement. Would it help? Who knew? Maybe it was no more than an illusion of control, but it gave me comfort.

The plastic sleeve with the document was in Florence's folder, just as I'd left it in the metal box. I didn't touch it. I asked the agent to remove it from the box himself. He did. All three of us could see the box was now empty.

We spoke in low, cool tones with civil but minimal words, including me explaining that the car was still in my garage and available to them should they want it. I would, of course, be available to answer any questions as needed.

When we were done, I made it back to Leland's car still breathing and walking. Barely.

As he helped me into the car, Leland said, "I've requested they contact me directly if there are questions and that you will respond promptly—through me."

"Thank you." I coughed. I'd hardly heard what he'd said. Now that the meeting was over . . . I was done-in too.

He handed me a bottled water. "Drink up, Leigh. You did well today. As we guessed, they do want custody of the vehicle. The tow truck will show up tomorrow morning. Until then, keep the garage locked and stay out of it."

"Will do, Leland, and with pleasure."

****

After I returned home, I checked the cats— they were fine —and then I changed clothes, intending to walk off the excess energy or the adrenaline drop—whatever it was that was making me feel shaky inside—before sitting down for lunch. I might even do a little gardening after. All the good, healthy things, right? Despite what Leland had said, I wanted to do a last check in the garage to make sure all was well in there. It was, but while there, and staying well away from the car, of course, I piled Florence's old gardening tools in the wagon and pulled it out into the yard to have it ready for this afternoon or whenever. I was fitting the padlock back through the bracket slots so I could lock the garage door when I heard—

"Leigh Ann."

He was there. Where had he been standing?

"Andrew," I said, with only a swift glance back, not wanting him to see my face until I could compose my expression.

"You weren't home. I thought I'd missed you." He paused, a slight smile shaped his lips, and then as he walked close to me he said, "Don't be angry that I'm here. I'm outside. I didn't go inside the house."

"Because you already returned the house key."

He made a noise of dismissal before saying, "Minor inconvenience."

Out here, in daylight and in plain view of the houses around us, I felt awkward but not in danger. There was something about the light in his eyes, the almost-shy smile that played on his face, that took me back to before it all went wrong. For a moment, I glimpsed the man I'd dated, had had feelings for. Had wanted to marry. A tender softening warmed my muscles, and while I could never go back to that time, I would welcome being able to remember him, and them, without the taint of everything else that had happened. But then, like a cloud's shadow on a sunny day, the sly look returned to his face, and something trembled inside me. I stepped back.

"Leigh Ann. I put myself on the line to protect you, you know that."

Been there, done that . . . I heard those words in my head. I said, "We've been over that before. It's time to move on, Andrew."

"Did you ever love me, Leigh Ann? Or were you just lonely? Was I just a convenience?" He made a noise and shook his head. "Until I became an *in*convenience?"

"I wouldn't have agreed to marry you if I didn't love you."

He sighed. "Maybe. Or maybe you thought you were. I'm not saying you were deceitful. But it didn't take you long to fall out of love with me, so there's that."

I would let *that* go. *That* wasn't open for further discussion. Old news, as it were.

"No," he said. "*Inconvenience* isn't the right word, is it?" He waited, possibly for a response, or maybe just to see whether his dig had hit a tender nerve. I said nothing, and he continued, "Or maybe it is."

He sighed. "Regardless, I'm here to help. I don't have any new info on your father's case, and since I haven't heard from you, I'm guessing you haven't thought of, or discovered, anything that might interest the authorities, so maybe we can do each other a favor. A small thing."

I tried to keep the words in, but I couldn't help myself. "What's that?"

He smiled. That Andrew smile. The one I'd fallen for right from the start. An approving smile? The be-a-good-girl smile I remembered from my early life when I'd tried so hard to please my parents to no avail? My stomach did its warning twist.

"So are you getting your car fixed? Or did you decide to get rid of it?"

Drawing in a quick breath, I continued to caution myself against saying too much. Per Leland, the authorities were coming in the morning to take the car into their custody. I was expected to keep it secure until then. But now Andrew was here.

That warning voice in my head kept repeating, *Drop this subject. Don't talk to him. Tell him to leave.*

But my lips moved anyway.

"I don't know yet."

"Leigh, I can take that car off your hands, no problem. You should start fresh anyway. Get a new car." His smile became engaging, like a man confessing to something silly. "You know I always liked that car. It's out of style now and needs a lot of work, but I'm game for it."

I looked at my former fiancé, now my nemesis. "I was thinking the same thing—a fresh start, that is. For now, the car will stay here."

Andrew moved toward the garage door just as I pushed the lock closed. He put his hand over mine.

"I respect that, Leigh Ann. It's your decision, of course. But if you don't mind, I might've left some stuff in the car. You left town in a hurry." His hand was gentle, not moving or allowing mine to move, but not so firmly that I couldn't have shaken him off if I was determined. He continued, "It will only take me a moment to check. I won't hold you up. I'll even lock the door when I'm done and leave the key on the porch or wherever you say."

He tried to sound low-key and open, but I heard tension in his voice. A tone that felt like a warning. I spoke slowly, thinking of each careful word before giving it voice. "The repair guy already cleaned the car out. It was just trash and random papers. There's nothing left." Let him assume the rest.

His face went pale, but his expression stayed the same, and then he nodded.

I said, "I have to go, Andrew. Take care of yourself."

He removed his hand from mine. As I moved to turn away,

he stayed close. Too close. Practically on my heels as I stepped toward the house.

"I'm surprised you aren't worried about your dad and the trouble he's stirring up. I remember when that's all you worried about. Not the present threat, necessarily, but ramifications of his bad acts and how they'd impact you." He grinned broadly this time. It didn't reflect in his eyes. Now he looked like the Andrew I'd glimpsed recently, the one I didn't love.

In a softer, teasing voice, he added, "Not inconvenience. Risk to comfort, risk to pride? That's what you were avoiding." He shrugged. "I don't care about the semantics. In the end, it means you aren't someone anyone can trust to have their back in times of trouble."

Above us, the breeze rustled Florence's tree, the one she'd spent her last days enjoying from her window while watching the change of the season and the squirrels and birds. I heard her voice distantly, telling me to slow down. I did slow for the space of a breath, and my head grew clearer. I grew calmer.

I said, "Your choices were your own, Andrew. I *do* worry, yes, but I haven't done anything wrong, not to you or anyone else."

"Leigh," he said as he grabbed my arm. "When did innocence protect anyone?"

This time, I tried to pull away, but his grip was harsher. He wasn't letting go, and I wasn't willing to see if he'd continue in a physical contest.

"Okay, Andrew. Here's the truth. The car has already been cleaned out. I told you that already. And what's none of your business is that someone is buying it. He'll be here to pick it up tomorrow morning. So whatever your fixation is with that car and with me, get over it." I glared at him. "The car will be out of your reach, and I strongly advise you to consider me the same—out of your reach."

He looked stunned. His grip relaxed enough for me to shake him off.

"Just go now. You and I have nothing to discuss."

I walked away, trying not to show that I was shaken. Because he'd scared me? Or because I'd lied so boldly and deliberately?

Turning back to face him, I asked, "Andrew, one more thing, after all. Was that you in my garage that night? You were searching for whatever it was that you think you left in the car, weren't you?"

He stared silently.

"Why did you break the porch bulb?"

He looked aside, his *Andrew* smile trying to re-form on his face, but he was maybe a little shaken himself at this point because he couldn't quite pull it off, and the truth was there on his face.

"Andrew, let me offer this as well-meant advice. Don't come back. Leave here and keep going."

He gave me a long look, perhaps trying to read my intent.

"Don't come back here. Seriously."

I walked away, going directly into the house. I moved from window to window, watching as he went to the passageway and then emerged out front to walk up the sidewalk until he was out of my view. I wanted to believe this was done. Finished.

Except I knew Andrew would give it another try because it seemed that he had even more at stake with these documents than I could know—but perhaps in line with what I suspected. If I was right about that, then tonight would be his best chance to get into that car trunk to try to retrieve his papers.

Time made it necessary to contact Leland immediately via phone. And in this case, unless Andrew himself was listening, I didn't think it would matter.

Pacing the house, I called Leland, explaining that he might want to pass the possibility of Andrew attempting to get into the car tonight on to his contact and that, if he did, to tell them I thought I'd be away from home tonight visiting friends.

"Will do," he said. "Are you sure?"

"About this? No, but yes. This must end—at least this part."

He started to speak, and I interrupted. "Oh, wait. I can't go. I forgot about my cats."

His silence was the question. I explained, "Harvey and the kittens. They are too young. I can't take them all with me, and I won't leave them here alone if this will go down tonight. If Andrew does get into the house . . . anything could happen. If I'm not here . . . Well, I'll *have* to be here."

Leland suggested, "Shall I tell my contact that you'll be home but sound asleep?"

"Okay." I wasn't sure about this. People knocking on the door—not just *any* people, but *those* people . . . The old familiar feelings—the racing heart, ringing ears, and a curdling stomach—rushed in. *I could leave.* The cats would be okay, right? I could lock the bathroom door. Put the litter box and Harvey's dishes in there . . .

"Leigh?"

For the moment, I was unable to answer. I dragged in fresh air and tried to reset my panic.

"Leigh—"

"Sorry. I needed to breathe. And yes, that's fine. Let them know that . . ." I ran out of words for a moment. "Oh, Leland, I hope this isn't a mistake, but let them know that if they arrive early, I'll let them into the garage, or I can leave the sliding doors on the front unlocked—however they think it will work best for them. If Andrew does come, I'm sure he'll enter through the loose panel on the side, just as he did before."

Leland and I talked awhile longer, and then he asked, "Will you be okay alone there tonight? If I was closer, I'd come over. I can send someone, though, if you'd feel better with a third party present. Legal help or security. I can arrange either or both."

"No, I'm good. I'm nervous, and yeah, I have doubts, but I'm actually okay." And I was. The panic had diminished. I was still standing. I was going to do this. Besides, I didn't want strangers here in my home, babysitting me.

"Well, then, if our friends are interested and will align with what we're suggesting, I'll text you a generic message rather than discuss this further on the phone. If, however, it seems necessary—whether for changes or concerns—I'll call you immediately."

We disconnected. For a very long moment, I was frozen. And then I heard a meow and felt pressure against my calf. Harvey. She was twining about my legs.

More cat hair. But it was also a dose of cat love. Or maybe her food dish was empty.

Movement in the foyer caught my eye. Baby Gray had climbed the stacked books. I'd added another layer, but there she was. Wobbly with the new height perhaps, like a climber reaching the Everest base camp, until she toppled over, unable to navigate the descent. Harvey and I both went to her.

Harvey nudged Baby Gray with her nose, seemed satisfied and walked on back to the kitchen. I picked the baby up. I held her close, her nose soft and cool against the crook of my neck. A few errant tears wet my cheek.

Why? I didn't know. Stress, relief, or because I wasn't alone? Just a cat. Or five of them.

We were together in this, whether they knew it or not.

Chapter Twenty-Six

"Sam," I said. "Can you drop by today? Like maybe early afternoon?"

"Will suppertime work? We could go out or I could pick up something on my way."

"Earlier would be better."

"I'm tied up right now, but if it's urgent . . ."

I didn't answer immediately, so even when I said, "Not urgent," my delay in answering belied the words. I hurried to add, "Seriously. It's a timing issue, that's all."

He said, "I'll cancel my last appointment. I can be there by three p.m. Will that work? Or for that matter, I can reschedule the earlier ones too. I'll come over as soon as I get that done."

"*No*, Sam, that's unnecessary. I only want to update you about something . . . timely."

"Fine. Okay. I'll call when I'm finished with the appointments and head straight over."

"Don't cut your clients short. I promise it's only an update."

We disconnected. I was disappointed—I couldn't deny it. I'd grown accustomed to having him around, either volunteering to be here or always available when I needed help or companionship.

Andrew had said no one could count on me. I wished I could say that was false, but it wasn't. I was quick to wash my hands of others' troubles. Well, I'd been taught that, hadn't I? Or maybe I was genetically unempathetic. Except that I didn't feel that way anymore. It scared me—this connected feeling. I was afraid of letting go and getting in over my head. It wasn't just the cats. It was the whispered prayers I'd found myself speaking in unexpected moments.

It scared me—this connected feeling. As if having more meant I also had more to lose, but oddly, at the same time, having them also made me feel lighter. Less dragged down. Less alone. More vulnerable, but more vulnerable by choice.

Well worth the risk.

****

Sam arrived. Guilt assailed me as I asked myself once again, what was I involving him in? Nothing, if I could help it, I told myself. I was still intent on keeping him out of it.

"I wanted to warn you since I can't be sure how this will go. I wanted you to know the plan."

"What are you talking about? The . . ." He glanced around the room. "The same thing as before?"

I already had my sneakers on. Boldly, I took his phone from his pocket and set it with mine on the foyer table. When he started to remark on it, I shook my head *no*, and he gave me a long look but cooperated. I led him back out to the front porch and then down to the sidewalk, where we found a nearby shady tree to loiter under.

Sam said, "Is it okay to speak now?"

"Yes. I hope so. I don't know if all this extra effort matters.

Sometimes . . . sometimes . . ." I sighed. "So this may be different for you as a guy? I don't know. But do you ever start to walk through a parking garage, or maybe to cut through an alley to get where you're going, and you have that moment of *hmmm*, maybe I should think about this a little more, maybe look around, or maybe even back up and find another route? Or wait to ask someone to walk through that parking garage with me?"

He nodded. "Sure."

"I don't doubt that sometimes that can get overblown, overly cautious and imaginative, and we just push through and it works out, so maybe next time we aren't cautious when maybe we should've been?" I stopped and examined his expression. "I'm not crazy. I may be risk averse, true, but maybe a little paranoia can be a healthy thing."

"But that isn't what you wanted to give me a heads-up about."

"No, it isn't. I was just feeling awkward about the phone thing." I shrugged. "These days I feel better talking about certain things outside the house where I can see who's around me."

"Actually, I think you have good reason given what you went through, and now this newer concern, which is . . . what?"

"Andrew came back. That document was his. He wants it."

"Is he dangerous?"

"I never thought so. Now I don't know. Andrew thinks this document is very important, so others may too if they're told about it, and that's why I need it to be clear to all concerned that I am not in possession of it. That whoever has it . . . it isn't me."

"Okay. That makes sense."

"Thank you." I nodded, saying, "So when he came today,

he surprised me in the backyard and I wasn't sure how to proceed. I insinuated that I hadn't found it . . . thus he thinks it may still be in the car. I believe he'll come back for it tonight."

"Maybe you are crazy. Or clever? Maybe both. Why would it be tonight anyway? Regardless, I'll stay at your house."

"No, that's the thing. You being here? If any questions or official conversations come out of what does or doesn't happen tonight, I don't want *you* to be part of that."

"I'm getting a headache, Leigh."

I smiled. I put my hands on either side of his face and pulled him toward me, kissing him smack in the middle of his forehead. "I apologize to your brain for making it ache. I'm not a devious person by preference, and just now I'm feeling all twisted and worried; otherwise, I could probably explain better." I took his hands in mine. "I would go away for the night and hope it gets resolved between Andrew and the authorities without anything going wrong—that's *if* he shows up. But I won't leave Harvey and the kittens, or anyone else, exposed to risk without being right there with them."

"Since you don't seem to mind a little hand-holding and kissing . . ." He slid his arms around me and pulled me close. He spoke near my ear, saying, "I'll stay away tonight, but only on the condition that you allow my father to hang out here. I want someone with you, not because something *will* go wrong, but because it *might*." After a pause, he added, "Dad is very steady and levelheaded in a pinch."

I didn't like the idea of putting Sam Sr. at risk either.

When I didn't respond, he said, "And one more condition."

"What's that?"

"While Dad is hanging out with you, I'll be at his house, close at hand in case anything breaks bad."

"I'm not sure—"

He interrupted. "And something else. I'm hungry. We'll eat

an early supper in your kitchen. We'll leave this particular discussion out here and revisit it later if the details change. For now, we'll bring warmth and laughter and good food into your home. Trust me, it will help bolster you later when you get to worrying again." This time he pressed his lips to *my* forehead, then said, "I promise I'll leave well before dark . . . whether I want to or not."

The comfort of his arms, the pressure of his lips . . . I felt guilty again, this time for underestimating him and his willingness to understand my worry and not diminish it or me.

"Yes, Sam. Thank you."

"Okay, I'll go talk to my father. How much can I tell him?"

I hugged him even tighter before I spoke. "Trust isn't easy for me, Sam."

"You trust me."

"I do. And your father too. I'll go with you to speak with him. He deserves to know what he's potentially getting into."

****

Samuel Marshburn was all in.

I hadn't doubted that he would be. The only doubt in my mind was how risky this might be for him. But in the end, as a neighbor, and being older, I thought his presence in my home tonight might be more easily explained than Sam Jr.'s if any post-discussions arose with the authorities.

Sam Jr. left after our meal. Sam Sr. showed up well before dark.

A couple of men I didn't recognize arrived. They didn't knock on the door. I followed their movements via my kitchen window as they entered the backyard through the alley gate, presumably having walked down the alley. They were dressed in blue uniforms as if they might be here to do repair work on something or other. Understated. Not too clean, not too mussed up. Not guys you'd remember unless they happened to walk into *your* yard uninvited. Though, in this case, they *had* been invited. By me.

They didn't loiter but moved directly to the sliding door on the front of the garage. I'd unhooked the lock earlier, just so that it didn't catch and could easily be slipped off, and that's how they entered the building, immediately closing the door again behind them.

Would Andrew show? My gut said yes. But not until dark.

"Leigh? You doing okay?"

I jumped. It was Samuel speaking.

I turned to face him. I'd come up here as daylight was giving way to twilight and had stationed myself in Florence's chair at the back window, thinking I'd be able to keep an eye on things yet be pretty much invisible if I kept the room dark.

"Can I get you a glass of water or tea?" Samuel asked. "Are you sure you want to watch this?"

"I have to."

He nodded. "Well then, since I knew we'd be laying low this evening, I brought some sandwiches with me. I have one for you."

"No thanks. I can't eat."

"Sam warned me about that. I'm on orders from him. He said the two of you ate earlier, but that was at least two or three hours ago. With this kind of *watching*, you'll need a snack. I'll bring the sandwich up. If you don't eat it, that'll be your choice."

I shook my head and turned back to the window, but then asked, "Hey, can you do me a favor?"

"What's that?"

"Can you check Harvey's dishes? Food and water, I mean?"

"Will do."

"Thanks."

"The kittens are okay?"

"Right as rain." He chuckled. "That Orange Fluffy fella, he's a hoot. He and his sis, Baby Gray, are bound to stir up adventure. Wait till they're bigger and faster. You'll see I'm right."

Orange Fluffy. I smiled. As he left the room, I called out, "Thank you." I was grateful for his kindness but also grateful that he'd stopped hovering. I had to focus. It was as if everything was coming to some sort of culmination and it was going to blow up in my face—and in my friends' faces—if I didn't focus, in effect *willing* it to happen.

Samuel brought the sandwich and a banana, along with a tall, fresh glass of iced tea. "Here's cookies too," he said.

I nibbled on the food as the sun went down and the sky darkened. It was a dark night. No moon was up, and the cloud cover was sufficient to dim what little brightness the stars offered. About an hour past sunset, I saw movement. The alley gate into my backyard opened. I saw that much because a neighbor's light illumined the edge of the gate and caught the movement. But the area between the gate and the bush that hid the access panel was heavily shadowed.

"Don't hold your breath, Leigh Ann. Breathe," Samuel said. He was standing near me and touched my shoulder.

"I'm okay," I whispered.

Samuel was right about breathing. It was important. So I made sure I did.

By now, lights had come on inside the garage. I heard nothing. I saw nothing more than the thin bright line around the garage door.

This waiting was tying me up in knots. I was now down on my knees at that window, hiding half my face behind the lace curtain for fear light would reflect in my eyes and give me away.

It wasn't at all like Florence's crime shows. It was quiet, and likely no one in the neighboring houses even guessed something was going down. When the sliding door was pushed aside, the interior light spilled out, briefly highlighting the two men and the one they were escorting toward the alley gate. When they passed through the gate and a car door opened, that's when I realized a large vehicle had arrived. The gate closed. The vehicle drove away. The gate opened and one of the men came through, but this time with a few others behind him. I presumed they'd go into the garage and do their thing—Florence would call it *processing the crime scene*. Fingerprints on the vehicle, maybe? No idea. That was their job, and I'd leave them to it.

I was left with a certain sadness. An emptiness that I couldn't define.

Samuel was suddenly there behind me. "Here," he said, offering me something.

"I ate some of the sandwich. Nothing more, please."

"Here," he repeated.

I turned and he put a kitten into my hand. They were close to a month old, still small but feeling more substantial, more durable than before. More vocal too. How had they grown so fast?

"It's Flo. Why did you bring Flo to me?"

"There's something about her that's calming, don't you think?"

I nodded.

"Leigh Ann, they don't need your help out there. If they do, they'll knock. Meanwhile, come on down and get a refill on the things worth living for. Harvey's a little fidgety. She probably senses the tension coming from up here, from you. That's not good for her or her nursing babies."

With Flo in one hand, I offered my other hand to Samuel. "I think my legs have fallen asleep. How about an assist?"

He nodded and fake-tipped the hat he *wasn't* wearing. "My pleasure, ma'am."

Chapter Twenty-Seven

Several days had passed since Andrew was taken from my garage and whisked quietly away. I'd heard nothing beyond what I'd seen, except for one short message from Leland stating that all was well—which suited me quite well. I settled into a simpler state of mind and being, hanging out with the cats, with Sam when he wasn't working, and even trying my hand at a bit of gardening in my tiny front and back yards. I thought I might set off a few square feet for a butterfly/bee garden.

Knees in the dirt, trowel in hand, I laughed, thinking I already owned the perfect butterfly and bee habitat a few miles away, just south of Mineral, Virginia, and along Cub Creek. In fact, I was planning to head out that way the next day to meet with Kris and Jen. We'd already talked about the things that I might be able to do to help them, as well as the reasons they might not want me to. A frank discussion. There was no other way I could consider stepping out into business again. By now, they'd have more questions and more to say, and I wanted to hear it.

I couldn't entirely put aside the worry and tension, but I

was getting better at it. After all, as Sam had said, stuff happened. It just did, and it would again. Might as well enjoy the good in between the chaos.

I went inside for a break, thinking all of those actions and sentiments sounded good and mature and healthy until put to the test—which was quickly confirmed when my phone rang and Leland's name once again lit up the screen—and I reverted instantly. Old habits die hard, and old scars fade slowly, if ever.

I grabbed the phone, afraid to answer and equally fearful of missing his call. "Leland?"

"Yes. Can you talk for a minute? I'm calling to update you on your case."

His voice sounded normal but stilted. I felt the old familiar fear rising in me. I tried to focus on connections. I wasn't alone.

"My case?"

"The situation with your former friend and the paper he wanted."

"Is there a problem? Should I come up to meet with you?"

"No. Indeed not. It's all good, Leigh. But people can listen in, even people who are . . . just nosy, so we'll choose our words carefully, shall we?"

My heart was racing. I tried to think clearly.

"Leigh?"

I coughed. "Yes, I'm here. I'd hoped this was all done."

"For you, it is."

I closed my eyes. My relaxed attitude hadn't held up very well. "Thank you. But I'm still confused."

"No, Leigh Ann. It's all good. I don't expect you to hear from anyone else about this. Anyone. They are, in fact, grateful to you. And your former friend is cooperating. Unfortunately for your father, it doesn't help his current effort.

Fortunately for others, the papers may be helpful in recovery."

Recovery. Leland was referencing the money Dad had stolen.

"Limited recovery, but some," he added.

"Oh, Leland. Thank you."

"However, the recommendation from them to you is that it's best not to discuss particulars with others. Things are still progressing."

"Thank you, Leland. Good to know."

"You know where to reach me if you need me."

"Before you go, may I ask your advice, as my attorney and friend? The young man who worked on the car. . . I need to pay him for his expenses. I didn't before because it might seem that I was trying to influence him in advance of any questions about. . .you know what. Do you think it's okay for me to contact him now and pay what's owed?"

"Yes. I believe the inquiry has been concluded in that direction. Just be sure to get an invoice and receipt, and as always, be discreet."

"Thank you again, Leland."

We disconnected. Talk about an adrenaline drop. *Whew.* I'd paced from the kitchen throughout the first floor and ended up in the library. I curled up in Florence's reading chair. The painting of the country property was in front of me, Florence's books were on her shelves beside me, Harvey and the kittens were rambling about, and Sam was due over momentarily.

I wasn't sure how this day—not to mention the week or even the month—could get any better. I closed my eyes and whispered *thank you.*

My eyes were wet and that was okay. I sat there and cried. And it felt good.

****

Once I had myself back in hand—I would attend to business. I didn't rush it. I'd earned a good cry. But I also owed something to Bill Mason—not only money but also a few words of explanation for the delay in contacting him. I washed my face and brushed my hair and climbed into my rental car. I didn't want to call him. This conversation would be better face to face.

I took a chance that he'd be at the car repair shop where he worked his day job. As fortune would have it, he was outside in the parking lot. He saw me, and we stood in the shade of the building.

"Ms. Sonder—"

I interrupted him. "Actually, it's Leigh Eden." If he was curious about the change in surname, he could ask. "I took the liberty of writing an invoice on your behalf so that I can pay you." I paused and frowned. "I'm sorry I couldn't give you a heads-up that people in suits might be coming to question you. If they'd asked you if you and I had spoken about you possibly being questioned, and if you'd told the truth, then it could've looked like conspiracy. Does that make sense?" I made a noise of frustration and shook my head. "Don't bother answering. *None of this makes sense.* It simply is what it is."

He offered a crooked smile. "I saw your face that day when I found the papers in the spare tire well. I knew it was a big something. Gnarly. Not something I want to be involved in. When those people showed up and showed me ID, I understood. That's why I didn't call or text you. Figured we'd sort it out eventually."

"Thank you, Mason. Also, if you don't mind, I'd greatly appreciate it if you'd keep this whole odd story to yourself.

I'm not saying you have to, but it would be good for all concerned."

"Ms. Eden, Leigh, no worries about that. I don't look to complicate my life even on a sunny day."

I smiled. I'd never heard it expressed that way, but I knew exactly what he meant. I handed him the envelope.

He pulled out the invoice and the check.

"I tried to account for the tow truck too, so if you will, please see that your friend is reimbursed out of what I'm paying you?"

"Sure. But it's too much."

I frowned. "Not *too much* too much, is it? I don't want it to look suspicious if anyone revisits the…gnarly thing."

"Oh, gosh no. It's fine. Just more than what I would've charged you as a friend. So, hey, if you need more repair services, just let me know and I'll work off the extra."

"It's a deal, Mason. Thanks so much for your help."

"My pleasure, ma'am."

Chapter Twenty-Eight

Don had called yesterday to make sure litter box training was in progress, and I was pleased to say yes, but we were early in the process, and so this morning I was on my knees in the nursery-bathroom replacing the stained newsprint with fresh paper.

Don had also explained that I should be introducing the kittens to solid food as they were weaning, and so we were now doing that too.

As for the litter training, I wondered if I might sacrifice one of Florence's old casserole dishes. It would be big enough for the babies, and the lower sides would be less intimidating to them than the plastic litter box that Harvey used.

Don had also warned me that the kittens would need to start inoculations in a very few weeks and that I should make an appointment to bring them in. I shuddered thinking of it. How could I bring the babies in for shots? They trusted me. It would be like a betrayal, wouldn't it? But I would do it. I was their adult.

The doorbell rang.

My Sam always knocked.

I peeked through the front window before my imagination could engage.

Marla and Sam Sr. were standing at the door. Two neighbors together. At my door. That hadn't happened before . . . But then I reminded myself that these days, when it came to my life, anything was possible—*even good things*.

Opening the door, I greeted them. "Good morning and welcome. Please come in."

They glanced at each other. Both looked concerned.

Sam Sr. said, "I hope we haven't come at a bad time."

"Not at all. Just watch where you step. Harvey's babies think they own the place now." I laughed softly, hoping to lighten their grave faces. "And maybe they do."

Marla looked at the kittens in the foyer, and a fleeting smile lit her face. "Oh my. They are so cute."

"That's Baby Gray and Orange Fluff. They are the most advanced and are often partners in crime."

I'd spoken in a deliberately light tone, making a gentle joke of it, but Samuel knelt, holding his hand out to the kittens. Orange Fluff bumped his head against Sam Sr.'s fingers. He laughed, stroking the kitten's back. He stood again, looking more solemn as he turned to Marla, whose expression was stricken.

Enough with good manners.

"Please, Marla. Please, Samuel. What's up? If there's bad news, I'd rather hear it straight out."

Samuel cleared his throat. "It's news. I don't know whether it's bad or good." He looked at Marla. "Go ahead and tell her."

Marla sniffled. "A man, fortyish, came to my house asking if I knew of anyone in the area who'd recently acquired a cat." She blinked. "I guess he asked me because everyone knows I have cats. He asked about an orange tabby." She stopped abruptly.

Sam Sr. said, "Marla came to me, worried."

I couldn't breathe. I tried to hide my anxiety, to appear in control.

She blurted out the words: "I told him no. I lied. I'm not a liar, but I just couldn't . . . I asked him for his name and number in case I *did* hear of someone recently finding or taking in a cat."

Samuel handed me the slip of paper. I was in shock, so he gently placed it in my hand.

Marla added with a gulp, "He said his aunt thought the cat was being boarded, that a woman was caring for the cat while she was away visiting family. Something to do with her house being renovated. But she started worrying about the cat, so her niece contacted the cat-sitter, who said she didn't have the cat because no one was there at the house when she arrived to pick it up." She pressed her finger against her wet lashes. "I didn't know what to do. I considered not telling you."

Samuel said, "That's why she came to me . . . to talk it through. Why don't you sit down, Leigh Ann? I'll get you a glass of water."

I nodded and sat, careful not to trip over Callie who was roaming, calling out to her siblings in a tone that sounded like, *Wait for me*. The runners squeaked as I leaned forward and picked the kitten up gently, but with sure movements so she wouldn't be fearful of falling. The chair rocked back as I pressed my cheek against the soft fur on Callie's head.

"Here it is, Leigh."

I accepted the glass of water and took a sip. It was helpful, but I was already breathing again and recovering my composure.

Samuel said, "We can forget this subject ever came up. Whatever you decide to do, we support it."

"We do," Marla confirmed. "Harvey was badly neglected. You took her in and gave her love and care. She's yours now . . . and you are hers."

The rest of their visit was rather a blur. I thanked them sincerely. I said I'd give this some thought. But once they were gone, I didn't. Instead, I gave myself permission to put the issue aside while my brain and heart came to terms with it. They were right about the neglect, but they were also wrong. Yes, I could lie by simply doing nothing. This was yet another temptation.

But there was an old woman who, whether she'd taken proper care of Harvey or not, had still loved her.

And there was love—but then there was *love*. Integrity and consideration of capability were also important, including the ability to care for pets properly.

But right or not, obligated or not, and regardless of the possible outcomes, if I had the power to ease the woman's worry, then it would be wrong not to do so.

****

Sam Jr. came by after work. I brought him up to date. His first reaction was close to my own. He looked shocked, and then he asked, "What will you do?"

"What I must." I nodded. "I'll talk to the man Marla spoke to. I'll see what I see and then decide what happens next." I looked down at Baby Gray, who'd settled in my lap. "But talk is one thing. The rest is uncertain."

****

The next morning I walked back to Floyd Avenue. There were signs of activity at the brown stucco house. Not much. Whatever renovations were planned, it must be early in the process.

My heart rate was up and my palms were damp—both of which I expected because this was so very important to me.

I knocked, repeating the nephew's name under my breath and practicing what I'd say to him if he answered the door, but there was no response. I descended the porch steps and was walking along the sidewalk when voices came to me. I stopped. The passageway was there, still shadowed. I had followed it a month ago. And look what had happened.

Yes indeed, I reminded myself. *Look what had happened.*

As I emerged into the backyard, I saw the fence at the rear of the lot along the alley had been removed and a large pickup truck with all sorts of gear and ladders and big white paint buckets filled with tools and assorted stuff had been parked where the wrought iron table had been. The table and chairs had been moved off to the side. A door slammed at the house. But before me, here in the yard, a man came around the end of the truck with a tool belt, focused on what he was doing or about to do.

Royce was the name Marla had given me on that slip of paper. *Royce Jones.*

Someone seemed to be in the house. Given that, I figured I had a fifty percent chance of guessing right, so I stepped into view, saying, "Mr. Jones?"

He stopped and looked my way. I'd interrupted his thoughts. His expression showed it, but only for a moment, and then he smiled. He had a pleasant face. I guessed he was in his early forties as Marla had thought. His T-shirt and oft-painted painter's pants said this man knew how to build and fix stuff.

"Yes, ma'am. Can I help you?" he asked.

"My neighbor said you were looking for a cat?"

"My aunt's cat."

I nodded. "That's what she said."

"A ginger?" His face lit up. "Name's Suzie Q? Have you seen her?"

Reluctantly and hesitating, I answered, "Yes, I have."

The relief that transformed his face nearly undid me. Instantly, my throat closed and my eyes stung. *No,* I told myself. *Her name is Harvey. And she is mine.*

I tried to speak and couldn't. I cleared my throat.

"Can I get you some water?" He smiled. "I've got several bottles in the cooler."

"Yes, thank you." Was I thirsty or only delaying this conversation by however many seconds I could?

He spoke as he went to grab a water bottle, saying, "Is she okay? My aunt has been frantic with worry ever since we realized Suzie Q wasn't with the pet-sitter."

I had to do the right thing. I just wasn't sure what that was. Hoping to manage my way through this, I chose my words carefully.

"She's fine," I said. "Quite well. Is your aunt here?" Was she the elderly woman or the middle-aged one?

"No, she's staying with family out of state during the renovation." He frowned in concern. "Are you all right?"

I cleared my throat and took a sip of water from the bottle, then another sip. *I can do this.*

I said, "Thanks, it's the pollen, I think."

"There's certainly enough out here. So, about the cat. Where is she? Not at the pound?" He seemed sincerely concerned.

"No, she's with me."

He frowned, perhaps reading the distress in my voice or written on my face.

"It was such a strange day," I said. "I was on my way home from the grocery store and crossed paths with two women, right here in this yard. They were in a hurry to leave, and the next thing I knew I was responsible for a cat."

"The airport. That's where they were headed. The younger woman was a redhead, right?"

"Yes."

"Deb. She was the caregiver." He paused, then added, "Definitely not a cat lover. She had her hands full with my aunt." He shrugged. "Actually, my *great*-aunt. We call her Nolly. Her husband died a few years ago. They never had children, so when she broke her leg, us *kids*"—he grinned—"stepped up to give her a hand." He nodded toward the house. "It was in bad shape. Worse than we knew. Mostly cosmetic, but some serious problems too."

I offered a small smile and tried to speak with calm dignity. "The cat and I have grown close."

Royce Jones's eyes opened wide and he laughed. "Seriously? No, you're joking, right?"

I shook my head, confused and, despite my worry, annoyed. "I don't understand."

"Sorry," he said. He gestured toward the iron chairs that were set off to the side. "Have a seat?"

I didn't move.

"Please?"

"Okay." I crossed over to the chairs and sat. He did the same.

The grin on his face showed a little embarrassment. "I see I offended you. It's just that . . . well, Suzie Q is the meanest cat I ever knew. My aunt is the only one who gets along with her, and even she . . ." With a firm change of tone, he added, "That cat has claws and she knows how to use them." He nodded. "But Nolly loves that animal."

271

"There must be a mistake. Harvey is a wonderful cat. Maybe she isn't the cat you're looking for . . ." But of course, she was. The old woman had, in fact, very clearly said *Suzie Q*, except I'd thought . . . Well, I didn't think she'd been calling the cat's name. "We get along quite well."

"Harvey?"

"I didn't know her name. That was the name written on the pet carrier."

"Wow. And you took her in and cared for her. Thank you."

"Mr. Jones . . . May I call you Royce?"

"Of course. Please."

"The house was empty. Totally vacant that day, though I didn't realize it until the next day. Why were they here? And with the cat?"

He chuckled, nodding, as he said, "Yeah. Deb, the caregiver, went on about that. Seems Nolly wanted to see the house one last time before leaving, going to the airport, and so she arranged for the pet-sitter to meet her here." He smiled again. "Yes, Deb was unhappy about that."

"It was all just a mistake, I guess."

He said, "Was it? Maybe. But if so, it was a fortunate mistake. Admittedly, my aunt is very old. She wasn't up to caring for an animal, but you know how people can be about things like that. They don't like to admit they're not able to do stuff they've always done." He'd been watching my face closely as he spoke about his aunt. Very carefully, he asked, "Suzie Q is with you now?"

I nodded. "At my home."

"Would you want to continue caring for her?"

"What does that mean?"

He shrugged. "No one in our family wants Suzie except for my aunt, and she'll be gone for at least two or three months, and that's if she ever makes it back to this house. We can reassure her that the cat is fine and well cared for. By the time she's back here—if her health allows her to return to her home—I think we can persuade her to leave the cat where she's loved and well cared for."

"Whether Suzie Q or Harvey—she *is* where she belongs. Maybe she simply didn't fit where she was before. I would find it difficult to give her up now."

His eyes were kind. "That doesn't need to be a problem, Ms. . . . ?"

"Leigh Ann Eden." I offered my hand, and he took it. If he gave an extra blink at the mention of my name, he didn't say anything to indicate it was due to my past connections.

"In fact," he said, "I've just had an idea. If you don't mind, a photo of Suzie Q—*your* Harvey—looking good might be just the thing to ease her worry."

"Photo?" All I could think of was the countless photos I, as Leigh Eden, had posed for back in my public days, and I felt that shrinking feeling inside again, but not for long. He'd said *your Harvey*.

He nodded enthusiastically. "Aunt Nolly would *love* a photo of Suzie Q looking happy and well. It'll ease her worry, and I think she'll come to the right decision all on her own." Staring straight ahead, seeing something I couldn't, he grinned broadly, adding, "Aunt Nolly likes it when things come together in neat, happy ways. Yeah, I think she'll like this ending very much."

After a long drink of water from the bottle, he asked, "What's the name of that movie? The one werc the gal and the guy keep just missing each other? *Serendipity*. Yeah, kind of reminds me of that."

I smiled in response. *Who doesn't enjoy a happy ending?*

"My phone number and address," I said, handing him my

own slip of paper. "If she'd like to speak with me, I'd be happy to do that."

My rules? My rules to break. Another one had fallen to the wayside as I'd just invited someone—the elderly woman who had complicated my life and could very well do that again —into it.

Epilogue

I walked slowly away from Floyd Avenue as I headed home. If anyone noticed me talking to myself, they may have wondered if I was having a breakdown, or perhaps they assumed I was speaking with someone on the phone with an earpiece they couldn't see. Regardless, I didn't care. Let them think me odd. Let them speculate or gossip. Leigh Ann Eden was officially out of hiding.

To the backdrop of rustling tree boughs, birds singing, and cars and service vehicles driving past, I indulged myself, telling Florence that I was happy with how the encounter at the brown stucco house had gone.

"You aren't going to believe this, Florence, but it will surely give you a laugh. On the day I was forced to take responsibility for a cat that wasn't mine, the old woman, Nolly, said, *Better late than never, Suzie Q. The cat's hungry.* At least, that's what I heard. But she must've been saying, *Better late than never* period *Suzie Q* comma *the cat* comma *is hungry.*" I laughed aloud, scaring a squirrel I hadn't noticed into taking his nut and running.

"So that explains the name thing. *But*," I said softly, "I'm not out of the woods with this. The nephew might be wrong about his aunt's willingness to part with the cat." I shook my head. "No worries, right?"

And yet, as I arrived home and climbed the front porch steps, what I saw stopped me in my tracks.

In the window . . . I gasped. Harvey was in the front window, only part of her showing as she appeared to be stretched out on the sill.

Had something happened? My heart raced as I fumbled with my key to unlock the door and get inside where I stopped short again, this time in the foyer.

The kittens were on the move. All four at one time. Baby Gray had made it up the hallway almost to the kitchen. Orange Fluff was about to disappear under the rocker. Callie was in the wide opening between the foyer and living room, looking lost and meowing for rescue. Flo had made it to the middle of the living room before falling asleep, apparently midstep.

Forgetting to slip off my shoes, I went for Orange Fluff first. Under that rocker could be a dangerous place. Next, I rescued little Callie and then hurried to the kitchen to catch up to Baby Gray. Lastly, I came back for Flo, who, when I added her to the mess of kittens in my arms, opened her sleepy eyes just enough to peek at me. As her blue eyes focused on my face, she purred.

Harvey lifted her head, gave me and my armload a dismissive glance, then put her head back down and closed her eyes.

Apparently, mama cat was on break.

The kittens squirmed.

I laughed.

Slowly, I eased down to sit on the floor, my back against the wall. How many times had I sat here over the past four weeks?

One month. Could it only have been a month since Harvey

came into my life? Her arrival, in effect, was responsible for bringing the neighborhood into my life, including Sam Jr., who hadn't technically lived on Hanover Avenue since he became an adult, but was part of this by default.

How would I have managed this past month without him?

One of the kittens wiggled from my arms and dropped to my lap. I gathered him back up realizing that someday, not long from now, these little ones would be ready for new homes. Couldn't I keep them with me? Harvey and all her babes?

Someone knocked on my front door, calling out, "It's me."

I smiled, responding, "Come in. It's unlocked."

Sam walked in and stood, staring down at me and my armload of Harvey's babies. He smiled and joined us on the floor. I handed him a kitten.

"It went well?" he asked.

"How can you tell?"

"You look happy. Peaceful."

I nodded. "I am, now." I smoothed a tiny furrow from Baby Gray's forehead. "The nephew thinks his aunt won't mind Harvey—a.k.a. Suzie Q—having a new home, but he couldn't speak for her, he said. Even so, he *is* pretty sure it won't be a problem. So I'll consider it done for now, and if they want Harvey back, they'll have to fight me for her. For them." I grimaced, a little embarrassed. "Though I didn't say all that to him." I breathed. "But I'll say that and more if I need to."

He nodded.

"Sam, it's just come to me this very moment that these cats are truly and wholly my responsibility. I can't blame my lack of plans for these kittens on mysterious women who passed Harvey off to me and then disappeared. This is a commitment. I'm okay with that, but look how mobile they are. These babies are a month old. Before I know it, they'll need homes . . . unless they all stay here."

"You could talk to Don about the advisability of keeping them all together, but I can offer an opinion. When they are a little older, these cats might be better off in good homes, bonding with their human families. Let them grow and socialize outside of their small litter group." He let that remark rest quietly as he looked down at the ginger he was holding. He gave Orange Fluff a friendly scratch under the chin and said, "Dad is talking about getting a cat. He hasn't had one since Cleo passed. Maisie is cat-friendly, so no worries there."

"Oh." I tightened my hug just a tad.

"No decisions today. Remember? A question or option doesn't necessarily need an immediate response. Tell the questions and worries to come back when you have more information. It's too soon to know the answer to this."

I nodded. "By the way, the nephew suggested I take a photo of Harvey-Suzie Q to send to his aunt. I didn't mention the kittens to him."

Sam said, "It's not likely he'd want them, Leigh."

"I don't think so either, plus he seemed quite nice."

"Did he?"

I heard the note in Sam's voice that sounded like a smidge of jealousy or suspicion.

"I've been thinking." I let it hang there.

He asked with a slight frown, "About what?"

"You've been over here a lot. You've been so helpful. I'm grateful, of course, but I . . ." I let the "I" trail off.

In a low voice, he asked, "But?"

"I think we should seriously consider going on that second date. I think it's time. Do you agree?" And though I'd been teasing him, implying there might be a question about it, I did hear a tiny note of tension in my own voice. "Are you open to an official second date? One that doesn't require brainstorming and strategizing and speaking in a strange sort of shorthand?"

Sam pressed his lips together, clearly in serious thought. He nodded and said, "Do I get to keep my cell phone with me? You know, just in case I need it?"

"Depends on what you'll need it for."

He set Orange Fluff on the foyer floor, then leaned toward me. He put his hand on my shoulder, which he then slid behind me to rest against the nape of my neck and touched his forehead to mine.

"I think it's past time, Leigh."

I nodded. "Agreed."

"We never finished that dance," Sam said.

A tiny moment of blankness stalled me, but it cleared as Sam added, "The one we started a year ago."

I pressed my cheek to his, whispering, "No time like the present, Sam."

He didn't speak; instead, he answered with a kiss.

And then the doorbell rang.

****

"Sorry," the man at the door said. "I know you've hardly gotten home, and here I am."

Oh, that familiar clench of the stomach. The speeding up of my heart. I went mute, and then there was Sam, moving to stand beside me at the front door, his hand finding mine and bringing me back to a thinking state, reminding me I wasn't alone.

The visitor must've noted Sam's movement, a movement that probably looked protective or possessive to him. He nodded and extended his hand toward Sam. "Name's Royce Jones. I was hoping to speak with Ms. Eden."

"Leigh Ann," I said. "Please call me Leigh Ann. Sorry for the poor welcome but I was surprised." I squeezed Sam's hand. "Royce is the nephew of the woman who owned the cat." Maybe I should've said "owns," but that was no longer the case, regardless of whether she or they knew it. I added, "Won't you come in?"

"I'd be pleased to. I'd like to explain."

I stepped back and gestured him in, saying, "Mind where you step, please."

He frowned. He looked down and beyond me and said, "Oh."

I followed his gaze, saw Baby Gray, and knelt to scoop her up.

"Are these . . . ?"

I grinned. "Yes, they are."

Surprisingly, he looked at his blank phone screen. He glanced back at me and then at Sam. "After you left, I called Aunt Nolly to give her the good news that Suzie Q was safe in your care. She was relieved and worried all at the same time, if you know what I mean."

I remembered my manners. "I hope she's doing well. Can I get you a drink? Maybe a glass of iced tea?"

"Yes, ma'am. Leigh Ann. I'd appreciate iced tea."

"Make yourself at home, please. I'll be right back. Sam, would you like a glass too?"

In the kitchen, alone, I stood at the counter, my hands gripping the edge of the sink, staring out, seeing the garage, the bush that camouflaged the access panel, and knowing that, hidden from view, was the gardening I'd been doing—gardening for the first time in my life. I was a city girl, right? City girls could garden too. And not all surprise visits were bad news.

The sound of the men's voices funneled up the hallway and

into the kitchen. I pressed my fingers against my eyes and drew in a breath.

I was fine. I'd *be* fine. It was all good.

I returned to the living room with the tall glasses of tea and set them on coasters in easy reach of the chairs. Royce Jones was seated in the gooseneck rocker. He had a kitten in his lap. Callie. He looked only slightly awkward.

He said, "When I called her, Aunt Nolly, she was excited. She wanted to speak with you. I told her that you were going to send her a photo and all that, but she doesn't take no for an answer well."

"No problem. I'm happy to speak with her." I knew my position on Harvey and the kittens. I wasn't sure of hers. But yes, I'd speak with her.

Royce looked relieved. But in truth, he also looked on the edge of miserable, like a guy who wanted to measure wood, cut wallboard, and estimate how much paint he was going to need to complete a job—not someone who'd volunteer to be in the middle of a potentially emotional, perhaps even unpleasant, interaction.

I smiled. "Is she waiting for us to call? I wonder if we might do it with video?"

"Yeah, actually, I think that's a good idea."

I nodded. "Then let's go for it."

"Thank you," Royce said.

Sam and I waited as the call connected and someone said, "Hello? Hello?"

"Hey, Aunt Nolly. Royce here."

"Is she there?" The elderly voice cracked as if the reception was iffy.

"Uh"—he glanced over at me—"yes. Suzie and Ms. Eden. Can you tell Sheila the phone camera needs to be turned around?"

Nolly's voice called out to Sheila, who was, apparently, near at hand and who flipped the camera.

"That better?" Sheila asked.

"Yes." Royce stood and came over to the sofa, sitting near me and holding the phone toward me. "Aunt Nolly, this is Ms. Leigh Ann Eden. The lady I told you about." He handed the phone to me.

I recognized the woman. So this was Nolly.

"Hi, I'm Leigh Ann. How are you? Your nephew told me you were visiting family in California."

"I remember you! You looked mighty confused that day." She squinted at the phone screen. "Sorry we rushed you like we did. A mix-up, it was, my nephew says. You've got my Suzie Q with you?"

"I do. And yes, it was pretty confusing that day."

She shook her head. "I don't know how long I'll be stuck here. You won't take her to the pound, will you?" She coughed and it seemed to shake her whole body. When she spoke again, her voice was croaky. "She okay there?"

Someone, presumably Sheila, handed Nolly a glass of water. While Nolly drank, I said, "She's fine. She and I have grown close. She's a wonderful cat."

"She is."

She seemed to stop to breathe, and I waited but only for a second, suspecting that it was emotion that had interrupted her.

"No reason to worry about her. She's safe here with me and will have a home here as long as she needs it."

Nolly sniffled and looked down.

I jumped back in to give her a moment to regain her control. A lighthearted story might help. "I hope you don't mind, but I didn't know her name. It's rather a silly story . . . but I'd seen the name Harvey written on the beige carrier, so when a neighbor asked the cat's name, I assumed that was it, but apparently, it wasn't. It took me a day to discover that Harvey might not be her actual name."

Nolly coughed again. She sounded like she was choking. Sheila patted her on the back. But then I realized she was laughing. "You telling me you've been calling her Harvey?" She laughed again. Her expression looked merry, even though the laughter sounded painful.

"Are you all right?" I asked.

Sheila said, "She's fine. She's always had a distinctive laugh, haven't you, Nolly?"

Nolly covered her face, and when she took her gnarled hands down, she was more composed. She mopped at her eyes with her sleeve. I waited again.

Nolly said, "Bought that beige case used at a thrift shop. You've been calling my Suzie Q *Harvey*?"

"Yes, ma'am." I smiled. "But then . . . well, soon after I realized I might need to change that to Henrietta." I stood. "Bear with me, Miss Nolly."

"Just Nolly, honey."

"I have to carry you via the phone into my foyer."

I hit the icon to flip the camera view on Royce's phone and panned the foyer. Harvey had paused there, perhaps having heard Nolly's voice, and the kittens, not quite weaned, had converged around their mama who was less obliging now as a food source, so the effect was that the quads were milling around her.

"Suzie Q-Harvey has a family now. Delivered the day after you left, right here in my house. That's Flo, she's the smallest."

"Oh my, oh my . . ." The words were repeated as I made the introductions.

"Orange Fluff, Baby Gray, and Calliope Calico, but we call her Callie for short."

"Four? *Oh my, oh my . . .*"

"I can't promise all four kittens will still be here when you return, but I'll know where they are, and I'll make sure you get to meet them."

"*If* I return. I'll hold tight to that thought, though. My Suzie Q's a mama. I can't hardly believe it. Is she a good mother?"

"An excellent mother."

"If you're stuck with them . . . are you okay with that? I mean, in case I can't return anytime soon?"

"Yes. Harvey and I are fine. We got off to an awkward start but became friends in no time."

"Then Suzie Q-Harvey must approve of you. She's particular, she is."

"Yes, ma'am. She is, and I think she does." I cleared my throat. "Would you like a picture? Your nephew can take a few and send them to Sheila's phone?"

"That would be lovely. That would be splendid." She nodded, still watching her screen, one finger pointing at it as if following the antics of the kittens.

"You know," she said, "life's been confusing lately."

"Yes, ma'am. Here too, so I know the feeling."

She nodded. "Just how life works, I guess. But I always love it when it comes out right, don't you?"

I moved the camera so that Nolly could see Sam and me together. He waved. I said, "This is Sam. And yes, ma'am, I agree a happy ending is well worth the effort and trouble of getting there."

After saying goodbyes, we disconnected. Sam and I exchanged a few words with Royce as we walked him to the door. When I closed the door behind him and flipped the lock, I turned to face Sam, saying, "Life and a happy ending are well worth the journey, aren't they? Especially when the right person travels with you and is still there with you at the end . . . despite unexpected complications and interruptions."

"It is, Leigh." He was slipping his arms around me when suddenly he stopped and looked down.

Harvey was twining through his legs, and now mine, leaving fur.

"I guess we're both members of Harvey's family now." I touched his cheek. "How about that dance, Sam? Before life interrupts us again. Because you never know what may be around the next corner, do you?" A moment of irony struck me and I laughed.

"What's so funny?" he asked.

For a long moment, I met his eyes and held his gaze. I said softly, "I'm convinced, Sam. I fought it hard, but I was wrong. Sometimes the unexpected—*the surprise*—can be the best thing of all."

****

Thank you for reading A HEART BEYOND. I hope you enjoyed it. If you'd like to read books set in Cub Creek or in a beach setting at Emerald Isle, NC, you'll find the list of novels you might enjoy on the last page.

Acknowledgments

To the Fan District of Richmond, Virginia, including Floyd Avenue and Hanover Avenue specifically, and all the amazing streets and scenic, very walkable sidewalks, the fabulous museums, entertainment, and shopping on Cary Street, and to the people who have lived and worked there from past to present—my sincere thanks to you all. I wish to acknowledge everyone who, through the past century and more, has worked to make this area an amazing, unforgettable, vital part of the city of Richmond.

Revisiting the neighborhoods in and near the Fan as part of writing *A Heart Beyond* was like traveling back to my younger years. It brought home to me memories of visiting my extended family there in the many different homes they lived in—Lombardy (that's the earliest one I remember), Floyd, Idlewood, West Grace, Spring Street, Monument, Laurel, and others across the city. The generations of my people who lived there worked in Tredegar, in the cigarette factories as rollers, as grocers, and as day laborers whenever and wherever work could be found, and they were laid to rest in Shockoe, Hollywood, Riverview, and Oakwood Cemeteries.

Thank you all for the care given this and surrounding neighborhoods so that many of them are still here to be enjoyed.

Special thanks to Jessica Fogleman and her editing expertise for all that she does to make mine and other books the best they can be.

Author's Note

In the Dedication and the Acknowledgments, I mentioned the memories I enjoyed reliving as I walked the Fan District while working on *A Heart Beyond*. Most of those memories centered around the people who were dear to me from years past, but I'd like to call out a book that when it was published in 1996 provided much the same experience for me and mine. One of my uncles saw *Richmond's Fan District* by Drew St. J. Carneal in a bookstore when it was first published. He told his brothers about it and they got their own copies. They were born there, and grew up there, and much of that book was almost a map of their lives. We thoroughly enjoyed visually strolling through the Fan District as we turned the pages and they pointed out where they'd attended school, where they'd lived, worked, and so on. I still have the sticky notes stuck in the pages of that book noting the details of what my mom and dad told me.

That was back then, of course, but what a joy it is to look through those pages now in 2024 and reread the sticky notes we scribbled on in 1996.

One of the coolest things I recall was my mother pointing to the photo of Retreat for the Sick (now Retreat Doctors' Hospital) and saying, "Grace, that's the window of the room where you were born!" A small thing, yes, but it is very sweet to remember the tender moments shared with my family these many years later.

Thank you to everyone involved in writing, photographing,

compiling, and publishing, *Richmond's Fan District*, by Drew St. J. Carneal, Copyright 1996 by Historic Richmond Foundation. We thoroughly enjoyed it—and still do.

Discussion Questions

1. Unexpected events can force choices—choices that spark consequences. Decisions matter, for good or ill, even though when we are in that moment we rarely have any idea how consequential the results may be. If Leigh had decided not to retrieve that can of tuna, or if she'd asked animal control to pick up the abandoned cat instead of bringing it home with her how might that have changed what happened after, for the cat and also for Leigh? What events flowed from her decisions that helped change her life for the better?

2. There are many similarities between Harvey and Leigh, most of which only became apparent to the author as the book was being written. Plus, the cats insisted on a larger role. How could they not? They were adorable. This author thoroughly enjoyed writing about them. What similarities do you believe Harvey and her litter shared in common with Leigh?

3. Leigh is quickly drawn to her cat family because of her own family estrangements—the realization of the emotional connection she'd never had with her parents and how much the lack of it impacted her other relationships. Observing Harvey mothering her kittens pushes Leigh to understand this and she consciously affirms it, thereby affirming to herself

the rightness of her initial decision. How did this affect the other decisions she had to make when past events returned to threaten her and triggered her fears?

4. One of the main themes in *A Heart Beyond* is trust, whether trust in people, family, or in the fairness of the world at large, including people in authority. Leigh's experience has taught her that you can't be too careful—even to the point of withdrawing from public altogether, and that sometimes a little paranoia is a good thing—a way of exercising control and protection, perhaps. Is she wrong? What do you think?

5. It's normal to feel emotional trauma when things go wrong, but it's hard to lessen trauma's hold and grow forward. How can Leigh trust today, much less tomorrow? But she changes. She has help stepping back out into life. Who helps her and how? Who or what gave her the greatest boost in terms of trusting herself to make bold decisions? Was any one of those more important than the other?

6. Cats are contrary. So is her mother, per Leigh. The scene in the middle of the night—a vignette with Mother and Harvey together in the gooseneck rocker—perhaps illustrates that. Leigh found that sight puzzling, yet also affirming. Why? Harvey's circle of magic is mentioned a couple of times in the story, but what was that magic really? Love? Trust? Connection?

About Grace Greene

Grace Greene is a USA Today bestselling author known for her women's fiction novels that blend heartwarming narratives with compelling emotional depth. Grace combines her joy of storytelling with her beloved characters to write books exploring themes of love, loss, and personal growth that resonate deeply with readers.

Residing in Virginia, and with strong ties to the Carolinas, Grace draws inspiration from her Southern roots for the scenic landscapes that serve as the settings for her novels. Her evocative descriptions of coastal settings, charming small towns, and forested countryside in the foothills of the Blue Ridge Mountains create vivid landscapes that invite readers into the heart of her stories.

Grace is dedicated to her family, story craft, and her readers. When she's not writing, Grace spends time with her family, traveling, and indulging in her love of photography, art, and gardening.

Grace's favorite themes explore the power and resilience of the human spirit, the beauty of the world around us, the tragedy we experience, and our shared hope—the core of which she credits to God and her faith. She hopes readers will find in her novels a journey filled with heart, hope, and the magic of storytelling.

For more information about Grace and her novels, check out her website www.GraceGreene.com

Also by Grace Greene

The Emerald Isle, NC Stories Series

Beach Rental (Book 1)

Beach Winds (Book 2)

Beach Wedding (Book 3)

The Barefoot Tides Series

A Barefoot Tide (Book 1)

A Dancing Tide (Book 2)

Single Title Emerald Isle, NC Novels

Beach Heart

Emerald Heart

Cub Creek Series

Cub Creek (Book 1)

Leaving Cub Creek (Book 2)

Single Title Novels in the Cub Creek Setting

The Happiness In Between

A Light Last Seen

The Memory of Butterflies

A Heart Beyond

The Wildflower House Series

Wildflower Heart (Book 1)

Wildflower Hope (Book 2)

Wildflower Christmas (Book 3)

Wildflower Wedding (Book 4)

For a full list of Grace's books please visit www.GraceGreene.com